PRAISE FOR

THE METHOD ACTORS

'Brash and fearless, *The Method Actors* is a self-consciously postmodern challenge to our perceived reality and its fictional depiction.'
—*New York Times*

THE LAZY BOYS

'Shuker captures the testosterone-driven verve of adolescent slang, and shows why this might be appealing to young men worried about their social standing. But he also makes clear how the limited vocabulary of these young men both embodies their emotional limitations and shields them from recognizing it.'
—*PopMatters*

THREE NOVELLAS FOR A NOVEL

'With its defiant difficulty, sly ambition and writing more than sharp enough to live up to its own hype, *Three Novellas* is an event . . . and a rare pleasure for fans of truly innovative local fiction.'
—*NZ Listener*

ANTI LEBANON

'One cannot help but be captivated by the slow, mournful mood and atmosphere of Shuker's Beirut. . . . Shuker has created a haunting and riveting account of war, loss, and exile.'
—*Publishers Weekly*

The Royal Free

Carl Shuker

Te Herenga Waka University Press
PO Box 600 Wellington
New Zealand
teherengawakapress.co.nz

Copyright © Carl Shuker 2024
First published 2024

This book is copyright. Apart from
any fair dealing for the purpose of private study,
research, criticism or review, as permitted under the
Copyright Act, no part may be reproduced by any
process without the permission of the publishers.
The moral rights of the author have been asserted.

ISBN 978-1-77692-214-7

A catalogue record is available at
the National Library of New Zealand

Printed in Singapore by Markono Print Media Pte Ltd

For Anna,
and Lotte

Acknowledgments

My deepest thanks to Imogen Pelham, who has stuck by me and this book forever.

Thank you so very, very much to Fergus Barrowman and to Ashleigh Young at Te Herenga Waka University Press who have done such heavy lifting on this book. Thank you for your characteristic vision, support, energies, good humour and intensely hard work. To Keely O'Shannessy for the gift of these covers. To Jack Shoemaker who has also stuck by me longer than anyone deserves.

To Damien Wilkins and all the staff at the International Institute of Modern Letters for the honour and boon of the Writer in Residence position. Thank you to Damien for shepherding and protecting and encouraging that wonderful, unparalleled freedom.

Excerpts of this novel have appeared in Britomart's 'Notes From Self-Isolation' and in *Granta*.

Robbie Fox, the great 20th-century editor of *The Lancet*, said that his method of peer review was to stand at the top of a flight of stairs with a pile of papers, throw them down the stairs, and publish the ones that got to the bottom. My friend George Davey Smith dared Richard Smith when he was the editor of the *BMJ* to publish an issue of the journal comprised only of rejected papers and see if anybody noticed.

'How do you know we haven't done that already?' replied Smith.
—*British Medical Journal*, 23 July 2012

Data is a singular noun

Dr Claudia 'the Goddess' Godwit, MD, FRCP, PhD, editor-in-chief of the *Royal London Journal of Medicine*—the third-oldest medical journal in the world—was not often to be found in the office on a Friday, and increasingly as the autumn light dimmed and the dangers in London grew, the incidence of Friday work-at-homers (WAHers) was growing. So, arriving latish this particular Friday morning was generally perceived to be a tolerable thing.

The morning of the night he would abandon his child, James Ballard, 38-year-old copy editor, recently bereaved husband and father of one Fiona Beatrice Ballard, aged six months and not much more, rode a quiet post-9am bus to work in Bloomsbury.

He disembarked at Euston station and walked the last few hundred metres past the County Hotel, through the park to the *Royal London* offices in their wall of grade II listed Georgian terrace. He walked, hunched, past the similarly hunched and verdigrised shoulders of the statue in Tavistock Square of Gandhi, who directly faced the building of the British Medical Association, home to the *Royal London*'s nemesis and chief competitor, the *BM* motherfucking *J*, and still got there early relative to everybody else.

James's hours were cut down this last six months, and he went freelance and ceased to pay his taxes or National Insurance in order to square the bills for childcare and rent and his upcoming visa renewal. He came in now 2.5 days a week, as early as he could though always, always late, to tech edit his allocated selection of columns for the *Royal London*, plus to mop up the clinical reviews going begging, technical papers, practise papers, 10-minute consults, and to basically try to make himself as useful as possible to keep this job. Because there weren't that many going round anymore.

Fridays tended to start quietly and slowly. A resigned slap of the ID card on the security gate. A resolutely cheerful good morning to the security guard. A tip of the hat to the apparently paralysed bug on the sanded stainless steel of the elevator surrounds—it had not moved for days now. In the elevator with him today were two people he didn't know, a man and a woman in their 30s. Sharing the end of some kind of anecdote.

The woman smirked and addressed the man, sing-song, up and down.

'"And so how did you get on?"' she said, waggling her head side to side and smiling. '"And swowdy-jew get oh-on?"'

'Hate that question.'

'*Hate* that question.'

'S'not that bad getting back in from Dagenham at the minute, anyway. S'not that *dangerous*. Don't know what they mean.'

'S'not that big of a deal. Got a bit of an elbow. Stole me phone. Decapitated. Be right, mate.'

'Lost me car, third-degree burns, punctured lung, srong wif ya!'

'"Swowdy-*jew* get *on*?"'

'Ugh. Goes through me like *that*.' He thumped his stomach with a closed fist. Their accents had normalised. They had an energy, an ease impossible to define, something facile, organic, undamaged and vital. A general air lacking any kind of neurotic drive or intensity. So they clearly weren't from the *Royal London*.

'Goes through me like a *dagger*.'

He left them at the third floor.

The *Royal Lond J Med* editorial offices on the third floor are formed in an approximate U around an atrium and terrace sometimes used for windwhipped barbecues and chilly, chilling private meetings with leadership (about your future here at the *Royal London*). So now, getting 'taken out on the terrace' had become *RLJM* code for getting the sack. James Ballard semi-permanently occupies a hotdesk in the furthest leg of the U, by the door to the elevators, from which he can see across the desks of editorial and production. His view is of the elite of the journal: the lieutenant editors, Barbara Jones, the three Trishes, deputy editor Dr Death and, ultimately, the Goddess's office—dark and closed this Friday morning, pre-Clinch. James sat at his desk, leaned down and pushed the power button of his Dell and watched his screen. Windows booting up. The functions in the system tray trickling on, bubbling up slowly, one by one: the clock, the volume (muted); the local area connection.

In the immediate local area, Susan was already in, hunkered down and recovering from the morning with her young son, with whom there were apparently problems. Julia ('Jyilliuh!' as imperiously pronounced by David 1) was already in. Julia was always there before everyone else. She was an online editor, one of the more precise and blankfaced people he'd met. He had a direct view of her screen, and

Harriet's beside her. Harriet—woolly haired, well-dressed Harriet, multimedia assistant—detoxed from her job of audio mixing of *Royal* podcasts and video by shopping for clothes, as did almost everyone, well-dressed or not. He can see her purportedly tweaking the levels on the sound app but in fact scrolling down an endless Yoox page, garment after headless garment. Her browser window perfectly matches the central audio editor window in its relative dimensions, and when someone passes behind her or rises from a nearby seat is thus clickable out of with a barely detectable nudge. But in his time there—a year on the journal proper now—James had never seen anything extracurricular on Julia's screen, past her precise and preppy ponytail. She had an accent that seemed to bespeak an upbringing of no little import, somewhat derailed. They were all, at the *Royal*, somewhat derailed. Her absence of irony seemed a hint of some terrible trauma a sense of humour doesn't survive. She did not self-edit or absorb discomfort or even radiate awareness of it. She laughed at jokes as if illustrating laughter. This morning she had said 'Hello' as if the word were a strange discovery to her. James had milked a smile once or twice and this had seemed to surprise her into a little girl of 6 or 16. He tried, as he sometimes did, to envisage the childhood that had created this beautiful, brilliant, blank young woman, and for some reason saw a terrible mother, rushing down a hill aflame.

    The icons bubbled up on his anonymous Dell: two little blinking monitors struggling to communicate, Graphics Media Accelerator, Sound Max Control Panel. Intel Active Management Technology Status.

    Simon Harriot, the head of *Royal London* IT responsible for wrangling these Dells, had a PhD in mathematical logic and could solve any CMS issue in minutes, but he was also a raging if genial homophobe—so, given the proportion of gay to straight men at the journal, he was a fascination to watch after drinks at *Royal* editorial functions. Old hands like John Mayer and Martin from digiprod like to get him drunk and ask inflammatory questions just to hear him say rude and dangerous stuff. 'What about David 1, then? Tell us what you think of David's new haircut. Goo-*waaaahn*...' for e.g. Despite the elite staff, all the history, the superlative impact factor, the *London* has these old Dells. With their cup-of-tea start-ups, their watercooler boots. Show hidden icons. Sophos Protection. Last checked for updates God knows when. The clock that only shows the date if you hover on it for an arcane and mysterious instant—too long or too short and the date won't materialise; a double or accidental click renders up a balloon: 'You do not have the proper privilege level to change the System Time.' And that hover's a fine thing to engender, when the caffeine and sleep dep levels are high.

James said hello to Susan. James is a single father and Susan is a single mother. She is approximately four feet high and lead tech ed on the Jobs supplement (which has its own site) and the university supplement to the *Royal*, and she sits in the farthest of far corners in the foot of the U, with a window onto the terrace and a view past him. She's thus collusive in his screen's extracurricular content. Her brief hello this morning was a clear signal (she likes an aimless chat) for them to subside into a mutual fatigued parental fug; a shared sense that being quiet together in this brief time before everyone else arrived was the only hope for them to survive the crushing boredom and exhaustion of the boredom he presumed she presumed he felt.

(Once, Susan told him, she'd had to go to the bathroom after the fortnightly tech ed meeting. 'It was so boring I had to have a cry.')

James opened up Firefox and yesterday's multiple tabs, plus Notes, Word and Excel for the journal make-up and his duties today. Know the difference between defining clauses (no comma) and commenting clauses (commas needed):

Medical staff who often work overtime are likely to suffer from stress.

Medical staff, who often work overtime, are likely to suffer from stress.

James sits beside the printer, which is beige.

Dr Claudia 'the Goddess' Godwit, MD, FRCP, PhD is the first female editor-in-chief of the *Royal London Journal of Medicine*. She is somehow impish and authoritative at once. Technically in her mid-50s, she is yet ageless and nearly six foot two and super, super famous across a certain stratum of the professional medical world. James had discovered the phrase 'tonsorial disarray' in an op-ed piece and it captured something of her hair, the important grey and bushy brilliance of her hair. The Goddess's hair had some of the unselfconscious virtues of alpine plants: an imperviousness, a hunkered-downness. As if it had a job to do—her hair had its mind on higher matters. Recent style guidance is not to begin sentences with its or theys or too many hes or shes. Because international readers of this very international journal apparently lose the antecedents, and thus the sense. So no floating its. She blushes sometimes, the editor-in-chief, when pleased; small round red spots appear in her fine, papery skin. She also murmurs '*Yes*' when people say the right thing. At farewell parties when the speaker says that right thing, that fine thing. '*Yes*.' These farewell parties are frequent: one is held every few months for the guest student editors, who rotate in and out again, back to med school. The poor young incumbent student ed has to farewell a crowd of articulate, high-level professionals who know each other intimately, for decades in some cases, and give a convincing speech, say goodbye to them. To the Goddess, too, who stands apart, always apart. Benjamin Subramaniam, for example, 22, student ed, an extraordinarily handsome Sri Lankan–Canadian student at Leeds, though extremely short and what John Mayer cheerfully calls 'a wrong 'un'. Benjamin was constantly unsuccessfully sarcastic then equally unsuccessfully earnest and jokey in compensation. He got weirdly antisemitic when he drank, and one drunk night had confessed to membership and intense study of several odd and somewhat worrying sounding men's advice forums. But then, as public speaker, he rose a foot, and last week delivered, to the incoming student editor and to the assembled *Royal London* (who were expecting a potential minor embarrassment to be finessed and a bit of a giggle perhaps), an amazing, rousing speech. He spoke about how much he had learned, how it was hard, how much work there was yet to do, how he was proud, that good was being done. 'And I'd just like to add that the incoming student editor has an enormous amount to learn,' he wound up, suddenly masterful, 'and, I think, an enormous amount to gain. And, having met him, clearly an enormous amount to *give*.'

The Goddess had blushed then, and in the silence before the applause began, murmured for all to hear, simply, '*Yes*.'

Heads inclined towards her. Gravitas and girlishness at once. This quality, this peace, that surrounds her: she made you want to be good. Standing in a little circle of grey light—no one comes near her.

James had once mentioned, in passing (and as if it *were* passing), an oblique appreciation of the Goddess's poise, quietude, idealism, and sheer physical *size*, to the *Royal* jobs editor at the time, Edward Woodward. Woodward was six foot several inches himself and abruptly blurted an anecdote describing what his equally Apollonian father had said when asked his mind on the Goddess. His father was a retired chest surgeon of some reputation and solidity, a professional splitter of human ribs, with a marriage of 40-something years and a grown family of five plus nine grandchildren. This old man had apparently blushed too (Ed said, and did his father's voice, with his own plum, and additional stutter and stumble), and had said, of the Goddess, just: 'Yes . . . yes. Well, *yes*.'

There is a ragged edge, sometimes, for the grieving; there is the onset of a strange confusion. An ontological dizziness that comes over him, crazed with lack of sleep, when in the midst of a day before press where he's edited four or five papers he happens across a bewildering verbal construction. These artefacts of human error present like some brutal modernist prose device. Like in the middle of the *Archers* omnibus on Radio 4 having William Burroughs or Gertrude Stein suddenly interrupt to hiss short, terrible, vicious yet somehow deeply personal non sequiturs right into your ear.

When errors creep into medical articles the tone doesn't shift. They continue to presuppose a plodding rationality and your resigned understanding. The owners is on you. Soley on you. To see what's wrong with 'inadvertedly'. 'Generally' for genuinely. This generally happened. 'Since I qualified I have also loved a committee.' 'We don't use patients we use people with.' 'Many year later.' Multiple causalities lying on the ground, scared for life. Scares for scarce. Statically significant. Sort-after. Near-do-wells and their non since, working at a snail space. Cosy not cozy. I would very much appreciated. Doesn't a 'not only' always require a 'but also', though? Afterword the whole tenure of the thing subtley changed. Louts Notes. The gasp in our understanding. Burned to aches around me.

James is aware, sometimes, of things going strange. He seems to have disassociations, blips of increasing tolerance for error. Like taking seconds—*seconds*—to figure out what's wrong with this: 'Winnicott was an psychoanalyst and paediatrition at Whittington Hospital.'

Or for several seconds not seeing what was wrong with 'publically', which Death caught, and copied the entire journal in on (all@rlondjmed.com) in a crack-of-the-whip-type name and shame: 'There is of course no such word, despite eight instances in the *London Journal* in the preceding 160 years.' When words go wrong for you. Primary-school stuff. The word *summer*. Capitalise it, if you like. *Summer*. Then look at *summer* in a sentence. Say *summer* out loud a few times. Write down *summer*. Do a sum, then say *summer*. Some *summers* sum to nothing. Some to something. Some *summers* bummers; some *summers* hum; some stay shtum. Hum *summer* in a song. Pretty soon there is no content to *summer*. Nothing in a *summer*, Mum. Like *daughter*, Mamma.

Looking long and hard at *daughter*, Mamma. Say *daughter* and write *daughter* down. *Daughter, mamma, laughter.* What is your *daughter, doubter*? How is your *daughter, laugher*? Where is your *mamma, daughter*?

Small clatters of keyboards, hums of hard drives. Jane, senior tech ed, soon to be re-crowned managing editor, appeared in the door. Darkly glamorous, supercompetent, pale and overtired in a full-length leopard-print coat, she blinked at James's proximity. He blinked right back.

'Morning.'

'Morning.'

She held the door for friend Vivien, 27, nepotiste but convivial new-hire tech ed, rescued from digi content editor on the doomed PoC project and revived on the journal. She sidled in behind Jane and began to unload strapped things from her shoulders—there seemed an unlikely number, more than four—onto her desk with a shamed, complacent grin. James was seated at the cold hotdesk by the printer, right beside the draughty door to the elevators and the freezing atrium there—his only boon is that he faces the office rather than away, so there is at least some scope for slacking off, browser-wise.

'Morning!'

'Morning.'

'Morning.'

'Morning. Is there something wrong with my face?' said Vivien. She pulled a pottle of yoghurt from her purse.

'What?' Jane laughed, then didn't and turned on her computer.

'Is there something on my face?'

'What? Like yoghurt or something?'

'No, there was this gangy kind of guy at Mornington Crescent who just stopped dead when he saw me.'

'Gangy?'

'Like, of a gang.'

'Perhaps he recognised you or thought you were someone famous.'

'He was carrying a cricket bat and a thing of shaving cream. It was really scary. At five past nine in the morning.'

'Oh dear! Maybe it was spray paint instead of shaving cream, though.'

'Someone did say once I looked like Felicity Kendal which I took as a strenuous insult.' Everyone laughed. Faces rising, turning to Vivien. She sounded incredibly melancholy. 'It was Mornington Crescent. Just up there.' Gesturing to the window, and to Camden. The anecdote subsided into the scrape of her spoon in the yoghurt pottle and faces fallen again.

The door exploded open again and Birgit rampaged in, guiltily grinning a huge mad grin for everybody and anybody's benefit. Seeing the filling desks and unaware of the snail space and sleepy 9:35am vibe, she adopted her brusque and shamed lateness shuffle, literally wobbling side to side in a show of weird infantile penance, over to her desk.

David came, and then came David. At the far end of editorial from the other door. David 1, recently promoted from op-ed editor to lieutenant editor; David 2, eight years younger, editor of online. David 2 paused by 1's desk as he sat down.

'Good morning?'

'Good morning,' David 1 countered.

'I had Thai beef noodle and rocket salad last night.'

'*Did* you?' David 1 said to his monitor. There was a silence and they both seemed to wait. What did it mean? The tone of that single syllable: brutal, scathing, awfully bored. But David 2 hovered. Today's first moves in the decade-long duel of their conversation were inconclusive, and each looked for the other to resume hostilities. When in, all of a sudden, came Kristian, tech ed. Kristian was losing his sight; it would be gone completely before the year was out and no one in the office knew. He was squinting, frowning, moving precisely in his footsteps. Did he walk like this because of the condition, or because he was passing the Davids? No one knew, so no one knows.

'Morning,' said David 1 as he passed. 'Morning,' said David 2. The latter looked over the partition testingly. There was an intimacy and a dare, sometimes, between the gay men in the office. Kristian looked at them both as if he'd just woken from a dream. 'I don't know what I was thinking about,' he suddenly said. Davids 1 and 2 laughed heartily, D1 never lifting his eyes from his screen. Kristian blinked and panned around editorial with exaggerated confusion, as if to demonstrate bemusement with himself, then proceeded on to tech ed. His face changed, James saw, once away from his masters, to an unhidden disgust. Both Davids immediately moved on, somehow; rose together to stroll to the Goddess's office for the Clinch, chatting amiably away:

D2: 'So did you eventually actually go and see that film you were threatening to go and see?'

D1: 'Yes, well we did and it was less armpittish than I thought it would be.'

D2: 'What was it then?'

D1: 'Coop in *The Fountainhead* at the Curzon.'

D2: 'Coop?'

D1: 'Gary Cooper! You don't know Gary Cooper? *High Noon*?

D2: 'High Noon?'

D1: 'I love Westerns. The combination of man, landscape, horse. You can't do it on the small screen or on stage. The combination of landscape, man, horse.'

D2: 'Did you *know*, in other matters I've just this morning learned, David, that "copy editors" is an exact anagram of "disco poetry".'

Was it having a baby that really showed him that you have to truly love yourself to truly be a decent dad? That this was a problem?

This was the kind of stuff that was coming upon him late in the morning or just after lunch and his stolen 15-minute power nap in a toilet cubicle, leaned back on the hard steel cistern, or underneath the main stairwell or in the park in summer. At his most vulnerable—under-slept or just awoken. Like now.

James knows he's really tired when he starts opening up jpegs of Fiona and looking at them for a few seconds and then hiding them behind his current document. He forgets they're there and finds them when he finishes a task and closes the doc and abruptly there she is, and he is overswept by the horrible sense of waking to a nightmare, having forgotten her, because she's so new and he's not new, he's been this way a long time and he knows how he is but not how she is, and here she is, new, and there's no one else to even know there's such a word as *daughter* in his world, and he's forgotten her and left her somewhere, out there in her buggy in the tall grass where the dark night hies and the dew begins to fall.

And thinking of the night, really early on, he'd crept in to watch her sleep (carefully, mind, for those massive creak-cracks of the nursery floor) and saw her right arm suddenly salute and belt herself in the eye. Her Jim-shaped arm in her jim-jams in a sudden salute; that moved him like nothing else. That hurt so good.

And his discovery of the swaddle, out of this, and how it changed everything. Standing in her nursery he'd watched her hit herself in the eye (winced, nearly laughed out loud) and wake up (which was less funny), and Google and *Between Parent and Child* had recommended wrapping the infant up tight. It was intuitive, of course: just like things had been in the womb. Suddenly the weird gauzy garment in the secondhand job lot of baby clothes he'd received off Freecycle made sense. He'd assumed it was some kind of African baby sling. For the first time some sense of achievement with her. He got pro—got so good with it he could lay her down half asleep on top of a mussed swaddle and straighten it beneath her, tuck her little legs in (in her plain white sleepsuit from John Lewis; against poo and plain laziness he'd bought no fewer than four five-packs and planned on more), tuck her hands down on her chest like curling fronds of fern and wrap and Velcro her in seconds without waking her up.

He didn't treat her as if she were made of glass anymore, knowing what needed to be done and doing it, like a daddy, a good strong daddy, a decisive daddy like he imagined he should be, not like the daddies on the forums, the MumsNet DHs ('Dear Husbands') who, absent, drunk, oblivious or just baffled, 'slept right through it, again'.

That first time, he had done it, wrapped the swaddle tight as could be, tighter maybe than her mother would have, if she could have, and laid her there. And she had been instantly quiet. He'd backed quickly out of her room with just one loud crack from the floor and she hadn't stirred and he'd turned down the dimmer gently and got out and closed the door without her waking again or crying out at all, and he had turned to the corridor with a great and boyish, open smile, almost laughing, and then was bewildered, utterly surprised and bewildered, to have to remember that there was no one waiting for him there at all.

'Morning.'
   'Morning.'
   'Morning, morning.'
   'Any trouble getting in today?'
   'All fine for me.'
   'I was on the train this morning and someone said to me stop coughing you eff-you-see-kay.'
   'Oh no!'
   'S' outrageous.'
John 'Lord' Mayer, production editor, 40-something, crisply dressed, five feet two and wiry as a twist tie, entered from the atrium, and said to James softly from the doorway, all east London, 'Morning, sweetie darling.'

Because on nearby Woburn Walk, the Serbian women behind the counter of the Sorrento Snack Bar (four of them, implausibly, given the size of the kitchen) greet all their customers in incredibly warm displays of endearment. 'Good morning darling!' one or more or all of them explode from behind the counter, mid boiling potatoes and bagging BLTs. 'Hello sweetie!' 'Hello darling!' etc.

James and John Mayer were regular patrons of the Sorrento's omelette and chips and of their sacred, perfect BLT, and they'd agreed, after long and arduous research, that the Sorrento Serbian staff's displays of endearment were actually possessed of an intricate elitist hierarchy. They had taxonomised this hierarchy, in ascending order of the true affection and warmth directed towards the customer, and they compared their own personal results after every visit. Thus:

1. 'Good morning!'—more or less utterly indifferent, possibly outright hostile, implying some prior bad behaviour on the part of the customer, or just frank dislike;

2. 'Hello sweetie!'—goodish but you might as well be spotty, foreign, UCL freshman foot traffic;

3. 'Hello darling!'—getting there; you've been recognised, acknowledged and gently fondled, verbally; this is often special enough for those who don't know about or have never experienced—

4. 'Hello, sweetie darling'—the ultimate and most deeply felt, authentic, warm and maternal greeting, sans tawdry exclamation or inflection—the gold standard; the double-blind randomised controlled trial of Sorrento regular love.

It was late, for the Lord Mayer, whom it was rare to see arrive at the office and rarer still to see leave.

'Morning, sweetie,' murmured James.

'Oh!' murmured Mayer.

'I know,' said James. 'Sorry. Not in the mood. *You're* a bit late.'

'It was the trains! The peasants are revolting out my way. I'll do better,' murmured John faux conspiratorially. 'Promise I will.'

James laughed awkwardly, feeling sick.

The riots. Now well into their third day, metastasising from Tottenham Hale all over London. A 29-year-old black man, Mark Duggan, shot dead by police in a minicab because they said he had a gun. The first, peaceful neighbourhood protest march from Broadwater Farm to the Tottenham police station met tooled-up riot squad, then the rage spread so quickly, to Brixton, Stratford, Croydon, to Oxford Circus, and then the north. Streets taken over in the dark and the windows smashed in of every Foot Locker and Cash Converters up Camden High Street. Cars set alight, then the shops, and hammers and converted guns dug up and motorcycle helmets, balaclavas, Twitter, Blackberry Messenger and athleisure and a hungry, angry glee, hitting and running and settling scores and stealing TVs and stoning firefighters and the fires thereafter visible from up Parliament Hill as the city stayed up night after night, considering their work-at-home options and watching the skies, the news and Facebook, to see if they were next.

Mayer, like James, was one of those perennially partner-less at work functions, like David 1. When David 1—a *Royal London* ten-year veteran—first brought his husband in to drinks at the Prince Arthur, Rob (young, gay, complexly bitter, news and reviews ed) had whispered to everyone, 'That's David's husband!' like it was a major deviation in a TV series' character's developmental arc, and had then been within seconds compelled to hiss, 'Well don't *stare*.' The Lord Mayer, everyone knew, but this was all they knew, was in a longish marriage to an 'eastern European' girl somewhat younger than he. The prevailing wisdom was the 'eastern European' girl was a mail order bride. No one had met her. Mayer never used her name, as colleagues were wont to do assertively, sometimes, or desperately; to drop into conversation the names of spouses who were otherwise utterly absent—and to their co-workers thus utterly unreal. Spouses dead, divorced or as unreal, as shocking and banal, as were their otherwise unreported and unremarked-on lives at home: their idiosyncratic cats, their cabbages, cancers, worms, their voles, their films, respiratory problems, their sick sons. All those sick sons.

Some of the women in the office got very stiff and quiet when the subject of John's 'eastern European' wife came up. The very few hetero men got oddly smirky. As if they'd all of them—single men and married—managed to avoid falling prey to that particular fate. As if it *were* a particular kind of fate. A temptation barely avoided or awaited, or perhaps the fate was not the marriage itself but becoming subject to the observing and judgement of the marriage that one knew would go on just out of earshot, forever.

This morning, bereft and having no wit to muster, James let the subject change and Mayer go, with his own smirk gentle and for all. The rest of tech ed briefly and collegially smiled their willing bafflement, then—being completely unfamiliar with the Sorrento.

'Morning!'

In came Harriet. In came Rob. Woolly-haired Harriet. Svelte and chinoed Rob silently uncoiled at his desk and let the Davids go. Friday Clinches were sometimes seen as optional. This, along with people WAH ringing off the conference line mid-Clinch, had led the vexed news editor—60-something epitome of ageing insouciant attractiveness Emily 'Pheromone' Firman—to write a ferocious, expletive-riddled email to the Goddess copying in the entire editorial team suggesting FFS why don't they give them up—Clinches—completely. The Goddess had had to intervene. For what was making the Pheromone furious, and what the WAHers didn't know, or had forgotten, as they lay in bed with their eiderdowns up to their nostrils or stared out their kitchen windows in flannel pyjamas with their handsets held upside down so as not to broadcast the idle chewing of toasted Hovis to the entire meeting, was that the conference call phone's officious male voice, with its jolly but unconvincingly assumed authority, as well as suffixing the caller announcing their own name with 'Has Joined the Conference' at the beginning of their call, also announces, after the pre-recorded name is repeated, 'Has Left the Conference' when they ring off, sometimes in the middle of something quite important indeed, to excruciating or weirdly ironic comedic effect, and to a strongly repressed and thus barely detectable collective wince in the Goddess's small, glassed and spartan office.

'Even the *Mirror* has come out against the strike,' Emily would be saying. 'Today's headline is—uh, so I'm holding it up; this is for you callers, I'm holding it up and I'll read it aloud—"Walkouts scheduled for Midsummer's Day, June 21. Doctors must resist this midsummer madness—"'

'Ah Neville Partridge!'

'Has left the conference.'

For example.

'Morning!'

Hum of hard drives; clatter of keyboards. Mourning, morning. Trills of phones logging in. Melodies, maladies; sniffs and sighs.

'Hi James, you have pelvic inflammatory disease, don't you? Or don't you?'

'Yes, I've got it.'

'Oh, good. And how's the stylebook conversion thingy?'

It was a task appointed to James, opaque, unplaceable James, baffled in his sadness, that in preparation for the conversion to an online wiki he must assemble all versions and amendments and appendices and addenda and postscripts and advisories even vaguely regarding the *Royal London*'s truly gigantic and authoritative style guide into a single folder on the shared drive. He named the folder 'Process legacy documents'. He was now collating all the really relevant style stuff into one Word doc as it once might have been when the stylebook was an actual leather-bound volume, and deleting the rest.

'I'm up to F.'

He smiled. The pause a kind of signal. Tech eds looked up for amusement.

'"Failure of the right heart."'

Everyone tilted their heads one way or the other and gently went *mwooaah*.

'Morning, morning, morning.'

Harriet, slightly slumped, standing at her desk a little dazedly, slowly took off her coat. Julia turned to her, blankfaced and distant and lost in the work, and said in a monotone, 'Oh. Nice dress.'

Harriet's whole posture revived. Her shoulders relaxed. She turned and smiled, and proudly looked down at her stomach. 'Oh thank you. I got it in a vintage store in Hackney.'

'Oh yeah?' said Julia. She was looking at the dress.

Harriet warmed to the theme. 'Yes. It's pure wool and it was £20 off.' She pinched two pieces of stomach fabric and pulled it taut to show.

Julia said, 'Isn't it itchy?'

Harriet straightened. 'No . . . no.'

Silence fell.

Julia turned back to her screen. The clatter of keyboards, slightly muted, continued.

Harriet looked at her dress, her desk, then the coat over her arm as if she didn't recognise it.

Then she sat down and started up her computer.

a, a's, A, A's similarly b's, c's, etc (but ABCs)
A-ha! not a ha
A level (not 'A' level)
a, an *Royal London* style is never use an before 'h'—always a historian, a hotel, etc. But an NHS consultant, an SD, a

URL. See **article, indefinite**

And James, typing, uncontrollably thinks—with a vividness he's often thought he should be able to do something with—of her sweaty brow when she's trying to get out of the swaddle. When she won't stop crying and the swaddle doesn't calm her and it's late, so late, and he goes in there, again, padding and limping down the creaky corridor to soothe her and she won't be soothed, and he swaddles her tight because it worked before but it doesn't now, and when he returns from standing outside her door for four minutes of screaming she's convulsing in her little straitjacket, pushing and heaving, and making tiny sounds in an adult world, like '*Nnngggggghhh*'. Sweat upon her brow. How long would that go on if he wouldn't or couldn't come in to set her free? How long would she last? Would it be the dehydration that killed her? He was working, today, on a piece about John Conolly, founder of the British Medical Association, first editor of the first-ever medical journal, the *British and Foreign Medical Review*. Conolly revolutionised the country's madhouses and mental healthcare forever when he wrote *The Treatment of the Insane without Mechanical Restraints*. In the news this week alongside all the phone footage of the riots was surreptitious footage of mental health nurses trapping disturbed young women under chairs and standing on their hands, and nurses beating babies with hairbrushes, and calls in the comments pages for more recognition of the routine kindness shown in the NHS, and he does it, can't help himself; thinks helplessly of the swaddling of her, the grunts and wrenches, the horror of power over her. But she cannot sleep if she can get free.

Editing an article on military surgery once, he'd had to lay out a Whitman poem. It turned out the poet had dressed wounds in the civil war:

On, on I go, (open doors of time! open hospital doors!)
The crush'd head I dress, (poor crazed hand tear not the bandage away,)

'Poor crazed hand', and he sees her, and is moved, invisibly, at his desk, for what is a baby if not crazed and badly handled, misunderstood, and wisps of hair sweat-clustered in flame-shaped clumps at her nape?

'Sirens are a bit louder than usual aren't they.'
'Yes, they are this morning.'
'Ha ha ha.'
And then here comes Simon Harriot, somewhat hungover, Birmingham maths prodigy and regular guy, once observed holding a handful of cherry tomatoes and holding forth in the cafeteria queue—caught somewhat awkwardly as he was between the two very quiet and smiling Davids:
'Hardly ever have these! Yummy. Jan won't have them at home because she bit one once in the antipasto at a gallery opening and the material within squirted right out of her mouth.'
(No one's met 'Jan' of course.)
'Tight as a snare drum! Aqueous humour of a tough little eyeball indeed, isn't it? When they're not quite ripe? HA HA HA. The vile jelly! Well that's your area. So now I rarely have them at all. Because Jan's, you know. We had to leave the gallery early. So these are nice!'
('Your area' presumably meaning the theatre but who knew.)

In the picture the health visitor had taken, Fiona was sleeping quietly in his lap, age a little bit and not much more. James was not working; he was looking at pictures of his daughter saved to the Documents folder. He hit next in Photo Viewer, and there was suddenly someone's speculumed eyeball rolling in a field of flesh. Fiona reaching out to touch a toy from full recline. Falling asleep flat on the sofa, laid out like a lightning bolt. Picked up and taken downstairs. Falling asleep nibbling gummily on his knuckle as he rocked the Moses basket and crouched further and further down beside the bereft bed out of her hopefully narrowing, gently dimming line of sight, her horizons meeting as he crawled on all fours out of the room. And editing this stuff, such stuff. Out of nowhere, horrible, a guidance allocated to him and he found himself almost starting to cry: *Bloodstained nappy: what to look for, how to respond.* Tickling the little fold of skin under her chin made her giggle. He remembered discovering he hadn't been drying in the fold properly at first and how it had gone red and he really needed to remember to do that, to dry it properly after her bath. 'Newborn resuscitation when the baby's father is there: qualitative study with healthcare staff. A series of interviews utilising the critical incident approach dealing with experiences of resuscitating an infant in the delivery room when the father was present.' A feeling like howling. Lost in sirens. Running was something that seemed to calm it. Running after something that slipped away and left you with yourself. Knowing you had done all you could to catch it, even if you failed. 'All healthcare professional groups said they often did not know what to say to fathers during prolonged resuscitation.' A child's trachea is tiny, the size of the child's own littlest finger. Like a straw, an electrical wire. Hard, round foods, curtain cords, bibs, television cables. Death by traumatic asphyxia when an infant is overlain by a co-sleeping partner. Death by traumatic asphyxia. 'Other mechanisms.' None of this meant he was working in the wrong place, at all.

'Since I qualified I have also loved a committee.' Either it was a simple colloquialism with which he was utterly unfamiliar or it was some piece of bizarro writing that had made it past editorial somehow. It could be true that under certain conditions madness was always just a word or two away, or a letter—a decent to in sanity—the void was always there, hard long beside in the snail space—slipping began with a space before a comma. Sliipng began with a space before a cmma .   ,

Then there was that terrible obituary of a hugely esteemed Chicago paediatric physician, who'd saved the lives of hundreds of children, their parents in dearest debt forever, who had as a civilian passerby unhesitatingly swum out into a rip in a stormy Lake Michigan to save two struggling boys and drowned then, in their place.

And of the passerby who attempted to resuscitate the dying physician, the obit's author wrote: 'His life savings efforts were in vain.'

James attempted to dilute the poisonous little joke that had clouded the clear clean sadness of the thing by emailing it to Jane, who was sanity itself, and she replied, 'Ha, mine certainly are.'

But he thought of that doctor, who had two young daughters, the good doctor, dead, and he thought of his own

£20,000 student loan, and his own six-month-old daughter and the feeling as though the little imp of error who punctures all that tries to be high and right and good was addressing itself directly to him. Your troubles and pain are an absurdity away from noise. I speak to you of tautologous and therefore redundant. Of teh onus soley on you. Scared for life. As was his won't. 'Here is my to-sense about this.' Irrefutability showed that it could. Of paediatrition. Life savings efforts in vain. Of per functionary abortions, ghastly things, things that hurt the mind and heart. Burned to aches around me.

Tech editors: Après moi, le déluge.

'Death is of course the ultimate hard outcome.'

James Ballard, writing at his desk, living in massive tables of data, a prison made of millions of cells of confidence intervals and p-values he dreamed about at night and woke with an erection; Fiona crying over the Angelcare. He had to wait for the erection to go down before he went in. Standing in the narrow corridor literally swaying, dizzy with tiredness.

And so sometimes here at work he could barely speak.

But actually most of the tech eds don't go to the Clinches; they're more a daily heads-up on news stories, press releases, relevant embargoes, *RLJM* traction in the broadsheets, and who's travelling at what conference doing what on what. The thickening web of the issues for future issues. In fact, noting which tech eds went to Clinches was a good way of measuring those ambitious for elevation. That number ebbed and flowed, since in tech ed land the pursuit of more responsibility and more involvement in higher matters of content and curation generally only meant more work tech editing for the same money. The hierarchy was extremely flat and no one had anything on Jane. Kristian Shattuck was the one at present learning this lesson. He'd had a sudden burst of blue-flame can-do and was volunteering for all kinds of things: page layout, extra sections. Soon after a rather bald and bold error he'd introduced into print and online a few months ago, with all the concomitant erratum-writing and low-grade guilt-tripping and humiliation (at the *Royal* this just means various kinds of silence) that go along with that, he'd burst into life and started volunteering to do layout on the Mac over by production, and was taking on Letters to the Editor as well as News and was the quickest on the reply button whenever Jane emailed a research paper going begging. He was turning up to Clinches with sheaves of paper and opinions. Arriving early and staying late and not laughing anymore. But soon—how soon?—if history told, when his duties grew too onerous his Clinch attendance would seem a luxury he could no longer afford; the extra papers and corrections and layout he was doing would get farmed out to others again, the chop would subside and the low and timeless calm of technical editing return to softly drown his brief temerity. Without the scientific literature there was no reality, only relationships. Seven or eight different versions of the recent interchange between Julia and Harriet were currently being compiled in brains around James.

'A foil to Occam's razor, which is the law of parsimony, Crabtree's bludgeon may be expressed so: "No set of mutually inconsistent observations can exist for which some human intellect cannot conceive a coherent explanation, however complicated."'

The bludgeon was a favourite contingency of James's Friday columnist and sometime bête noire Dr Desmond 'transposable' Bernard, a youngish (30-something) practising GP and prolific *Royal London* author from some tiny fen-fettered Scottish town.

The problem with transposable Bernard was that his bons mots were recycled—factoidish, pseudo-learning-type apophthegms from La Rochefoucauld ('To refuse praise is to wish to be praised twice'), Marcus Aurelius, Cocteau ('Cherish what others criticise about you—because that is you'), that sort of thing, a couple of couplets of Alexander Pope, a bit of less-strident Nietzsche. He used them repeatedly, these gobbets, and however sparkling and refreshing they might briefly be in the journal's wider context of papers with titles like 'Protein oxidation at different salt concentrations affects the cross-linking and gelation of pork myofibrillar protein catalysed by microbial transglutaminase' etc. (something, perhaps, to do with pork scratchings), they were in fact a bit limited. He bent the data of his stories to fit the somewhat small pool of witty things he wanted to shoehorn in. James had seen the bludgeon bit in completely different contexts in pieces for *Pulse* and *GP* magazines going back a couple of years. It was like hearing your favourite famous person saying the same thing verbatim in different interviews, but worse, because it was as if Bernard were pretending anyone reading his column in periodical X was only going to read periodical X. Not Y or Z. And somehow self-defeating, or self-hating, or criminally out of touch, because he didn't seem to be bargaining on anyone following up his stuff, being a fan, *googling* him.

The other problem, the real problem, was that he sent in his pieces by iPhone and they were autocorrected all to shit, and the punctuation—an all-consuming horror.

Some tech eds fall under the illusion that they are involved in the content of what they edit. That they do not merely edit; they possess, somehow, through their expertise, their knowledge of, familiarity with, osmotic absorption of, whatever, beyond grammar and usage, the material they edit. They fall for the illusion that they are more than what they are. They fall for the illusion that in their powerful, authoritative editing—editing that may indeed save a piece and its author from utter incorrectness, incoherence, the bin—they are as critical as they feel they are. For the illusion of ownership; of importance. That somehow, deeply, fundamentally, they are editors. Or worse: *authors*.

A great calm pervaded, a peaceful working hum. It was very quiet but for the sirens outside. Everyone typing into a private lull. Two forty-five loomed.

'Jane—' Margaret said.

—the tone of her voice and abrupt abbreviation revealing she somehow knew that now, mid-afternoon on this Friday of all Fridays, was the wrong time to say something or ask anything, and she was both realising that and but had to, anyway—

'What's the best way to address an associate professor? I never know.'

Jane knows everything but, musical, dull, descending without condescending, she sighed, 'I—don't—know . . . *either*.'

'Heeheeheeheehee,' went everyone breathily, then went away back to their machines.

She wasn't cross; she'd sent an email to everyone at more or less the same time that read: 'Ha ha ha. The o has gone from the County Hotel sign. Guess which one.'

John Mayer ambled up to James.

'The editorial . . . ?'

'Working on it.'

'Working on it as we speak.'

'Yep. Just about there.'

'Some white paper . . . with some . . . black writing on it?'

'Yerhss.'

'On qualifications for authorship or something—?'

'It's entitled, "Should peer reviewers become authors if they make a significant contribution to the article?"'

'No.'

'Having read it closely, would you like me to blow your mind on this subject now or . . .'

'No, no, I'd rather wait.'

'Yes?'

'And post a quick reply online—'
'—yes—'
'—"fuck off".'
'Yes.'

Hard rain and hail came about 3:20 after the weird long warmish week and Rob went to the window softly, thoughtful. Everyone commenting on the smell.

'Such a strong smell.'

'There's a word for it,' Rob said. He looked post-coital somehow. At the window, the faint mist, the net curtain, his distract.

'For what?' said Birgit. He was near her desk.

'The smell of rain on hot . . . hot . . .'

'Rain smell,' Hamish said.

'No.' He sounded dreamy. Rob's family had disowned him when he came out. More than ten years ago. He had half the DPhil in physics at Oxford, then he quit. 'There's a word for it. The smell.'

Hamish was laughing, smiling up at him.

'Rain smell?' someone else—Birgit—said.

'No . . .' Dreamily out the window like a little boy. He went back to his desk. Searched. Said gently, '*Petrichor*.'

'What?'

'Petrichor.'

Birgit got up and came round to his desk to see.

'From the Greek roots *petra*, stone, and *ichor*, blood of the gods,' she read. 'The rain activates the blend of oils in the stone and cement that plants secrete during dry and arid periods.'

Hamish got up and came round his desk to see, too.

'Oils in the cement.'

Heads in the clouds, utterly soft, the manager of the process review the *RLMJ* was currently undergoing had called the staff.

It was really quiet for a while.

Nearer the close of play, Birgit, whose chair backed on to Rob's, ooched herself backwards and swivelled round to him. She rose and took a pronounced and actorly step forward. Hands clasped behind her back, she bent towards him.

'Hello,' she said.

'Hello,' he said, a bit subdued.

'Nice to *see* you,' was all she said.

'Mmm,' was all he said.

But his face had changed. Softened.

And they went back to work.

'How was your beef, David?' someone ventured at last.

'It was on MasterChef last night.'

'Was it?'

'Looked just like it. Thai beef noodle.'

'Re-eally.'

'It was very rare.'

'*Blee*-ding and *moo*-ing.'

Even later, James opened an email from Dr Death, duty ed last night on a jokey occasional piece by a regular obit writer on useful music to which postmortems might be performed: composer: the Czech, Bedřich Smetana:

Dear James,
I'm mystified why you've knocked the capitals off the composition *Má Vlast* (My Country).
Cordially,
T.D. Death

James could remember distinctly the decision not to capitalise the second word—*Má vlast*, he'd put; something about foreign language title case being a *special* case somehow—but the reason why, the exact justification, escaped him. He couldn't remember why and there was a low-grade panic feeling and dread. Slipping. No one knew for what the D in Tony D. Death stood. A huge repetitive banging sound began from upstairs. You've held it together and now you're slipping because it's your time to slip. A siren rose in response, choked as quickly, died.

The last email of the day was in fact a small cluster, with the first empty but for Harriet's signature, the subject line reading 'Polish coconut biscuits on random table by Ibrahim'.

Geoff: does that mean that the biscuits are Polish, or that you want us to polish off the biscuits?

David 1: or simply, somehow, polish them, in which case I don't like your tone.

Stuart: Sorry or that the biscuits are made out of polish and coconuts

Geoff: or that the biscuits are made out of coconuts that grow in Poland

Harriet: Oh for crying out loud just eat the bloody things

Geoff: If you'd just said macaroons all this could have been avoided

Harriet: Next time I just won't bother, and they're obvi not macaroons, they're zlotesdiuhskowiczs.

The conversation died as either the bit had run its natural course or the more astute had clicked to the fact that Klara Cyrankiewicz was cc'ed in the editorial cluster.

Ibrahim, the Syrian doctor seated next to the Polish biscuits, was with the *Royal* as a visiting editor. He was known for watching shaky and graphic YouTube of what looked like beheadings and tortures and field executions on his Dell a lot of the time after he first arrived until Trish Gravely had a quiet word. The gentle laboriousness of the replies to Harriet's biscuits seemed to trace the mood of the dying Friday afternoon. Across town, as rioters crossed the Barking Queen's Road flyover, right at this particular moment a young man was delicately lifting the PlayStation, phone and lunch from the unzipped backpack of a Chinese student who was amazingly still standing though disoriented and confused after head trauma and a broken jaw sustained from the repeated punches of several different other young men. The Chinese student still had his backpack on at the time. This in fact was a copycat crime from a YouTube video that had 633,462 views.

Home, James

avulsion usually surgical: a forcible separation or detachment: as a) a tearing away of a body part accidentally or surgically b) a sudden cutting-off of land by flood, currents, or change in course of a body of water

The low white mystery of the Mansfield Road estate was the last of Camden Council's Golden Age follies. The 73-apartment building by Benson & Forsyth lay on Mansfield Road, NW3, on the border between the middle-class Gospel Oak at the foot of the Heath to the north and the increasingly stab-happy Lismore Circus and Queens Crescent estates to the south. Just half a mile away to the west were Hampstead, the Royal Free and £2 million flats above the nicest, cleanest Marks & Spencer in London. A year ago, when James had taken the job at the *Royal London*, they had decided to move north of the river to prepare for the birth of their child. When they'd first seen the very rectangular whiteness of the Mansfield Road estate, its boxy, ragged and graffitied slab, he'd sighed for the wasted afternoon's viewing. But the estate agent pressed on, and led them past the burned and melted recycling bins at the zebra crossing. Past the exploded Styrofoam tub and shrapnel of lustreless chips scattered over the brick-covered way. Past an IKEA frying pan full of rainwater, leaves and the oily corpse of an incongruous eel, perched on the fence. Led them wordlessly, eyes averted, past the steel sheets riveted over the street-side windows. Wordlessly, because as the agent would later tell James, inside the strange, multilevel maisonette with all its sleek balconies, clean lines and false dead ends: 'Once they come in it's straightaway mate. They hate it or they *have to have it.*'

A third of the apartments still had council tenants; the rest had been bought, with trouser-chilling mortgages, by a statistically significant number of young architects. They are strange three-storeyed contrivances resting on the south side of a minor hill. Finished at massive expense in the early 80s and then found riddled with asbestos, causing further delays and withering cost overruns, they comprehensively signalled the end of the Neave Brown golden era of architecture and of Camden's interest in progressive public housing.

He should really move out now they were only two, but the costs of moving were prohibitive in the short term. And the long term, with a six-month-old, is hardly an imaginable thing at all.

Now here he was on Friday night, 38 years old and starting again, again, standing alone in the dark in his white work shirt and sensible slacks on the covered way outside the cage of the front door of his apartment, waving goodbye to his babysitter and his prostitute, who were the same person.

A hundred metres down Mansfield Road—Tatia, 23,

Lithuanian, 'economics student'—turned in the light spilled from the gates of Gospel Oak station, watched over and safe from harm, and waved back.

James waved yet again, cheerily.

She turned and her hair gained sudden definition under the fluorescents. She went on through into the white-lit tile and the traffic muttered past her down Mansfield Road.

It was 7 o'clock, home from the *Royal London*. Beneath him in her room Fiona was successfully down and asleep. The flat quiet and dark. It was a Friday night and he was not sleeping with Tatia tonight, had paid her only for the week's babysitting.

James sighed, and turned and went inside.

He climbed down the first flight of stairs to the living room all in darkness, all in quiet. Feet splayed carefully wide to keep the loud steps from squeaking. Round and down the next short flight of stairs to the middle level of the apartment: the kitchen, a dining alcove, his office, the bathroom and the nursery. Where her door was closed—FIONA it said on the door in cut-out paper letters—and all was quiet; all was still. He stood and listened and looked about.

Even through the steel panels over the streetside windows he could hear the digestive murmurs of heavy traffic, the odd, hopeless siren.

The mess in here. Used wet wipes piled on a wet-wipe packet on the table by Fiona's highchair. A square of once-transparent vinyl underneath that chair now like a crushed cheesecake of crumbs and slushy stuff. In the kitchen two cupboard doors were open and all the dishes dirtied and gone to parts unknown had left a stencil of lighter and heavier grease on the empty shelves. The kitchen bench under the crockery cupboard was now permanently devoted to clean laundry, washed and dried and piled and shoved in there haphazard as bones in the Parisian catacombs, to be rummaged in daily before work like a tender of the dead, or like a bodysnatcher, pitifully late. Sometimes Tatia might fold up some of the linen but she wasn't paid to; neither was she paid to clean. She was paid for sex and childminding.

Under all the laundry there is an archaeology of snail mail dating back six months, much of it Antipodean: cards, letters, in heavy-GSM stationery discreetly embossed, some of it pink, some of it white, some of it a sober grey. All of it unopened.

Upstairs the living room in darkness, the TV aerial still unconnected. Silence from Fiona's room: she was asleep. Downstairs the double bed, unmanned, unmade and unchanged for months, a laptop on the other pillow, hard drive full of quarter-watched seasons of torrented HBO. Beyond that, the manged, unmanaged lawn and the great honey locust grown out of control through which the London sun might occasionally embarrassedly peer. It was silent down there, the air thick and chill. Where all cold sank.

He stood in the empty hallway for a further full minute, figuring his options. Another computer screen. Gin in the freezer. Photographs. Thinking. *A book.*

He looked about himself and sighed again.

He went downstairs to the bedroom. In the bookshelf on one side: *Between Parent and Child. The Baby-Led Weaning Cookbook. Healthy Sleep Habits, Happy Child. The No-Cry Sleep Solution.* A rogue *Sound and the Fury. The Soft-Spoken Parent.* On the other, in a little stack in a tidy corner at eye level: a Karrimor shell jacket, £17 delivered from Sports Direct, shorts, two identical T-shirts and five balls of paired white slipper socks, from a prior life. The £120 Nike trail trainers from the season before last were waiting at the door. Down here is where he dresses for running. It was now a necessary thing, a vital thing, running: he gave up cigarettes and most of his bad drinking when Fiona was born. Now he tends to drink in a transparent monotone: gin or vodka, tonic or water and lime. No mixing. On a Friday night like tonight when he battens down the hatches he won't be in bed until two, unless he's really killed himself running, and he'll be up several times during the night, and up for good by five, or six or seven at the very latest. It's simple pragmatism: he needs to drink but cannot afford hangovers.

The baby books were dusty now. Didn't have to feel guilty about not reading them anymore. That distinction between guilt and shame someone somewhere made—one came from within, the other from without. The other from without. He struggled to make that distinction. And did not read the books and blundered on.

The act of pulling on the old shorts, lacing the trail trainers tight, right, and zipping the cheap shell jacket up to his Adam's apple excited him—he could feel the serotonin uptick straightaway.

Fiona upstairs didn't say a word.

dark
dataset; datasheet
data is not a singular noun

He stretched his hamstrings out on the security wall in front of the Mansfield estate. He stretched out the right, hips squared, bent low over his leg, gently pulling on the ball of his foot. The streets shining. He stretched out the left. To a count of just 15 seconds. To get going, get on the Heath, do it quick and get back, 40 minutes running off that lactic acid of days of editing. He heard something, stopped his stretch and listened—was that crying? A far-off siren or an injured dog or a TV or his daughter alone in her room?

In order to deal with the rage and funk of office—his hurting heart of work—James Ballard discovered running late in life, at 38. Like a meal before running, there's no place for second thoughts or even first—one vomits out the day's editing as one grinds up the slopes of Parliament Hill. There to float over the rough ground into the dark trees, free for a time. Watching for danger ahead without a conscious thought in his brain. Thinking about it is exciting. It used to be when the office was empty and around 3:30pm and there was no Tatia in the evening that a huge depression sank in; sugar crashing, solitary, sedentary. But not when you have to run home, after work, with your wits about you. The promise of pounding, panting, bounding home alone. All those thrown elbows and dropped shoulders of Camden hostile. Up the slow crawl of Chalk Farm, past the hospital, past the ponds and up and up and under the frail ancients of the Heath trees over darkened Parliament Hill—it elevates, it thrills. It simplifies.

(Something he's become aware he does when he gets to the foot of the hill by the ghostly band rotunda—and as he bounds closer he stares at the ground and though he knows he does it, doesn't consciously try—James, every time he hits the same first piece of gently sloping cement, prepares to give up. But every time, he mutters *go fuck yourself* with a gritteethed sigh and then a kind of half-grin and even a laugh in the form of an exhale in the dark, whether to himself or the hill, who knows—and heads on up there, into the nothingness. *Go fuck yourself.* Every time.)

The first stretches awaken something. Like a dog who hears the clink of his lead and smells the night, his mood shifts automatically. It's not a particularly sophisticated or dignified pleasure and doesn't seem to say much for his sophistication or his dignity, but you take it where you can get it. Nothing quite like a six-month-old baby to adjust your expectations of yourself.

He listened for the cry to come again. Confirmation it was televisual or animal or something other indeed. He couldn't hear the sound again and so there it was: he was maybe 80% sure his daughter was still asleep—and still it seemed he was stretching; still it seemed he intended on going for this run. Was he? It wasn't very comfortable when you gave it percentage odds, was it? But it wasn't very comfortable not running either. It wasn't very comfortable in a cage.

James had sprained his ankle six months before and the weakness still remained. He'd been bombing it home when he did it (*go fuck yourself*) on freshly mown grass on the floodplain alongside the men's pond, east Heath.

Twilight—maybe there was a darkness to the longer grass of the pothole (some famished rabbit's dying dig), but he didn't see it. If the grass had been unmown he would have, because if you're looking and you've the eyes to see, you know that holes tuft up; maybe it's the extra water. At full sprint along the smooth mown grass beside the asphalt path he had stood on the lip of this particular hole and his whole weight had gone over the ankle and in and down and he had heard the tendon go. Even sprinting, as fast as he could go, he had felt it and heard it make that tendon sound. The wet quick crack of a chicken leg twisted off a carcass hard and fast. And he went down, straight down almost like a dive, in part because he'd tripped, but mostly to get off it as quick as he could. To get off the violated thing surely hanging by a tendon-thread. Darkness falling all about, he had rolled and rolled around in the grass, roaring at the pain—not screaming but roaring at it. And was there not something kind of funny about it—funny boneless, floppy, broken and useless—something funny in the way it was so irrevocably gone? Trying to hold on for the pain to ease. He had to just hold on a bit and the worst would ease. An old woman was passing by, walking two dogs of incongruous size. 'I had that happen to me once!' she'd called out good-naturedly, and then off she hurried into the dying day. He'd continued to roll around in the first agony of the major sprain, half of which was knowledge of what had been done. Fucked for weeks. Not walking properly for days. Not running for weeks. Mustering the strength to wait out the first pain so he might essay a limp home before the darkness was complete and he got in trouble on the Heath. Because he had to get back to make her dinner, massage her shoulders, read the hypnobirthing mantra to her in bed. She was nine months' gone then and James was still limping pretty bad when Fiona was born, a hairy head, a water birth, at the Royal Free.

The phantom ankle still aches, after runs, when he wakes, and when to bed he goes, alone.

There was a low mist. A glow in the sky over Savernake Road's Georgian terraces from the lit athletics track. He was going to return soaked, maybe even shirtless, from sweat and rain, barbaric, limping. Utterly fatigued to the point of comedy. Not a thought in his head. His daughter asleep. This was the goal.

He started off.

Bounding down the covered way, down the brick steps and on into the night. Thrilled every time, because after six months of joyless flabby plod and grind he had mounted some plateau and running suddenly became this thing, with acceleration, with spring and grace. He could turn it up or down. He could bound.

To the end of the estate he went, past the standing traffic back to back from Fleet Road to Highgate, heading towards the station. The night in his nostrils exhaust-blue, high and clear. Only 40 minutes or so, maybe 35. Pulled to a halt by traffic at the darkened crossing by the Old Oak where the wood-framed windows were boarded up with riveted steel. Wasting these precious minutes. While she crept closer to waking, crying alone. He slipped between commuters and the railings, inches from the air red and smoking with brake light.

'Speah some *chain* sir. Ahm *ahngry*. Ain't had nahfing *teat*.' A homeless man whined from a shroud of blanket in the lights of Gospel Oak station. 'Speah some *chain* sir.' All about was a darkness of oozing brick and overgrown undergrowth, and as the traffic picked up in a sudden pulse the great doubled bridge of the Gospel Oak railway tracks over the Mansfield Road tunnel took sudden bracelets of headlight into and out. Crowded about with dripping brush under the skeletal poplars behind the Heathview apartments, the pavement suddenly opened up too. He pounded down Gordon House Road, stamping flood-muddy puddles until the ragged concrete gave onto the gateway to the Lido.

CORPORATION OF LONDON HAMPSTEAD HEATH GOSPEL OAK ENTRANCE.

Three paths opened emptily into the Heath: one straight past the school to the rotunda and the path up Parliament Hill. The middle path was a gravel promenade through stately ash to the Lido: shuttered, winter-silent.

The third path turned left past the Shack Café, burned out last summer. This path hugged the route of the Richmond tracks above and went into premature darkness in the thick trees back towards Hampstead. He ran past the sagged carrion of some roasted rubbish bins. Just metres from the noise and eyes of Mansfield Road it went quiet. Carrier bags and crumpled cans of Żywiec lager marked the border of last spilled light. After that lay 50 metres of deep and forested darkness before the athletics track and playgrounds.

James rounded the corner off the main road at speed, and on a whim ducked left onto the darkened track, favouring the right ankle.

The concrete was sprung with roots and sprain-dangerous, and he ran lightly, each footfall noncommittal.

The path's shadows split in sudden bright shards from the lamps of the station above.

The leaves in silver negatives.

Immersed in sudden separation, sudden silence.

Three figures in hoods stood in the tree-dim, awakening as he passed.

Fahrenheit (F) Do not use. Convert values to degrees Celsius (C).
failure of the right heart is correct
falciparum malaria (roman)
fall off two words: to deteriorate; to become detached and fall. As noun: deterioration
fallopian

Sudden fear.

    Sudden fear was not correctly what he felt because he was moving at some speed. He still had his wind, his legs were fresh and stretched, it was the beginning of a good run. Three stooped and hooded figures like pious novitiates were suddenly beside him in the heavy dark of the penultimate and ultimate oaks. Shifting, waking, seeming to come alive as he passed. He had time to register the hoods, three of them. The word GRA VIS on a chest in a stilled shimmer of blues and greens, split by a zip. That they were all young and that one was conspicuously smaller than the others. That his passage had spurred movement in them and that they were turning with him. These data came to him as he ran on. Just kids from the Lismore hanging out in the darkness on the Heath. The GRAVIS one had turned with him and begun to move. Now James was metres out from the last tree and up ahead the One O'Clock Club's buildings, venue for children's playdates and birthdays, were deeply enshadowed opposite the silent railway tracks. There were at least 200 dark and empty metres in which to die alone. This small calculation was made without any confirmation they were coming. It seemed ridiculous. His mood too good. It could not be true. He'd misunderstood the sinuous turning, the fluid uncurling. He had to not sprain his ankle again. The stadium lights were up. Making the shadows deeper here but also meaning runners, people, over there.

Two hundred metres of ambiguous ground.

'No, *don't*—'

He heard a voice behind him say it.

It was all in moments. It was an afraid voice, a small, dreading, pleading voice, and he instantly connected it with the youngest, smallest figure, possibly even female.

And just as instantaneously the scenario was clear.

He had seconds to get away.

There were three. They'd waited in the shadows of the last tree, well away from the Gospel Oak gates and lights from Mansfield Road. But they were not looking for solitude for a smoke or a grope—the entire Heath stretched away. They were waiting by a jogger's path for someone to do. They'd seen him come; it wasn't a rape they were waiting for, so they were likely armed. They were coming after him. There were two older who'd brought a younger. There was an element of dare, of a plan, or test. They'd been debating it and the younger's voice was afraid, and something in that fear bespoke a storytelling, a waiting and a disbelief at an end in dread. These data came to him as he ran on.

If these facts coalesced into a beating—if he tripped; if they caught him here—he was in darkness equidistant, and thus done: as far from the Lido entrance and the Roderick Street bridge and the stadium clubhouse as he could be, in the shade beside the stadium lights that blinded the runners' eyes to the night out here. Done. They would do him in the tall grass by the fence and he would lie or die in the shadows and the dew and Fiona was velcroed tight in her swaddle, asleep in her Moses basket. She would wake at 2, at 4, or 5 or 6 and cry. There would be no one. There would be no one who would gently open the door and limp to her across the creaking, cracking floor and lift her from the basket for a cuddle. No formula and no nappy change. Why the swaddle so tight?—She cannot sleep if she can get free.

Dog walkers would find him in the tall grass at dawn, Fiona perhaps by the end of the day. No identification on him. Sweat rising on her brow.

She cannot sleep if she can get free.

He veered off the path abruptly, over the rough ground, stepping lightly, stepping high. Heading for the edge of the football pitches. Heading for the running track, and trying not to trip.

He looked back once and fast over his shoulder. The small hooded figure was standing under the last oak, watching him go.

But the other two were by this stolen glance momentarily frozen and ranged over the rough ground towards him. The first with a low, fey hand, an odd and open gesture, on a weird, idle angle. The weight not of a knife but a fully extended steel ASP baton swinging freely by his leg.

James turned back and bombed it over the football pitches, looking ahead where he must circle the gleaming, muddied triangles of the keepers' boxes because he might slip, slip once and die.

Running for his life towards the lights.

A Patient's Tale

'It's a vile world we live in,' said David 1.

In his usual way he was both ironic and deeply serious. David 1 did not hunt, but with his bifocals on a plastic chain was wearing a hunting-themed tie with small, intricately embroidered shotgun cartridges floating on crimson silk. Since the promotion there were new aftershaves, braces, cufflinks, new fabrics for his shirts in butcher's stripe and contrast cuffs. Waistcoats. The piece he was holding, pincered at the corner as if it were pristine and antique lace, respectful and delicate, was what was called 'A Patient's Tale': a regular column, not IMRAD in format (Intro, Methods, Results And Discussion), very much not a scientific paper at all in fact, but featurish, told in the first person, designed to broaden the perspective of practising doctors to encompass the ineluctable alien: an actual person's view of what is wrong with them. To encourage empathy and understanding in medical professionals. The narrative voice was flat, simple and unaffected. The translation had been made by the young narrator's doctor at the clinic she'd ultimately made it to, in the strange refuge of the Democratic Republic of Congo. The piece had been gently shepherded about the office from editor to editor to tech ed to duty ed and all the way back again, each solicitous, caring, quiet.

#Patient: We don't usually say 'patient', we say 'consumer' as in 'health service consumer' or 'person'—though 'A Person's Tale' didn't have such a reader-friendly ring—with vesicovaginal and rectovaginal fistulas. The young woman had asked for her real name to be used—Mary. Who in London offices could weigh true that gravity? Her voice, though free with terms like shock and hope and horror and dignity, was affectless and deliberate. It was like some strange and awful fable. They all felt it best left that way. Mary was a Nigerian girl of 21, pregnant with her first child. The editors moved about the office quietly and efficiently, discussing the needs of her piece in the simplest, most economical terms. Soft of voice, collegial, brisk, decisive. The atmosphere clinical and gentle.

I began my labour before arriving at the clinic. I was there a day while the pain steadily increased. A nurse came and told me to push. Later a doctor came and said my labour was not progressing. The next day a nurse said to me, 'All the other mothers have had their babies and left. Why are you malingering? Are you lazy?' I was told to go outside the clinic and walk around and do squatting exercises. The pain was very great. In the car park something burst and black water ran down my legs. My mother called and the nurse came and said to me maybe now you will give birth.

Papers: they come in twos or threes, or they come alone. An email is sent. A self-deprecating and apologetic request is made. Refusal is an option only in the most desperate cases of overwork. Imagine the faces emptying of sympathy and feigned pain. Susan, anyway, is the tech editor who likes to say yes. 'Yes, of course!' she says brightly, adds her initials to the Excel file, and with an undetectable sigh and a rolling, sluggish wave of grey depression drenching her CNS goes to the folder that Quadrivium automatically creates upon acceptance for publication, to assess the damage.

For the wonder of Microsoft Word and of budgets to employ real people is such that the *Royal London Journal of Medicine*—the third-oldest medical journal in the world; impact factor: intimidating—sends its final submission papers to a form of text sweatshop, in Guangzhou, China, to be cleaned up prior to technical editing. This business, a text launderer, an automated editor, staffed at some tier by humans or completely by code, no one seemed to quite know, was called 'Molesworth', and was thus apparently a dark and now largely unmentioned joke amongst the better read of the lieutenant eds. ('The prunes are openly revolting,' muttered D1 in the Clinch, and D2 snorted horsily. Everyone else just blinked and did the wide-eyed side-to-side of WTF, public schoolboys.)

So there, in Guangzhou, at this business improbably named Molesworth, someone—or someone using something—or simply something—strips out the junk and the footnotes and the field codes and special characters and all the other Microsoft clutter that impedes the translation of healthcare professionals' prose into clean and parsable XML. The goal is pure, pristine, verified text where every character has a precise and vanilla Unicode equivalent. Where every block of text is tagged appropriately for the building of a document worthy of the name, worthy of publication in print, online and PDF (for doctors, like all academics, like to print out and lug those anonymous, adless bundles of paper home to read by the fire). Where every space contains only that:

space.

But in Guangzhou, they don't read the text so much as clinically investigate it for purpose. Scripts and algorithms interrogate the content and tag it as the code finds appropriate. What looks like an address by placement and relative shape of numbers and words is tagged as an address. It is writing reading writing.

Papers arrive from authors in all kinds of fascinating distress: entire texts of super-serious thinkpieces about medico-ethical lapses in hyper-stressful situations by and about otherwise stainless, high-functioning surgeons, written in gigantic-point-size Comic Sans. Papers written in, as Jane might whitely, politely put it, English as a second language. Papers with not only Word's hideous and bewildering fields function used for the footnotes, where the fields cling to the text and fail the XML through Clear Formatting and through every possible countermeasure bar pasting whole suspect blocks of text into a new document, Clear Formatting, then pasting back in again in the most extreme available textual scorched-earth policy, with the then-requisite and tedious replacing of italics and allowed special characters—not only this, but with *nested footnotes*, footnotes to footnotes, *and also using fields*. Clinging to the text like poisoned, invisible barnacles latched on to other poisoned, invisible barnacles. There are a thousand ways to fail XML—Molesworth removes most and then adds their own crazy. The papers come back with all kinds of strange—clearly what was someone's name posted as the title, job and address of author on a clinical review of basal cell carcinoma.

Brian Hairweatherer
by Brian Hairweatherer[A]
consultant general surgeon
[a] Brian Hairweatherer, Brian Hairweatherer Brian Hairweatherer Brian Hairweatherer Brian Hairweatherer, Brian Hairweatherer, London UK

A list of patient resources turned into references. The authors of 100+ references, unstyled and without page numbers (the *RLJM* uses Vancouver, more or less), lifted out for no good reason and rendered into a single-spaced paragraph as if it were something one could read, like a tone poem, in the middle of the same, long, gruesomely illustrated paper:

Toyka KV, Drachman DB, Griffin DE, et al. N Engl J Med. Patrick J, Lindstrom J. Science. Dau PC, Lindstrom JM, Cassel CK, et al. Hertel G, Mertens HG, Reuther P, et al. Giraud M, Vandiedonck C, Garchon HJ. Ann N Y Acad Sci. Hohlfeld R, Wekerle H. Adv Neuroimmunol. Drachman DB, Patton CJ. N Engl J Med. Jaretzki A 3rd, Skelton RW, Yarnslo K, et al. Ann Thorac Surg. Benatar M. Neuromuscul Disord. Hoch W, McConville J, Helms S, et al. Nat Med. Shoffner JM, Shoutbridge EA. Karpati G, Hilton-Jones D, Griggs RC, eds. 7th ed. Brais B, Bouchard JP, Xie YG, et al.

Etcetera. Visual nightmares a human tech ed would recoil from, seeing and feeling something very wrong indeed, but not Molesworth. They too face a process review, and Jane, on behalf of Charles Boddington, vicious, peerless consultant and reviewer of processes, has asked that their transgressions be logged.

(One would think that the tech eds would be pleased by this. But this wasn't action, just the promise of future action. News of the log was met by a series of patient, smiling frowns around the tech ed meeting table. As someone once said: 'It's just more *stuff* I have to do now.')

So the tech ed opens her newly assigned paper with a sense of resigned trepidation; no matter the state of the document, she has the same limits on her time. She sighs, or not. Then she applies the *Royal London* template, cites the paper top and bottom, and tags the text whether Molesworth has done so prior or not. Applying auto-formatting and XML tags for font and size, titles, authors' names and addresses, paragraphing, indentations, references, appended tables, figures and sidebars. It is oddly soothing. From the chaos emerges a paper. Order comes. Word crashes. Is restarted. Autosaved document recovered, reviewed. Retagged. Competence, sanity, persistence, the accretion of measured and proven modes. The essence of the purpose of a medical journal. From the actuality of contingent well-meaning and the limits of individual knowledge and experience, even genius, the new limits of the edit, the peer review, the dialectical investigation, time spent, argument, disagreement, compromise, presentation, arbitration, *publication*, emerge:

Parsable text.

After six days in the ward I lost consciousness many times and my sisters and my mother feared that I was going to die. They begged for me to be referred to a different hospital to have a caesarean section. I think the clinic nurses were glad to see me go. We took a bus. It was an eight-hour journey. When we arrived at the new clinic the doctor there asked my family how they could let me stay in that condition. By now the baby had died as they could feel no heartbeat. After a week at the post-operative clinic they removed the catheter and I felt myself make water in the bed. I was shocked. My mother tried to absorb it with a towel and asked me why I had spilled water on the bed and I said that I didn't. I said that I think it is urine as I can feel it coming out but I can't control it. My mother screamed because she knew that it was a fistula.

The editors had debated briefly with Susan over the word 'absorb'. It wasn't colloquial and it sounded officious and translated. But the alternative, briefly mooted, 'mop it up', had been felt indelicate. Fistulas form during a prolonged labour when the baby's head presses against the pelvis long enough for tissue to die and necrotise. This causes a hole to form as the tissue breaks down, which acts as an abnormal tract between the bladder and the vaginal vault, causing an uncontrolled leakage of urine. In the Nigerian girl's serious and complicated case, there was such a vesicovaginal fistula, and a rectovaginal fistula.

I knew it was a terrible thing because in our town there was a woman who begged at the side of the street into her old age. As children we made fun of her and called her dirty. My mother had known the woman when she was young. She had a fistula from her first pregnancy when she was seventeen. Her baby was stillborn. Her husband and family rejected her because of her condition and she could never have another child because no man would marry her. The rest of her life was spent begging on the street.

In the next town there was a group of women who suffered from fistulas. They lived together in tents in a park by the lake. Many of them had suffered from their fistulas for ten years or more. Around the park the trees were full of blankets hanging out to dry. The women begged for money to pay for clothes and, to trap the urine, nappies.

The day the piece was due the duty ed was Death. Susan stood lost in thought over the printer waiting for her proof to return from Death and the proofreader. Staring up spacey at the bookshelf over James and Margaret. James looked at her, at the bookshelf.

'I worked on some of those books,' she said. Acknowledging the prolonged stare, James's noticing. Dreamy, lost in some fog.

'Did you go for a run today?' James said, half-smiling.

Susan was running in her lunch hours. With her young son waking her all night, it was pretty impressive.

'Yes.'

'And how are you feeling?'

'*Turrible.*'

Scarcely a grin, and she went back to her desk and back to work without another word and everyone laughed.

I was in shock and very distressed. How would I see my friends again at university wearing a nappy or urine trickling down my legs? Would I ever be able to try again to have a baby? At night in the post-operative ward I cried in my sleep.

Only my mother stayed. She helped me to stay clean. At night the urine would trickle through the sleeping mat and onto the floor. Urine and faeces were coming out freely. My mother tore up a blanket for me to use as pads and washed them during the day. But I would wake up every night cold and wet. I stopped eating because I would pass everything I ate and I stopped drinking before I went outside. I became very thin and anaemic. After the diagnosis my husband went away from the hospital one day and I have not seen him again since then. I wanted to die from the wound but I didn't.

The doctor came and diagnosed me with two different fistulas, rectovaginal and vesicovaginal. He said that there was a specialist fistula clinic near the Democratic Republic of Congo (DRC) border. A lot of fistulas are caused by the war crimes of soldiers. This clinic had become very experienced dealing with refugees from the DRC with fistulas caused by rape, and in doing fistula repair surgery. There were European doctors and trained staff. He recommended I go there.

Editors, two, and three, standing around Susan's desk, examining the text. Scrolling through the proof, one finger on the gently clicking wheel of a mouse. One's eyes bright with tears. The quietening all about in tech ed, as the others gathered something was up. Editors reading the final draft. Everyone who'd had a part. Editors consulting on an image for the cover of the *Journal*: two slim black hands, one wedding ring, resting resolutely on the brilliant white of a hospital-gowned lap. The cover filled to the trim with bright hospital linen, and those two young hands. Editors ensuring the res was so high that there was the weave of the material; there were the dabs of pink polish half grown out on the fingernails of one hand. There were the gowned sleeves and elbows on either side of two more women of how many more, waiting in that line. Editors concurring. In a semicircle they leaned this way and that about the screen. Death had sourced the image and would brook no dissent. Mary had explicitly asked for her name to be used, and at the time of publication was 22. She hoped to return to university and to be married again one day.

Editors, in all things otherwise adversary, sending back one-word emails that read simply:

'Yes.'

I have had four surgeries to repair the extensive damage done to my body. I trust my surgeon and I feel good when I think about him. I am always waiting for the last surgery but I know that it is a complicated case and there are many different things to consider. I look back and I think that I am lucky that my mother stayed with me and that I was recommended to the fistula clinic. I am grateful to my doctor more than words can say. It is wrong that so many women suffer from fistulas that are never treated. I am 22 now and I have a chance to get married again. I am lucky that I am educated and that I know what a fistula is. There are many thousands of good women of childbearing age who lose their babies and husbands and families, and dignity, and are turned out on the street through ignorance of the problem and that it can be treated, in some cases very easily.

My situation is not fixed yet. I hope to return to university one day and one day when my surgeries are finished and my body is fixed, I will be able to have a baby.

The proofreader found no errors in Susan's copy edit. It passed XML on its first try, probably due, as much as anything, to the spare tone and absence of mathematical characters and any particularly complex content. Just a patient's tale. Godspeed into the CMS. An afternoon well spent. Publication still to come. Everyone on to the next thing.

'It's a vile world we live in,' David 1 said, shaking his head.

The process review

Halfway up Parliament Hill he had at last looked back. Out in the gloaming—past the joggers still jogging, past the lights of the athletics field, down the path, out upon the football pitches. There were three figures, blurrily, gone into the darkness towards Highgate. Was that them? Heading home? Looking for another contender? Would they walk the same if he were bleeding out unconscious in the dark grass? Life went on, after all. Or would they be excited, skipping, comparing notes. Cajoling the younger one. Who knew if it had even happened. What if he had halted, turned, waited for them to come. Who was qualified to say? Just a story to tell in the morning, the pitch and intensity dispelled in the telling. If your death was always that close and instant and contingent, how real was your life?

So he'd just run on.

into turn them in to the authorities *v* turn them into the authorities

intra partum or intrapartum two words adverbially (she

bled profusely intra partum) and one word adjectivally (severe intrapartum bleeding had been noted)
it is clear that clearly
it is likely that probably
it would appear that apparently or seemingly

'Neither a sweetie nor a darling today.'

It was hot. The editors were gathering for a meeting in the Heatherington boardroom about the process review. Tech ed weren't invited, but some of the tech editors were finding excuses to spy, to walk past the doors, to walk right in and hand proofs to Death, duty ed today.

'He's still not arrived,' Susan informed them, after dropping in a news story to Death, of the still-absent Charles 'Worzel Gummidge' Boddington, commander-in-chief of the review in question: 'Half an hour late. Stuck in Reading because of the stuff that's kicked off round Battersea. There's someone's started a fire, 'parently. Clapham Junction closed. Trains are down again. They're all bored and talking in German in there.'

The latter was actually true. All of them. James hadn't known it either until one day Helen Jackson came in late from an unexpected summer downpour in a damp dress that started low and ended high and very grumpy about something or other. She crashed down at her exploded desk.

'What's the weather going to do do you think?' said Rob beside her, staring out the window.

'It's supposed to be 25 degrees,' said someone.

'Well you're dressed for it, Helen,' said Benjamin

Subramaniam, and allowed himself to sound admiring. Then appeared suddenly panicked as if he might have sexually harassed her.

'I've got to stop reading all these apocalypse books, hu-huh,' said Harriet. 'Supposed to start with the weather isn't it.'

'I don't care,' Helen growled, raw and guttural and muttered. 'I don't care about a bit of rain.'

Birgit was on the phone to someone, in German, and holding forth gaily.

Helen turned on her Dell and glowered at it. After a while, as she leaned back and listened during the long wait for the Dell to boot, her expression began to change.

Birgit hung up.

Then Helen swung around with a sudden big bright grin and said, in German, '_____!'

'_____!' Birgit said.

'_____,' said Helen.

David 2 popped his head up from behind his Dell and said, '_____.'

'_____,' said Rob.

Birgit: '_____.'

'_____!'

'_____!'

Then they all laughed cheerfully.

So they all spoke German as well.

'It's not right you know,' said Margaret. 'We won the war.'

Boddington had a makeshift office among the hotdesks of what had once been a closet, alongside a small meeting room (now nicknamed the Holding Pen, which has its own door, one of only two, onto the killing floor of the *Royal* atrium's windy terrace) on the west side of the building beyond the digital production unit, with four other hotdeskers on unrelated tasks, including Sophie, the Junoesque IT consulto-specialist with whom Stuart and Geoff were once obsessed to the point of poetry.

Where the Holding Pen had once been a destination approached with some nervous excitement for the exciting changes Boddington and the process review were bringing to the *Royal London*, it was now the site of much tedium and leaden dread.

John Mayer and Martin from digiprod and even Hamish and Harriet had been invited to the process review meeting too. The uninvited tech eds sat around the tech ed end of digiprod. The feeling was mutinous, and the mutinous feeling expressed itself via a sort of miniature impromptu street party. Everyone stopped typing and stopped working and stood up and hovered at the ends of their desks. It was Margaret, Jane, James, George, Susan and Vivien and even Kristian. They gathered in the aisle by the printer where the shared snacks live. They ate the last of the least-liked chocolates from the last tin of Easter Quality Street that everyone was sick of (the clammy pink cream of Strawberry Delight, with its melancholy rumour of menthol). They talked about which flavour was their favourite and then other things they felt guilty about liking, like Hobnobs and chocolate digestives, and clothes-related discussions bloomed and died and they talked about who they'd heard was going to be fired.

Next they told small self-deprecating stories. They wanted warmth.

'So I went into the Regent Street Apple Store to buy a Magic Mouse for Kevin,' Margaret was telling James, 'and I didn't know how to buy it! I picked it up and I carried it around for ages looking for the till and there wasn't one and

I didn't know what to do. I didn't understand it at all. I'm *British*. I want to *queue*.'

None of it was serious but it was serious too. Margaret was over 50, a freelance single-income working-class hotdesker and a brilliant ironist in desperate danger as well.

'Who's going next,' said Jane. She meant to visit the meeting on whatever pretext. She had a wild look on. Beneath it all, this anger. Newly crowned as a managing editor, and still. 'Shall we draw lots?'

'Hoo hoo hoo! How many times can we just walk past the door?' said George.

'We need to put someone *inside the room*,' said Kristian with sudden viciousness.

'We need a spy.'

'You could go in with a pen and pad and pretend you're a stenographer.'

'You could take in the tea and just stand there in the corner and serve it.'

'You could pretend you're fixing the conference lines and get down under the table and then stay there, unresponsive to queries.'

Boddington had told tech ed, as part of their particular process review, and in the weird, confidential manner he had with them that seemingly arose from an otherwise rare lapse in his shark mode, in that he appeared to believe they shared something—something to do with a shelved novel he'd apparently composed, something to do with language, idealism, corruption, a horribly English emotion like a relaxing, shared defeat—one that no longer endeared him to them at all—had confided in them that he considered the culture at the *London* 'soft'. The way they dealt with each other, and with their authors, with their *audience*. 'All quite brilliant, heads in the clouds, utterly soft,' he said. Grinning, delivering a compliment. He seemed genuinely affectionate towards them, even and perhaps especially towards Jane, who—as the review dragged on and resources were lopped off and reallocated, as budgets shrank and she was forced to police more and more spreadsheets logging not just hours and papers and word counts and turnovers but numbers of actual edits, misspellings, corrections that Molesworth didn't make, as well as the errors Molesworth did, against the tech eds' various 'scores', plus sick days, errors missed, error/hour ratios, money to words published, etc., etc., and who, as she perhaps began to realise she was being forced to collate the case for not only Kristian's but also quite possibly her *own* dismissal—was growing very impatient with Boddington indeed.

And who in turn—Boddington—being the experienced and consummate professional process reviewer he was, grew friendlier and more convivial and chummy and charming. Baring those terrible teeth.

'I noticed something funny the other day, well I think it's funny,' Jane said.

'Meyehhrrss? What's that then?' said Susan.

'Well, somehow David not that David the other David, has gotten to whatever age and station he is thinking emeritus is pronounced emmer-itis. As in emmer-itis professor.'

'*Is* it then? Pronounced that way?' Margaret did her ingenuous blinks.

'Like it's some kind of condition.'

'David 2?' said James.

'Myeah. David 2. Emmer-itis. Like an inflammation. I know it's stupid and mean but it makes me laugh.'

'In my school,' said George, full-time, 50, and who

seemed to do nothing at the *London* but fix Word templates and was thus irreplaceable, 'there was a well-read boy who in his rare conversation referred to the *Nationalsozialisten* as the Nayzies.'

'I used to remember someone I worked with like that who pronounced banal like anal but with a b.'

'You never forget things like that do you.'

'The baynalitty of evil.'

'Like the boy who wet his pants. Even if now he's an MP or something like that, he's the MP who wet his pants.'

'Baynal Nayzies.'

'You could trick him into saying it out loud.'

'You could take him in a message to make him say it out loud in front of everybody.'

'I'd do it,' James said.

They gathered around his desk and roughed up a message for D2. There was a certain muted glee as they stood there, heads bent, hard at work. And because the Goddess's handwriting is, like her, singular and inimitable, they then typed up the message and printed it out and James carried it upstairs himself.

In the gloaming home he had run, then down the corridor of the Mansfield he'd limped, the cudgel he'd wrenched from an old oak still hanging from his hand. Filled to the skin with the run and the night, his shoulders square, his belly taut. That old paradox: he could go on forever, but he could go no farther. He had known that this was the last night, for the coming season of rage, his last night out on the Heath.

In the Mansfield ten years ago, a neighbour told him, you knew where to buy weed by the front door alcoves that had additional steel cages built on. Now everyone had the cages, even the last council places. He had unzipped his collar pocket, slipped out the hidden keys—two for the cage, two for the front door—and unlocked his gate and his door. Sealed it behind him—with deadlock, London and Manchester bars, one low, one high. He had laid the cudgel under his yellow Skellerup raincoat in the corner behind the door, with the baseball bat and the Husqvarna axe. The axehead in a leather sleeve and the metal box over the mail slot. The raincoat like a person hiding behind the door.

The apartment had been in darkness, just the streetlight coming through the kitchen door two storeys down, playing over the floor of the living room. Silence. He had descended the stairs—the ankle crackling and throbbing; the stairs creaking and cracking like Nijō Castle's nightingale floor. In the living-room darkness he had stopped and listened—nothing.

He had stripped going down the hall to the bathroom and nursery. He had showered as quickly and quietly as he could. Had made a burrito out of a Sainsbury's burrito kit and a very stiff gin and in his bathrobe eaten and drunk at his computer. It had begun to rain heavily outside and he hoped it would not wake her. An hour of the new Bond film and two more stiff gins. The possibility of masturbating to some YouPorn abandoned. Had rinsed the dishes, brushed his teeth, gone downstairs.

You should not have left her alone.

The windows of the Heatherington boardroom look out on the plane trees of Tavistock Square and their springtime loads of hayfeverish spores. From right down the institutionalised Victoriana of the hall—past HR, past the exec offices, the portraits of all the *Royal*'s past editors in chief, the big glossy wooden doors with their scuffed quarter moons of expensive mauve floral carpets laid down in a pre-internet New-Labour 90s with not a care in the world—he could hear the voices of the combined forces of *Royal London* Editorial: bored and loud and carrying on.

He broached the doors. An idle head or two turned his way and Death raised an eyebrow—James gestured a no. They were locked in a polyphony that even once resolved from an ambient roar into individual voices James couldn't quite fathom the oddness of at first. He circled the atoll of editors surrounding the lagoon of the immense pine veneer conference table, in the centre of which floated malignantly the dead black squid of the conference phone apparatus. Ibrahim al-Rayess at the corner nearest the door. The heavy hitters clustered together. Barbara Jones by Death. David 1. The three Trishes in an actual row. Helen Jackson. Hamish. Birgit. Rob. The skinny registrar. Beaming Benjamin Subramaniam and smirking Oliver Reed. He circled them. The Pheromone. Annabel Pitti again. Stuart and Martin from digiprod. John Mayer. Noticing that Mayer might have only been five foot five but he was built under his Oxford. Or not built but: *hard*. Compact and hard. The commando stuff with Helen on Clapham Common, then. Mayer looked up with a vacant grin, and mouthed for only James to see, bared teeth, pouty kiss and tongue, an idle, noncommittal *sweety dah-link*. Until he came to the shining white head and gingham shoulders of D2. He placed the message down in front of him, and D2 looked up coolly: 'From Claudia,' James said, and shrugged, and began to circle back, negotiating a route through the chaos of chairs and legs of editors at ease.

The message they'd roughed up was supposed to be a covert limerick, designed to entrap D2 in a public shaming over his elocution, with a mass group-laugh as a punchline that he wouldn't see coming, and would humiliate him, and it read: 'David can you please read aloud to all ASAP? John McIndoe has, after an op—right iris—contracted severe blepharitis. He cannot make it to the meeting as planned, and asked that I deliver this msg by hand: he'd like to invite us to his coming conferral—he's now prof emeritus.'

Already the stupidity of the idea hitting him. The waste. It was then he realised they were speaking to each other more or less in poetry.

'My mother is a fish,' murmured Helen Jackson.

'A pacifist is one who uses his open hand,' said Rob.

'Physicians value *fame* and *wealth* above the drooping patient's *health*,' said Oliver Reed smilingly.

'*Arva, beata petamus arva*! As Horace would have it, yacuntya,' said Hamish, looking gleeful and sounding actually Scottish for perhaps the first time ever.

'Hay-*mish*,' said Harriet. '*Rude.*'

They were bored, radically, brutally bored, impatient and idle in the face of severe and life-altering change, and Boddington the agent of this particular manifestation of the unrest still not present. Of maybe 30 in attendance a third were locked in deep conversation—the rest were communicating solely in literary quotes.

'And if,' pronounced the Lord Mayer faux-ponderously, with one of the confidential grins of a little boy post-fart, 'after the manner of men I have fought with beasts at Ephesus, what advantageth it me, if the dead rise not?'

'I would prefer not to,' murmured Martin.

'La la la. La la la la la. La la la,' said Hamish. 'S'Kylie, innit.'

'O wrangling schools, that search what fire,' said Barbara Jones very thoughtfully, 'shall burn this world, had none the wit unto this knowledge to aspire that this her fever might be it?'

'Oh well, very good,' sighed Death mildly, looking away. As if routine brilliance made him weary; its familiarity slightly disgusted him. The piecemeal, edgewise futility of high aspiration.

'Donne, innit,' said someone.

'Myerhss.'

The windows were open and from outside came a quite audible scream, followed by a voice which said, 'Ah me ears, shit fucking shit.'

The editors barely paused.

'The tip of the tongue taking a trip of three steps down the palate to tap, at three, on the teeth.'

'Lo, plain Lo, in the morning.'

'Myehhrss!'

'And I am the arrow, the dew that flies, suicidal, at one with the drive, into the red eye, the cauldron of morning.'

'Yes, well. Bit much, isn't it.'

'*My* favourite poems are set in Nantucket and Devizes, respectively.'

'A cricket team in their hospital whites—from far away doesn't a cricket match look as if someone is inefficiently being rescued?'

'With a heigh-ho, the wind and the rain.'

'Their relationship consisted. In discussing if it existed.'

'I always misspell it Syliva when I type. Saliva Plath.'

'Okay. There was a young man from Nantucket. Who put a Nazi bastard in a bucket. Daddy didn't buy me a fine, featureless pony. Black shoe I do not do me. I want a pony I want a pony I want a pony.'

'It's all degenerating. Denigrating. What's the word I want.'

'David knows his Chaucer. Do your Chaucer.'

'S'not that hard really is it?'

'No he does it in the Middle English though. Do it David.'

'Well it's quite easy really. Just do a Middle-English James Brown. Lots of suffixed uhs and ahs. Than-nuh pain I me to stretch-uh forth the neck-uh. Roll your Rs and stretch out your vowels. And east and west upon the people I beck-uh. Mine hand-is and my tongue goon so yern, that it is joy to see my busyness-uh.'

'Bit rude isn't it.'

'Go, little book, go little mine tragedy.'

'You've got to do the *accent*.'

'Life is a dream a little less inconstant.'

'Teach us to care and not to—'

'Nope. No Eliot, ever.'

'—care, teach us to sit still.'

'Shan't.'

'Do your lecture one.'

'Noooo.'

'Do it!'

'Since Merit but a dunghill is, I mount the rostrum unafraid: Indeed, 'twere damnable to ask if I am overpaid.'

'Auden.'

'Meyeehrss.'

'Physicians know *everything* and *do* nothing.'

'Hit me.'

'Myeehrs?'

'Baby one more time.'

'Surgeons know *nothing* and do *everything*.'

'Auden used to pee in his sink in his rooms at Christ Church, didn't he. You didn't have those rooms did you Trish?'

'Psychiatrists *know* nothing and *do* nothing.'

'Oh everyone does *that*.'

'Has anyone ever noticed how little difference there is between Coleridge and Agadoo?'

'No. Yes! No.'

'Pathologists know everything and do everything a day late.'

'In Xanadu did Kubla Khan a stately pleasure-dome decree: aga-doo-doo-doo, push pineapple, shake the tree. Where Alph, the sacred river, ran through caverns measureless to man, aga-doo—'

'S'cuse me. Thing here from Claudia she wants me to read aloud. Excuse me!'

As David 2 interrupted and everyone quietened and looked up to listen and he began to read aloud the forged message from Claudia, James turned again and looked at John Mayer. They met eyes. John nodded. Winked effortfully. With one hand he discreetly made the sign language for 'Y': thumb and pinkie extended, the rest of the fingers curled. Tipped it, like a pint, a couple of times. James nodded too, and smiled sickly, realising: though he had to carry on like this he couldn't carry on like this.

Ibrahim al Rayess sat in the corner of the room by the door, completely silent, watching it all.

Rising water

Dong.

James lay in bed in utter darkness.

Dong.

The sound that woke or stirred him. Utter dark. Had he heard it? It was viciously cold on his cheeks and feet. The faint hiss of the engaged Angelcare monitor. Sss. It had heard something. It flicked off. Or had it. Was that the rain. The endless, selfless rain tonight, neither abating nor settling in—a downpour unEnglish. Moving in? Strange thoughts. Living in a bell like a spider. A bronze tent. The canyons of Kotsifou in Crete. Goat's cheese and honey in the comb in the sun on a flowered balcony overlooking the valley. A thimble of violent raki. With her. A holiday a life ago. Debt. As irrevocable as myeloid leukaemia. You are your dead father. Have a child and then listen to yourself parrot him. Half-thoughts like unfinished bridges collapsing. He thumbed the alarm clock—it was not the apparent minutes ago he'd lain down. It was 4:20. What could make that hollow, ringing, metallic sound in this house? What was made of hollow steel? His crumbling thoughts moved slowly though the darkened, empty apartment, reaching out blindly for some purchase, for some other shore.

Dong.

It came again. It was right before him in the bedroom. Then *ssss* went the intercom, one pixelated red bar lit up. Far away, he heard it. The answering echo from her room: *dong*. It must be the radiator. She must be hitting the radiator. Where was the radiator in her room? At the corner of the Moses basket by her feet. She'd got free of the swaddle and she was sitting up and she was knocking on the heater. With her little fist. Fingernails like onionskin. Calling to him. It had echoed through the pipes to ring—*dong*—in the radiator down here.

Dong.

There was no way that could happen.

Someone.

He climbed out of bed on freezing numb feet and stiff legs and he limped in pyjama pants and T-shirt to the door and pulled his bathrobe on inside out. Desperate for more sleep; a delirium like being drunk; cognisant of his own impairment; the flowing slowly of his thoughts. Darkness of the house. The rains poured on. He climbed carefully up the lower stairs. Tried the familiar and muscle-memoried elaborate straddles and shuffles down the creaking corridor. Reality flickers—there are thoughts which don't make it to anywhere where there is capacity for action. He thought—*if I think there is someone in the house I need to move quickly in there and I need to bring a weapon*, but he didn't or couldn't, and simply went there.

Dong.

It came again, from the nursery (FIONA on the door, the A beginning to peel away) and the sound came again from the monitor below in a dopplered eerie echo.

Then the *crack*, the special crack of the floor from inside her room.

Someone.

He moved suddenly quickly and well and utterly awake, pushed the door open wide so they couldn't slam it back on him, an open stance, his fists raised, ready for—

—smell of cold. Violent wet and cold. Darkness. The Moses basket was a shaded ivory object oblong in the dark. Was she not in there? *Was she not in there?*

Not in there—but—a white shape. The swaddle. She was there. She was lying on her front, a little black bead on the white; her hair.

She had not got free; she had not touched the radiator at all. She was sleeping.

His freezing feet he'd thought snarled in ticklish muslin left over from a nappy change were colder than cold, and he turned up the dimmer very gently to a softish light.

The floor was full of flickering water. The floor was full of river water inches deep and he was standing in it up to his ankles. Plastic toys, a rubber ball, floated underneath her Moses basket and her swaddled sleeping larval form.

And leaves.

Leaves were floating all over the water filling her room. Great beech and birch and plane and ash tree leaves from up upon the Heath, leaves, flat and shining, rippling in sympathy, floating, floating everywhere.

literature the scientific literature, the medical literature, is OK
little, less, least as great, greater, greatest. Do not use lesser in ordinary prose.
live birth but stillbirth
live born a liveborn infant (but, the infant was live born)

Morning with Fiona

And then suddenly it was the weekend, and, for the single parent, the weekend stretches on.

Fiona woke at six with a gentle coo, a call, and some considerate murmurs. He woke immediately, calves stiff, about as rested as could be. He opened her door, pulled two towels from the shub's curtain rail, and slopped them down on the flooded floor to little avail, and sloshed across to her. She was fully swaddled but strangely content, contemplating him. He pulled the curtains open and she heaved gently once at the swaddle. He unripped the tab and opened it at her chest and her warmth came toasty from the white sleepsuit in the chill room. A smell that he'd forgotten, like Weet-Bix, rising off her. Her arms rose stiffly in jagged increments, and he saw that spooky echo again of how he felt the stiffness in himself. He recognised her again and did not know it would be that way—both selfish and not—that she would be so known. He bent and grasped her at the ribs, her armpits in the webs of his thumbs, and she heaved helpfully to get up, for him, a tiny *Nnnngh*. And he stood on the sodden towel with her, looking down at the flooded floor and the leaves he'd scooped and piled in the corner and then left there overnight.

'Good morning darling,' he said into her cheek.

She did not answer, but seemed to wait. They looked down at the water, and the creeping dark in the coir matting of the hallway.

'What are we going to do about this?' he said. His father's voice there. And what was this false confidence? This bravado? It wasn't some simple problem. A question like that implied an answer already known, didn't it?

She sneezed abruptly, her whole small body tensing then subsiding into him. A warm capsule in white towelling from his cheek to his bellybutton. 'Has this leaked in from . . .' he tried and then stopped. He didn't want this to be one of those days where he talked bullshit to her until he was exhausted. He'd read that single mothers ought to keep up the chatter, talk about real stuff, not baby talk, to make more bearable their time alone. Articulate your problems aloud, the books suggested, especially those with the baby. 'Now are we going to have X or Y for breakfast? Let's have X because it's good for your A, B and C,' and etc. It helped with your sanity and it was calming for the baby. James, however, started pretty badly with half-remembered nursery rhymes, then bastardised and bowdlerised popular songs (Beatles, Beyoncé, Beastie Boys), and wound up in totally inappropriate film quotes and fragments of song lyrics like the barely visible peaks of an iceberg of mental fatigue and inability to focus.

Because here it comes—he'd forgotten. He needed to go to the bathroom. He had to empty out all this water on the nursery floor before she returned for her morning nap, and figure out what it was and where it came from. He had to change her and feed her breakfast, which was now part solids or supposed to be (NICE guidance says six months). He then had to shower and get dressed without her leaving his sight (making plans here for the bouncer on the bathroom floor, door open to let out the steam, probably she won't have patience for him to shave). But most pressingly he had to take a shit, a pressing shit that would take at least five minutes, at *least* five minutes, and now he'd got her up she was too awake and alert to be laid back down in the Moses where she'd howl and scream in disappointment and distress and he wasn't going to put her in the Baby Bjorn within his sight and therefore within her sight, too, of him taking a shit. Sitting bouncing lightly on the bathroom floor as he sat looking back at her, making the various faces he supposed he made. So he'd have to wait until first nap, around 10 or 11 hopefully, and that seemed a long way off.

'I have to go to the bathroom,' he said experimentally, 'but . . .'

His feet were freezing and he stepped off the soaking pile of towels and carried her—high, proud, she looked ahead—down the creaking hall, up the stairs to dawn light coming up. He pulled the sliding door to the chill, chill morning and stepped out onto the welcome mat on the balcony. Josephine, the black-and-white cat from next door, erupted from the garden and leaped the fence. He hugged Fiona tighter in the cold. Steam goldly flowing from the air vents of the next apartment, and the next and the next.

To smell and love the morning.

She looked about.

'Birdy,' he said and pointed and she looked. 'Tree.'

There, a kind of grace.

The nursery had no drainage. It was a small room, about the size of a long double bed, and was designed to be a nursery, storage or study only. It was countersunk an inch or two, so the leak into the coir and the rest of the house was not serious. He fed her, and changed her, poo-less, and put her in the bouncer in the hallway, and started work: scooping up and bagging handfuls of leaves, then bailing out the water into the bathroom using her nappy bucket then the dustpan and dripping broom. 'Down at the fire station. Early in the morning. See the little fire engines. All in a row.' She watched him silently from the hallway as he sang and the lines were surely wrong and he repeated them because they were all he could remember.

He dropped all his towels into the flood to mop up what could not be bailed out. Still wearing his rolled-up pyjama pants and T-shirt, still shitless. Fiona was in the front pack, and he was bending sideways and leaning right and holding her tight so she didn't slip out, and carrying the towels to wring out in the bathtub, when the doorbell rang.

The plumber was here.

Fiona watched him as he investigated the room.

'Hiyo,' she said gently.

The plumber, a thin white Englishman in his mid-20s, in an orange Dyno-Rod Plumbing polo shirt several sizes too large, turned from his crouch at the base of the radiator he was exploring and said, 'Ha ha ha! Hiyo!' and both he and James looked at Fiona, and then James looked at him, and was obliged to smile—in his pyjamas, a mess.

'Ooweeaah,' she murmured, and looked around. 'Bldah, bldah, bldah.'

'Ha ha ha,' the plumber said. 'Yeah well you're gonna say that incha. Have to wait round for us to do our work.'

James laughed at that and her face changed. He stood sidelong so she could watch and her forehead cleared and she stared up to see what was funny to him, the whites of her eyes luminous and clean. Then she coughed, then she sneezed, and then a long line of drool fell from her mouth. The plumber laughed again distractedly, and started feeling his way up the back of the radiator.

'Sort of thing happened before?' he said to the wall.

'Never,' James said. 'It's been a nursery six months and it was storage before then. We've been here a year and I've not seen anything like this. I've been here a year.'

'Yeap.'

Fiona moaned terribly and moved sideways in the front pack.

'And another thing,' James said, 'while you're here. The washing machine's making everything stink. Comes out stinking musty.'

'Have to log another call mate,' the plumber said. He was brisk and bright. 'But I'll tell you what it is. Leave you a bag of boric acid to put it right. Run it through a cycle and you'll fix it. Water round here. It's heavy.'

Fiona grasped James's arm, then his hand, and drew his knuckle into her mouth where she gummed it hard.

The plumber turned to them. 'She got an appetite then! HELLO!' He shouted at her, a huge grin. 'HELLO!' Then, to her, or as if to her, 'Run a bag of boric through it, empty. Couple a rinses to make sure. Don't let her near it.' He made a mad face at her. 'Burn her up if she gets it in her eyes. It's a fiver.'

'That's fine,' James said.

'Look mate, I'm sorry I've got no idea where this lot has come from.' He looked then genuinely apologetic, sorry and a little wary. 'It's not from anywhere I can see in the baseboard or the wall and I can't see any kind of rising in the flooring—look here'—he indicated the seam of wall and floor right around. 'Good tight joins and there's no actual plumbing through here!' He sounded suddenly incredulous. The great act of English manners. 'There's nothing to leak! Pipes go through the wall over there. The pan's outside. Only thing I can think of is there's problems with groundwater in the area 'cos you know the old Fleet River's down there somewhere always looking to come back up.'

'Yeah,' said James. 'Under the Fleet Road. Past the hospital.'

'That's right. That's right. One of her ways. But she comes down both sides of the Heath. Just about right under you. Follow the ponds—the east Heath has a branch too. Always looking to come back up.' He looked a bit troubled.

'D'you want a cup of tea?' said James.

They stood in the living room sipping their tea and looking down at Fiona futzing about on the floor. Her legs in a soft white horseshoe, she moved a doll from hand to hand. They stood there at an oblique angle to each other. James had paid him for the consult, for nothing, and it was embarrassing to both of them.

'Yeah,' said the plumber finally. 'Nope, I'm sorry. Because I know for a fact round here there's been cases where someone's excavated out their basement and it rains the next day and they go downstairs the whole thing's a pond. Because your river's just there somewhere innit. Bloke out of that band wanted to build a studio. And that's just about all I can think of 'cos there's nothing else there that could put that kind of water in there in that quantity, do you know what I mean?'

'Yeah,' said James. He was still wearing his pyjamas and it was getting on to 10am. 'What can I do about it then.'

'Issue for your landlord mate.' He looked down at Fiona. 'Clean it up. Tell your landlord. Hope for the best!'

'Well all right then.'

A small slightly uncomfortable quiet fell.

'Biscuit?' said James, uselessly.

It was approaching an ambiguous time, towards 11, when Fiona threatened to nap, or not to nap. He had formula and nappies but now otherwise no food in the house. So here was the plan: put the heater on in her room to dry it out somewhat, forget the shower, forget the shit, put on jeans and jacket, get Fiona outside for some air to help her nap, to the off-licence for kielbasa, hotdog buns and Colman's for lunch, home for a nappy change, hopefully full of poo, then formula in his lap on the daybed and down for a nap, in a cleaned and warmed-up nursery, a hugely relieving visit to the bathroom with the Angelcare in hand, praying she won't wake, then a shower, maybe, and hotdogs for lunch if time allowed and if lunch was interrupted, unfinished when she woke, that was all right. They could eat together. And it would be all right. And then it would all start again and go on forever.

So he carried her and the front pack downstairs to the bedroom and dropped her a comedic inch onto the bed, squeezed her thighs and upper arms and put on some clothes before she could pull herself to the edge of the mattress. He put on the front pack and lifted her in, and sang gently to her as he arranged her legs. 'Hey, Fiona, what's that sound? What's that sound that's goin' round? Hey Fiona?' This was a portmanteau of 'Stop! Children, what's that sound?', a Dusty Springfield anti-war song he half remembered from *The Muppets*, and the melody from the chorus of John Denver's 'Calypso' that got stuck in a loop from which it could not escape. He sighed, and sang it again.

Outside the cage the street was leafy, sleepy and damp, the sun at 11-something a white, soft explosion above the estate. Down the other, Gospel Oak station end of the estate's covered way—a sort of dead, elevated end for pedestrians but one with three distinct exits—there were four or five kids, smoking and hooded, and a big dog. The other way, too, there was another group, at the off-licence end. With their own big dog, a Rhodesian ridgeback. A bundle of Fiona warm and attached to his chest, still borne up by the infant insert, in a cuddle round his ribs. He headed down the corridor towards them; halfway down he'd drop down the steps to avoid passing them and the dog. Just avoid it—the tiresome thing of avoiding eye contact, of dealing with the smart comments, the tiring bullshit of always, always passing them by. Each apartment had a terraced window box full of hopeless soil. Some had ivy; most were dead. One had three perfectly round and topiaried shrubs, which were plastic. This morning one plastic shrub was missing. Fiona's eyes were wide and she looked about and James sniffed deeply the morning and said, 'Mmmm! Smells good!' He sang her two more verses and then he stopped. He approached the kids, three white, one black—16, 18, he didn't even know anymore. Eating kebabs; off the street. The huge dog at their feet.

And he didn't go down the steps this time.

The problem and the boon of the Mansfield covered way was that everyone could see everyone else coming a hundred metres off. So back at the Gospel Oak end they could see the feds pull up and be away down the steps, down the wheelchair ramp at the other end and behind the estate, or back down the corridor, depending. They could scatter easy, divide the boydem, and be on the Heath or lost in the Lismore in minutes. Here at this end you were funnelled in and it was getting like this: more and more it was becoming a place to sit, shelter, to smoke and drink. And so, for the residents, a place to negotiate and to fear. James always said nothing. Nothing or sorry. 'Sorry,' he would say, and turn slightly to sidle through the group. Because he never knew if it was going to be kids from the Lismore or real trouble, since the fires and the rapes last summer. So when he had to get past he prepped himself, generally, put on a cold, cold face, and said his 'Sorry' tonelessly, with a faint air of withheld threat. Always, always waiting for the first thing to happen, and he wondered how it was for the council tenants, the old woman in 23A who claimed to have been married to some famous 60s musician James hadn't been able to locate online, or the ancient Irishman at 49B who only ever went out to Morrison's.

There were two sitting on the wall and two standing facing them with the dog at their feet and he would probably have to pass between them, by the dog, not go around, but this was a decision they would make for him by whether and where they chose to move. The big young ridgeback lay on the ground watching him over its paws, concerned eyes a shade of tobacco brown darker than its coat. James was the father of a baby, he was a nearly 40-year-old man, and he was sick of this shit and wished he'd brought his knife. The two who were sitting looked his way, then away—then so did the other two. He had to be calm. He could handle himself. What kind of fucking little rotter hassles a man with a baby. And they were almost finished their food so he was probably all right—full belly, who wants to start something? These are the kinds of computations he makes. He had at least briefly forgotten he needed the bathroom. Noticing then that the left-hand seated one wore the black hoodie with hologrammed letters that read GRAVIS.

Myasthenia gravis. *Myasthenia*: muscular weakness. *Gravis*: serious. He'd edited it for a clinical review. 'A chronic autoimmune disorder of the postsynaptic membrane at the neuromuscular junction in skeletal muscle.' AKA 'rag doll' syndrome. Usually initial presentation was fatigability, and ptosis—drooping eyelids. Old men who have to hold an eyelid open in order to read the *TV Guide*. A woman who feels guilty when her hand feels too heavy to hold a cup of tea. Goes to bed earlier and earlier until she sleeps more than she doesn't. And slurring her speech when at long last she phones her daughter for help. To work hard and to be valued for it. To make some money. The clouds above full and rich like something lost, a dream of RAF skies.

Two girls on the street below the wall suddenly came into view, only 12 or 13, and one of them was singing. The dog lifted its head, dark muzzle and furrowed brow smoothing, to smell him. James passed between the boys, stepping over the tongue-cleaned tubs of their chips, over the big dog's paws, concentrating on the hair of Fiona's head, her eyes rolling towards them. Three of the boys swung round at the girl's voice. '*Cunt,*' the youngest boy said, to the girls or James he didn't know. Almost involuntarily fast. Like a line he had studied hard to deliver, his first and only, and here his cue had come at last, and it was over, and he was almost surprised his job was done.

He passed through, holding his daughter, giving the boy who'd said the word his back, placing his body between them, watching the one with the GRAVIS hoodie to see if he was recognised.

At the off-licence his hunger was gone. Sick, achy and empty in his stomach. From the scratched metal shelves that seemed to be emptying before him he bought the supplies—the old fruit, the yoghurt, the vacuum pack of cheap, fatty Polish kielbasa packaged in Birmingham, the empty, stale hotdog buns, the jar of faithful Colman's Hot English. Milk, just two pints to keep the carry bag light, and Fiona was wriggling now. Gently heaving up in the front pack, letting him know she wanted to be free.

The Turk who owned the off-licence was the father of a daughter too, and though fluent in English he seemed to cycle in his monolingual male friends and relations to staff the tills in the endless hours the place stayed open. The one who'd stayed the longest they'd nicknamed Shrek, back then. He was big and soft-eyed, gentle, a little dull. He murmured only 'Hello' and the price and that was as far as it ever went. Even when James came in almost every day. Even when the recycling bins on the far side of the street were on fire, he could not be summoned to action—'Do you have any water?' James had said, pointing to the smoking bins. There'd been a queue. The Turk had pointed vaguely to the 330ml bottles of Volvic in the wall fridge.

'Seven pound. Fifty pee.'

James paid and left. The girls were gone, the four were still there and he would have to go through them again. If he went down on the street beneath he'd be obviously avoiding them and might be spat on or, worse, recognised from the night before and what then?—but really the point was fuck them, that's why.

He remembered coming to Camden the first time, fresh off the boat—he didn't understand the street markings, what those alarming jagged zigzags meant. He crossed the road, and turned to go up the ramp. Low half-light, white, and puddles. Leaves on the concrete squashed and waterlogged to a gelatine.

Now there were only three, plus the dog; the GRAVIS one had gone, where? And they'd moved—deliberately?—together to block the way. He couldn't get through.

'Sorry,' James said, toneless, as he approached them.

'*Thawy*,' the young white one said automatically, imitating him in deepened voice, his tongue stuck out through his teeth, his head hunched down and the other two laughed and one said, low and mildly, 'Koff you cunt, I'll fucking eat that baby, I'll bite his whole arm off.' The third boy's face, so closed he had hardly any eyes, leaned forward. He kissed his teeth. He said what sounded like '*Killa da Babylon*' and it was a Saturday morning and boys get bored.

The eyeless one twitched at the dog's leash. But James passed through them then, stepping carefully over the dog's ragged paws and he'd left them well behind when at the top of the last steps before his apartment the fourth boy burst abruptly up beside him out of the stairwell and James only had time to turn his back.

The GRAVIS boy thumped into him sidelong, and James protected Fiona, his back to the boy, bending away and looking over his shoulder.

'You fucking muppet,' said the boy, coming out of his hunch with a hand on his upper arm. 'You dizzy, blud, you fucking muppet, come on,' he said louder and shoved James high on the shoulder, his arm stiff, his face a washed mask.

Down the corridor the dog sat up to see.

James didn't say anything. As if programmed he put down his shopping, wrapped his right arm tight around the baby and did a stupid, stupid thing.

A fox in the garden

There was a fox in the garden. All muscle. Dark and tawny.

He'd watched its progress over the fence of each apartment's yard. Up above was Josephine, the cat from next door, high in the honey locust. She was crouched and wary, folded up like a fist, watching it too. The fox had climbed the fence and spotted James standing motionless on the balcony smoking his first cigarette in six months. James had kept his last stale half-pack of Bensons when he quit, like someone in a film. The fox got stuck halfway, struggling, scrabbling, hanging on his belly over the rail, eyes rolling up at James, who didn't move, smoking.

Sent back how many times, a fox?

The cat watched from the tree, as close to death as she might ever come. In time the fox fell over in a clumsy tumble, and paused in the garden to look up at James. Dark gold and watchful. They stared at each other. What it couldn't see was that it had three more apartments, four more fences to go, each higher than the last. And after, still, the dog and the despoiled street to come.

Holding her safe and away James had reached out quickly with his left hand and seized the meat of the boy's neck as if his fingers were a claw. His nails caught in the skin under the boy's jaw and bit in and then he'd crushed the trachea hard. The boy had made a squealing and a creeching sound straightaway and James clenched his fist as hard as he could till the boy didn't make a noise but a scraping and something moved quick and liquidly under his fingers and the boy was pulling away, twisting his body, falling beneath him. James had held Fiona tightly with his right arm and leaned with him, pushing him to the ground. He'd looked back, checked the dog. The other boys hadn't noticed what had happened yet and though the big ridgeback was standing at attention, staring his way, it had not chosen yet to move or bark.

Then James had picked up his shopping and walked away down the corridor.

James dragged on the stale cigarette, looked at the colour of the stuff under his fingernails. The rattling and clanging on the cage and the shouting had stopped 15 minutes ago. He'd go out there later in the full dark to clear and wash away what they had thrown, whatever they had left.

The Angelcare was silent.

Fiona was asleep.

They would come back for him.

The fox jogged across his garden to the next fence to the next yard to do it all over again.

Swollen pussy tonsils

'Swollen pussy tonsils,' Trish said.

James almost said something awful like 'My wife is dead and gone' but instead he managed, 'Mmhmm.'

Trish Gravely was at James's desk with the marked-up proof of a Des Bernard piece. The piece was about patients who lie to their GPs, and managed somehow to incorporate Wordsworth, water polo, and trace amounts of broad-spectrum antibiotics in Indian rivers.

(Patients apparently simply *demand* antibiotics in India, no matter what the issue, and snub doctors who don't or won't prescribe. Which with a population of 1.2 billion leads to massive overprescription, big and under-regulated pharma factories, drug spills, and dumps of expired stock directly into water sources, and thus ultimately the rise and rapid spread of very bad drug-resistant bacterial pathogens indeed.)

Trish was duty ed and however strict on stats and medical content usually rather relaxed on syntax, diction, punctuation. Each duty ed had their own MO. With the tech eds as their minions and editors as their underlings, duty eds formed and shaped that arcane and uncategorisable thing, with Claudia at the head, that is the *Royal* style.

Dr Death, senior amongst the lieutenant editors, was

infamous for his hack and slash, a violence to authors and to sloppy prose, to questionable content and poor editing. He had hips like a matron and a boxer's swinging shoulders. Though no family was extant and no unsavoury comments or behaviour recorded, he had an enigmatic and somehow aggressively heterosexual vibe. A man with tastes he had the charisma to indulge. He liked to spike, unmercifully, articles that had been on the books for months, years; 800- or 8000-word papers that had gone through three or four peer reviewers, that had been back and forth to author from editors, tech editors and proofreaders. That had been described as 'in press' on CVs that got people jobs. He undid all their work in a moment, usually in person. He *liked* it. He reamed; he reversed elegant variations. He axed; he struck through. He liked it linear, factually correct and to the point. He was the journal's hard and spiky, fishy spine. Though his rostered days as duty ed were met with tired dread and a great and weary mustering of attention and focus and preparedness for last-minute substitutions and reshufflings and rewrites and he was seen as a make-work and a hassle and a witch in the bracken, the truth was that Death was good-humoured, frightening and patrician and almost always right, and you'd better listen closely because at the very least he always had a very good point.

So, depending on the article, Trish Gravely as duty ed was refreshing. But editing as a job meant—because of all this, and because of the process review, and because one didn't do much actual talking during a working day—tech eds can seem or in fact be pretty defensive and prickly when approached. And here was Trish at his shoulder with some severely marked-up copy from transposable Bernard who'd been using some Wordsworth that James hadn't seen before in his stuff (he ought to keep a log of his quotations) but that the proofreader had already signed off on and that should have been ready to build to CMS and be basically done and dusted by now.

The piece had dialogue; in part it was a mock consultation between the author-surrogate doctor and a patient who is lying about what's really wrong with him, and at one point the increasingly impatient doctor character rather gruffly says to the patient character, 'Don't stutter.'

'It's a bit bloody arrogant but—' said Trish.

'Yeah, ha ha, well he always is—'

'And I think cut the line about—what does it say. "Don't stutter." The doctor's talking to the patient, saying—'

'Don't stutter?'

'Yes, I think we'll cut the "Don't stutter".'

'Yes, don't stutter, ha ha—'

Trish was grinning and engaged. At the end of a Friday James was living in Word templates, intricately worded email queries. He was on the edge of a sour-tasting sweet spot, the outlands of the Zone, commencing the burnout after a ten-month run of editing form where he could catch bold and unbolded periods, roman or italicised commas, where he could see an en dash where an em dash should be without even *reading* the page per se, just by glancing at it. Just glancing at an A4 page like it was a freshly painted wall (a hair raised and wavy, a shadow in the enamel) or a piece of sculpture or fabric and he could see the flaw in the weave, from a distance—without requiring the involvement, the emotion or engagement, *the complication*, of actual reading. James was at the stage where he no longer tolerated a space after a period at the end of a para. It doesn't matter that it was invisible and didn't trouble the XML. The contempt he sometimes felt for authors who can't put their periods and commas inside their quoted dialogue, who can't seemingly close a parenthesis, who can't distinguish which and that—it's *vicious*.

The *contempt*, and then the *self-disgust*.

David 1—classics at Magdalen, not a medical doctor—had managed to make the transition to lieutenant editor well enough; gently, firmly and somewhat distractedly, with a certain weary flair, he tore massive holes in technical editors' grammar, usage and self-esteem. It's probably not very common knowledge that most tech eds are very instinct-guided and seat-of-the-pants, certainly as they advance in their careers, if not when they get started. They're readers, primarily, and often as not they are or were creative writers—novelists, poets, playwrights, usually the first—on indefinite hiatus, failed, or unbegun. Most editors are failed writers, but so are most writers, as Eliot had it. A lot of failed writers were failing editors too, these days. It was hard work, on a Friday, having David 1 up in your face saying—quite gently for David 1, given his general mode of slightly fey uptightness, of total yet gentle aggression in service of the correct and the to-the-point, though however sweetly and winningly counterbalanced by his complete and utterly charming willingness—even gladness—to be corrected—but having David 1 at your desk at 3:30 on a Friday, gently reviewing your copy edit, gently asking incredibly involved questions, gently and rapidly telling you that well *he* was taught that the use of *polysyndeton* is really only a bit of a mannerism, isn't it, sort of designed a little bit isn't it to affect what could you call it a bit of *pseudobiblical* authority and gravitas off the back of the King James the prose wouldn't or couldn't otherwise muster on its own but oh well if you think that's all right, fine, fine!—and floating off leaving you ostensibly deferred to but also dazzled and humiliated somehow, like he did with everyone.

It was hard work.

(A series of conjunctions, you found out later, googling it; like this and then this and then that and then that.)

James had seen it in others, in Kristian and Susan, and felt for them, and he had felt it in himself—the total blankness that comes when queried on a specific decision after fixing all these tiny things:

Although at the time of course convinced I was right I cannot now summon for you a justification for what I did there.

There's inevitably some idiosyncratic verbal obfuscation, then, as the tech ed concerned got his or her head into gear. James quickly learned to say, 'Can I get back to you on that?' and to deploy only half-ironically the classic bit of passive-aggressive call-centre semaphore: 'If you could just bear with me a moment.'

But the most common response was the one most satisfactory to all, the one with total authority, that stood behind and beyond decisions that might seem bizarre, arbitrary, wilful and foreign to everything you'd ever been taught and relied upon and comfortably assumed unassailable fact:

'Check the style guide.'

Royal Lond J Med style: so discursive, so ranging, evolved, dense, deep and broad, no one person can claim to represent it or know it exhaustively. It's Borgesian, encyclopaedic, labyrinthine. *Guardian* style, for e.g., is a 362-page large-point actual hardback book. Generous of margin and for sale: £19.99 at Waterstones. *Royal London* style is over 500

10-pt Verdana single-spaced pages of virtually zero-margin Word doc. *Not* for sale. One of James's tasks on the side of regular editing is the conversion of the whole doc and associated tracked changes to an online wiki. *Royal London* style is the product of 140 years of not only medical and surgical but of medico-lexical evolution—from griping in the guts and impostumes to positron emission tomography; from dropsy and falling-sickness ('period' hyphenation, please, and lowercase) to gluten free (no hyphen) and gammaglutamyltranspeptidase (one word); from the Doctors' Plague (caps, and append 'maternal puerperal fever' in parentheses unless clear from context) to disintegrations per second (DPS), to DSM-V (spell out), to dotcom, DOTS and DXT to DOIs, dB, DBCLT, D Day, DDR, DDT and never, ever, ever say 'doctoring'—but also rapid, comprehensive adjustment to imperial expansion, aseptic surgical techniques, antibiotics, post-imperial contraction, the discovery of DNA, meta-analysis, worldwide publication, web and mobile. It has a feel, a taste, an authority. It's unimpeachable—it has arguments with itself any dissenter must first try to absorb in order to mount any sort of challenge. Which it, in turn, absorbs. This all goes on out of sight. You'll never know the influence it has. The rumour goes: the first editor to compile the stylebook was blind or blinded during the Blitz; some frail and ailing Miltonic figure lying full-length on army stretcher in darkened basement offices dictating key initial axioms in laboured gasps to a devoted secretary leaning over candle and lend-lease Smith Corona. The stylebook itself has track changes activated. It's so big and dense that every time it repaginates, your current document as well as your browser become completely unresponsive. It's a corporate secret, subject to nondisclosure and espionage agreements.

It's unpredictable. You start to gather a feel for its rulings but you can never know until you check that specific entry, and then when thus punctured, corrected, you find yourself nodding, hunched, receding quietly, murmuring slightly pained assent. Even the most experienced copy editors here, when in dispute, will go to its pages tumescent with certainty and return flaccid and quietened with a third completely unexpected, authoritative ruling. It's surprising. It's Delphic, oracular, paternal, testamental, lapidary and yet still dynamic and fluctuating and alive. Its first line reads, 'Please write in a clear, direct, and active style.' (That '*Please*'.) It has a fossil record. It contains traces of the many editors who've come and gone, ghosts in the tracked changes of those whose contributions have been deleted or updated. Experienced disco poets here can cite particular entries as being in the style, the certain tone, of this or that head copy editor from decades ago. It is the stylebook: it is civil society, the model institution, the great modernist novel, organised life, man as an ordered political animal, civilisation, and its critique.

Just off Gray's Inn Road, a dozen 14-year-old boys rounded a corner into Mecklenburgh Square to find the other group of young boys whom they'd been seeking there. They called out, 'Manor House, Manor House, bitches,' and had at it for not much more than 30 seconds before they scattered.

The last boy to leave was dragged from the corner by his parka's raglan shoulders with a 10-inch serrated bread saw firmly embedded 5 inches deep intracranially along the right infra-orbital margin, beneath the globe and passing directly between the two internal carotid arteries, fortunately for him.

That is, a nearly foot-long bread knife jammed halfway into the bottom of his eyesocket.

Attempts by the other boys to remove the knife were hindered by inadequate purchase on the item due to secretions of blood and clear liquids from the wound and the very public sounds and urgent movements of the boy's protests, and ultimately resulted in the handle breaking off. The boy, otherwise alert and orientated, was then walked by his friends right past Great Ormond Street Hospital, past UCL Hospital's emergency services (blinking slowly at wide-eyed Spanish tourists over the blade along which he looked), past the Portland Hospital and the entire two and a half miles to the Western Eye Hospital on Marylebone Road because it had eye in the name and one boy's grandmother went there once.

There the boy and his squad of 11 sat down quietly among the dozens of stately, ancient sufferers of diabetic retinopathy in the day-case clinic waiting area for 20 minutes or more before the receptionist noticed the white boy with a bread knife stuck in his face—

—'bruv it's *itchy*'—

—and ushered them all off round the corner to A&E with hoarse exhortation to for God's sake get him in *there* you silly young buggers.

'"Don't stutter",' Trish said. 'You could put something like, "Now, think before you speak," couldn't you. Or couldn't you?'

'Yes, we'll cut that.'

Her idea was a bad solution. He could see it wouldn't work and so could she. He would think of something better and she would like it, but *just not right now*.

'You're not going to stutter if you don't have a stutter, and if you *haaaave* . . .'—she drew it out long and parentally assured—'. . . that's cool.'

James smiled.

Trish: 'Now . . .'

Indicating the phrase.

'HA HA HA,' said James not very convincingly.

'"Swollen pussy tonsils".'

'"Swollen pussy tonsils".'

'"Swollen pussy tonsils". I googled it, which you really don't want to do.'

The passage read: '"Earth has not anything to show more fair," said Wordsworth, "than a big pair of swollen pussy tonsils." *Ubi pus, ibi evacua*, as they say. It's always a welcome sight to us general practitioners because it means we can fire ahead and prescribe antibiotics with a clear conscience and avoid yet another draining fight.'

'Pus-covered?' said Trish.

'Pustulent? Purulent? Pus-covered? Is "draining fight" meant to be a pun?'

'Pus-covered, I think.'

'It's not very elegant.'

'No.'

'All right.'

'Done.'

Annabel Pitti

Emily Firman was, as mentioned, in her mid-60s, and she had a new amanuensis whom she was vigorously grooming to replace herself ('Goodbye tension—hello pension'). This new apprentice was promoted out of tech ed. Her name was Annabel Pitti and in her new position she'd been promoted out of several complex relationships and one case of low-level sexual harassment.

And promoted far out of her admittedly smallish comfort zone, Annabel Pitti. From the world of tech ed, where real-life conversational interactions might be managed down to:

Death [returning a proof of a pretty dubious article they were having to go ahead with anyway]: Annabel, that's brilliant. Absolutely, totally brilliant in its composition.

Annabel: Hu-hah hah hah!

[utter silence]

Death [pointing]: And after consultation of the style guide I see 'non-' here takes a hyphen but 'anti-' doesn't, apart from a couple of baffling instances.

Annabel: Hu-hah hah hah!

[utter silence]

From this cool and quiet world, promoted into a land where she was required, as assistant news editor, to be a proper journalist, on the phone to high-level personages sniffing out stories, penetrating mystifications, puncturing facades, announcing her surname very quickly in hyper-Italianate pronunciation, teasing out unravelling threads, dispelling smokescreens, reading twixt lines, etc. Probing. Seeing if people were lying, for example, evading or misrepresenting or judiciously editing. She was required to milk stories out of hardbitten and hardbiting economic, medical and political brains accustomed since kindergarten to fighting off PM's-questions-level weakness-probing. She was not long in the job and her coldest fear was that she was possibly not long *for* the job, and her ongoing efforts to manage the stress and give the new position a good whack, her best foot forward, were being watched not just by the Pheromone but by Editorial at large, just as closely as they were watching the slow-motion Morrissey implosion (on which more later), though with substantially more emotional investment, and hope for the future.

That is, she was teetering, and they were cringing, but with her as opposed to Adrienne Morrissey there was at least a *chance* of a happy ending.

Annabel had had to develop a phone manner. Most of her interviews were done over the phone, directly across the desk divide from her new boss and within earshot of a good third of Editorial. And how she was managing it at present—hunched and whispering—was doomed and completely unsustainable. It added (her terrible phone manner) to the collective sense, in Editorial, of the weird vicarious dread and embarrassment and hope that surrounded her. To the extent that one single and rather oblique mention of the idiosyncratic qualities of her dutiful, mirthless, *enounced* and unmischievous laughter— laughter that sounded like nothing less than the forlorn cry of a tame bird marooned at sea, blighted by the loss of its mate and masters in some spontaneous and ridiculous ship-sinking ('Hu-hah hah hah!')—a single mention of Annabel's ghostly, terrible laugh, made by the delicate and subtle Rob, who was usually highly attuned to such gossamer social moments, a mention made at the Cider Tap in front of Euston station to a select crowd the previous Friday had, instead of a brilliant flurry of vicious and energising repartee, brought about a rapid and barely detectable exchange of glances and averted glances, followed by sipped drinks and a complex silence that spread and settled like a flung white flannel sheet. Silence, even from John Mayer, high priest of quiet, witty cruelty. This silence might have been interpretable as either he'd gone just a bit too far, been too mean, failed to really imagine her life and her history and the very strangeness of people and the struggle her laugh represented, or that 'there are just too many of us here and thus too many unknowns for this sport to safely be indulged in', a loose lips and volatile relationships situation, or, what was more likely, really:

—that there was an attractive quality to the fine edge of her desperation. To her increasing dependence on cycling and other forms of extreme physical activity and elaborate discussion of said extreme physical activity, coupled with a new thing, her out-of-the-blue smoking. That there was something, in fact, in her desperate and high-English awkwardness that caused a delicious and pleasurable pain for the staff of the *Royal London*, like pressing a healing bruise (and for which there was a medical trope in the palpation of an abdomen: exquisite tenderness). She prolonged the agony, her own, and this was the essence of her exquisite comedy, and her tender drama.

It was essentially relaxing to watch her suffer.

The last clean teaspoon

James left work at 6:03pm and walked across Tavistock Square. He did not pause at the 168 bus stop there but continued north on foot. He waited at the lights on a teeming Euston Road and crossed. Past the Cider Tap to the south entrance to Euston station, where he queued to withdraw £400 from an ATM and then walked on to wait at the next stop for the 168. Three 253s halted before a crowded 168 rolled up. Two thirds of the bus disembarked there and then he got on, went upstairs and took a seat. He read his novel on his Kindle as they drove.

Up Eversholt Street. In Camden the traffic thickened. Coaches held up the lights and the bus came to a halt. James looked out his window. On the street outside the plywood shutters of the windows of the wrecked Foot Locker was a man. An average-looking man, a dad, friendly, maybe 50, broad and thick in the chest and belly. He stood on the pavement half smiling down the street at the oncoming people. He singled out a girl of around 20. As she came towards him he stepped forward and smiled and almost bowed, and he spoke to her. She stopped, her face inquisitive and polite. He held up his wrist and forearm and he spoke. She swung her backpack round, reached inside a side pocket and pulled out her phone and showed him the screen. He appeared to thank her and she smiled and appeared pleased and then she edited the emotion and went blank and walked on. As she passed him, his head went sideways and he turned to follow her, watching her body moving, leaving him. He was grinning differently. Then he turned again and looked up the street into the foot traffic. James watched him. Things just fail and fall down, don't they. Just up there some years ago a William Hill sign fell off the store front and killed a man. Things fail and get torn down. Just down there on the Hampstead Road the sign frontage of a failed service station had been peeled off and all that remained of the business were swirls of dark, cracked glue that looked like a message in that Sri Lankan language, Sinhalese: all those serifed hearts and kidneys. Things get destroyed and the new thing revealed. Just up there and back a street, the frontage of a failed real estate agency had been ripped down to reveal a joyous, foot-high graffito on the raw wall behind that James loved, and that read in its entirety: WILSON YOU NUT. Another girl came along, about the same age, 20-something, in running gear. The man's face went smiling and paternal again. He inclined towards her out of the crush, and raised his wrist as he spoke, and half bowed, as courtly as a man from a dream of another century asking for a dance.

He'd done the same whole thing three more times before the 168 moved on. All girls, all in their 20s. Tie-dyed tapestries big as a wall. Orange juice squeezed fresh. Kebabs. *Good girls go to heaven, bad girls go to London* read the T-shirts for sale at the stalls by Camden Lock.

Up Haverstock Hill. Halted in traffic at the Belsize Park shops James saw the Syrian doctor Ibrahim al-Rayess amongst the clumps of raincoated commuters emerging from the tube station. His arms were full of expensive-looking shopping bags in sober racing greens and navy blues, brands in gold and serifed fonts. The doctor moved deliberately and economically. At the pavement he turned and went back down the hill like a child's idea of a robot, different from the Camden dad, his head just following his body.

James disembarked at South End Green loomed over by the Royal Free and bought a bottle of Tanqueray, a baguette and a tub of tomato soup from the M&S. Where he'd normally buy a bottle of Gordon's and have a half of Guinness at the White Horse before taking the route of the old Fleet River down to the Lismore end of Mansfield to get a kebab and meet his babysitter, he took instead Constantine Road, a block back from his street, and crossed the train tracks at Roderick Road onto the Heath. He walked fast in the twilight down the joggers' path by the overgrown children's playground. All the way to the Lido and the long grass behind Gospel Oak station. He came back out onto the street where he stood anonymous among the comers and goers outside the station. Across from the closed-up Old Oak he stood and watched his building from the other end of his usual approach.

After a while he walked quickly up Mansfield then took a right, opposite and away from his door and up Savernake Road and round the bend to Estelle Road, where he walked quietly and slowly down the obscured side of the street back towards the estate entrance. He stopped under the last tree outside the doors of the off-licence and watched the estate corridor and the approaches from the Lismore for ten minutes. He got his keys out of his pocket. There were two barrel keys for the barrier and the front door, an Abloy for the padlock, and a four-sided Yale for the deadlock. He fitted the base of the first barrel key firmly into the palm of his hand, with the barrel and teeth protruding an inch and a half from his fist between his middle and ring fingers. Locked in place by the fold of skin at the base of his palm, and the wedding ring he wears on his right hand instead of his left. Which she never understood, and ribbed him about. *Are you pretending you're not married?*

He walked down the block back towards the station with his head down. Halfway there he crossed the road at a jog, his fist down at his thigh, ducked between parked cars, climbed the stairs, unpalmed the keys and quickly let himself inside.

It was all dark and quiet as he descended the creaking steps. This meant Tatia was still putting Fiona down. He closed the living-room curtains and turned on the lights. The day's mail was piled on the coffee table: a catalogue from Hilditch & Key, a *Royal London* payslip, junk mail, and a piece of unstamped printer paper unevenly cut to the size of a postcard on which in black capital Times New Roman in a generous point size, like it was a ransom note, was printed the words CHEYNE STOKING.

In the kitchen the formula was still out on the bench and the sink full of the day's milky bottles. He put his dinner in the fridge.

Then he stood there—the living room lit, the kitchen dim. Stood there listening to Tatia putting his daughter down to sleep. Waiting to pay. £150 he owed her for the two and a half days' sitting. Another £150 for the sex. The silence of the apartment all around, the good thick walls full of non-asbestos insulation. Being virtually underground: they'd have to bomb him out. The waste of time of it all. He looked around at the evidence of childcare, what passed as his family. The big soft blanket on the floor by the kitchen table. Leopard-print jacket draped on the kitchen chair. The toys made of soft tied fabrics, fringed and tasselled with bells and mirrors. A rattle made of a cane ball with a bell trapped inside. Wet wipes left in strange signs that some forensic scientist of his new life might read: milk spilled, left of mouth, sitting on another lap, plus late vomit—late afternoon. You were editing a piece on thrombolytic complications in heart failure to pay off your debt. Leaky nappy change at 4:05. You were editing a sensible and worthy thing on why the devolution of basic dermatitic care from GPs to hospital-based specialists in the UK, unlike, say, Sweden, resulted in higher costs and worse care. You were planning a route home such that you'd see them before they saw you. You were fucking useless. *You should never have left her alone.*

He made as if to go to the fridge, and stopped. He made as if to go to the cupboard, and stopped. He took a long breath and shakily exhaled. He grinned and his face felt like plastic in patches, warm and liquid elsewhere. He took another long breath, then another, and listened.

The murmurs in there. The occasional crack of the floor.

Tatia was putting her down.

He went quietly downstairs to the bedroom, turned on the lights, closed the curtains and straightened the bed. He went into the bathroom and washed his face and brushed his teeth. He came back upstairs and located an envelope in the third drawer down: 1: cutlery, 2: everything else, 3: stationery, 4: haberdashery, that's how it usually goes. In the last six months the little plastic hollows of his cutlery drawer had gathered debris: toast crumbs, breadcrumbs, biscuit crumbs, anonymous grease, semi-transparent shavings of hard cheese, coffee, crumbs in all shades brown to black, undisturbed unless wiped into the occasional stripe by a fingertip dredging for that last clean teaspoon. He put the £300 in the envelope and tucked down the flap like a birthday card and wrote 'Tatia' on the front in biro. Then he went back into the kitchen and waited for her.

Heart starting to gently thump in these few small preparations. All the fantasy falls away. The whole landscape of the *Royal London*, London, the buses and the rain and the fear shrinking down in rapid contractions, heartbeats narrowing, like the city falling, retreating anaesthetised into a dream—all context closing down behind a rising black in a *puff, puff, puff*.

He waited.

Creak, crack went the floor. Crack. The door opened and the door gently closed. Her footsteps coming along the hall. He knew then he'd give her a scare, waiting there, so he said, quietly, 'I'm here Tatia.'

Like *Ta-sha*.

'Oof,' she said from round the corner. And she stopped and came on, creak, crack, gently shaking her head side to side.

'Sorry,' he said.

'Oof, that was a fright,' she whispered.

He smiled and they hovered there together, listening for Fiona. The traffic passing by outside. They met eyes when a siren rose and fell.

No answering cry from her.

'How's her nose?' said James.

She waggled her head side to side: 'Running, running.

I don't know.'

'Was she all right today?'

'Oh she was *darling* always.' She did her smile. A smile she always did when he asked. Far off, private and dreamy, half away from the asker. Their own love affair was nobody else's business.

'Thank you Tatia.'

'Oh *no*,' she said, and waved a hand. She straightened then arched her back, and smoothed at the baby creases in her white blouse. 'Oh I'm a mess.'

'Can I make you a drink,' said James.

She heard him, and looked up at him, differently, and seemed to see him for the first time.

Emerging from one self, in the threshold, crossing in to another. A Lithuanian part-time economics student at a barely listed and barely accredited London university, holding down, just barely, three jobs, one of which, the most but still insufficiently lucrative and promising, at an office in Fitzrovia, doing ambiguous comms work of some kind or another that troubled her. Wearing rubber gloves on the cleaning work to protect her hands for the public job.

'Gin, please, if you can have it,' she said, courtly, knowing he always and only did.

'Neat or tonic?'

'With tonic, please and ice and lemon rind.'

He put the envelope on the counter and she took it and looked inside and then put it in her purse on the table, as he mixed the Tanqueray like it was a date. Not a peep from Fiona. What did it matter, £30 on gin, when you're £20,000 in debt. An hour and 12 minutes' work for two or more nights of relief. Still in the dim quiet light in the kitchen, refracted, ghosted from the other room: lunar and spacious. They sipped their drinks in the far-off sirens, the half-bunkered feel of these strange and flattering apartments.

'*That's* what I meant to not,' she said suddenly, and gently beat the air with her hand.

'What?'

'I left her bottle in there, James.'

'Oh don't worry about that.'

'I left it on the shelf of drawers in there.'

'That's okay,' he said. 'I'll get it later.'

She took another sip of the gin, her second. She looked down at her blouse. 'I'm all a mess,' she said.

'No,' he said. 'I'm all a mess.'

'All creased up,' she said, smiling at him as if warning.

'You look really good,' he said, smiling back.

That moment then—heart banging hard in there in his dusty chest like a crazed bird, he just let himself stare at her body, let himself look her up and down and breathe. The baby asleep, that's all that matters. And this feeling to throw it into relief.

'Have you had a very hard day, then?' she said, and went to put her glass down.

'Not so bad,' he said, half smiling.

'Oh James, you are a hard worker,' and she looked around for where to put her glass, and put it on the table on a baby wipe for a coaster, and came over to him completely changed now. She moved in close, one hand to his thigh and one to his waist like a dancer, and they kissed once like civilians as if to familiarise her again with her role. He put down his drink too, and she placed her hand on his crotch and with the other started to undo the buttons of her creased blouse.

The very strangeness of this moment, forever, was the best drug. The transformation, the alteration was everything and they kissed again a little longer.

She looked up at him and said, 'Shall we have our intercourse now?'

She was well gone when something woke him at 3am. He lay naked under sheets, deeply slept. He must have fallen asleep around 8:30, like a young boy, and dozed through her leaving.

Listening to the apartment. Something out in the garden? Pillowy sounds of the wind. From where he lay, he watched the LEDs of the Angelcare. Nothing moved, just the temperature in her room: regulation 18 degrees Celsius. The front of the house was secure. They could post as many postcards as they liked. The cage was impregnable to anyone without the requisite tools and time, and the nursery's small windows had long ago been bricked up. The bedroom and living room, he guessed, were vulnerable from the back. But, like the fox, they would have to climb four six- and seven-foot fences to get to his garden, and that was a big risk and a lot of noise.

And there it was. The realisation. He was now always to walk in fear on his own street.

If I had the time and inclination to hunt a single father tied down to his house and to his job, how easy would it be to find my moment and how long would I wait? Where was he vulnerable? Tatia. They would do her. He'd have to find a crèche in the city, or around here, either of which would cost much more. He would give her up. But Fiona?

He could do nothing about the house. It was in fact a

strength. He couldn't move out. Take a holiday? 'Leave town'? And imagine the return from your BnB in fucking Whitstable with your arms full of Fiona and travel cot, to find what? Exactly what you fled, and worse. Help. Who could he ask? Someone from work? The fucking Davids? Kristian? *Death*?

No, you are alone.

He lay awake making his plans. Around 4:30am he got up to urinate. Then he patrolled the house. Astride the creaking steps he went from room to room. In the kitchen he drank a glass of water. The peace of Tatia—that was the hardest to give up. However temporary it might be. The thing of oblivion. Face in her thighs; perpetual newness; he never thinks. Hand in her crotch, fingers deep inside her, he thinks only in the monosyllables of how she responds. Giving her pleasure, he can disappear. So it is another escape; is it craven?

It was time then, to manage this. He tidied the kitchen by the light from the Xpelair. Put away her toys and binned rogue wipes and folded up her rug. When all was neat for tomorrow he went down the hall to the nursery to check on her. FION on her door in cut-out paper letters. The A was gone to parts unknown. He grasped the handle, pulled the door into the jam slightly to release the tongue and opened it in silence. Into the darkness and the warm Weet-Bix smell of her. Only illumination a soft green glow of the ring of the night light on the Angelcare monitor under the basket. He measured his steps and barefoot strode to the bearer's joint in the middle of the floor; to where it creaked the least. He stood over her in the Moses basket. Swaddled to her earlobes in white terry cloth. Fierce dark head of hair. Turned away to the wall. He could make out the fine bone of her nose. The faint feather of an eyebrow. He leaned down.

Pfff. Pfff. She breathed. Heaved once, gently—he watched her for that long—and breathed. A slightly different smell in here, a winey note to the warmth, and he sniffed down at her waist for a poo, but there was nothing in particular. The deep intimacy with her poo was an unexpected but in hindsight obvious fact. As was the pride that went along with that; knowing everything. Fibrous, mashy, crushed banana poos, in all the camouflage shades, now she was having some solids. Variation over the nappy, clusters of poo-froth, liquid paint, foul cream, a grape skin (carefully pre-split with his own teeth). Wipe the buttcheeks of the worst of it, then her butt, then the creases of her thighs, her labia front to back, then her butt again, then her buttcheeks once again. The amazement of human skin—how perpetually cleanable it is. He'd learned on the journal how heavy was human skin. Slippery and heavy. It falls from your hands. It had got so that when the luck of the fall of the folded wipe was right, he could clean her up thoroughly with only three, sometimes two wipes. No matter the size of the deposit. He smiled in the dark. Unless came the welling as if from angel-sprung aquifer of that abrupt and tiny spring, carrying off the flotsam beneath her as she half smiled who knew where. And then you'd need light. He turned around and there was a dog in the far corner opposite the door.

A Rhodesian ridgeback was sitting in the corner of the room.

The hair on James's neck went erect in a series and a wave of silver shiver went down his back. Adrenaline began to pump in long smooth floods. The dog from the boys. Their dog. The big tobacco ridgeback. The big tobacco ridgeback sitting in the dark. Facing slightly away from him, as if thinking about something else.

A dog in the corner of the room.

He stood there. He could hear Fiona breathing. His heart going *talker talker talker*.

He not quite immediately took one step. Placed himself squarely between them. The dog seemed to eye him obliquely. Quite dark in the pale green play of light from the Angelcare up one facet of his iron chest. But didn't move. Sat on his haunches at the foot of the daybed as if waiting for her to wake.

He could hear her breathing.

In the half-dark he stood there watching it, eyes wide.

He slowly raised his arms to hip height and as wide as the Moses basket behind him, as if laying a blessing. Dozens of seconds. His heart went *thoughter thoughter thoughter*. An acidic streak of sweat ran down his ribs. Fiona snuffled and the dog turned slightly to look, then turned back as if to the wall beyond him.

'Good dog,' James croaked, and watched it. He stepped one foot closer and stopped. The ridgeback was watching him back now. He could smell it. Winey and rich. It licked its lips and panted once then closed its mouth again and watched him.

James cleared his throat. 'Good dog,' he said.

A metre and a half away. James held out his hand in the passive, palm-down posture he'd once been taught. He wasn't close enough. The dog ignored it.

He stepped closer once more and reached out.

The big dog extended its neck slightly and sniffed his knuckles, so close he felt the wet.

Then it turned idly away again.

'Good dog,' James croaked. Without moving from between the dog and the baby, he reached to the door handle and turned it and pulled the door open. Then he reached down and very gently grasped the dog's collar. Trying to be gentle but firm. Trying to be ready to not let go if it fought. To drop the door and go for the eyes with the other hand. The dog let him. He softly pulled at the collar and the dog stood quietly, and then he led it down the hallway. He led it up the stairs, and the dog waited patiently by his leg as he opened the front door and then the cage door to let it out into the night. It stepped out and stopped.

He pulled the cage door shut. 'Off you go,' he said bleakly. The ridgeback eyed the entrance to the apartment. And then it jogged down the covered way, slightly sideways like they do, to the right, 20 feet to the first steps down to the street, looked back, checked James once, and disappeared, towards the Heath.

James stood at the threshold of the cage watching the corridor through the bars. There was no one and nothing. No traffic at all. The night silent, the air thick and chill as frozen gin. Great darkness of the Heath up there. A void impenetrable and an old, old cold rolling down off the hills.

And then he heard Fiona start to cry.

Search history

Ectopic pregnancy
Ectopic pregnancy overview
Ectopic pregnancy clinical guidelines
Ectopic pregnancy royal college of obstetricians and gynaecologists
gynaecologists
Confidential Inquiry into Maternal and Child Health
Ectopic pregnancy images
O wrangling schools, that search what fire
Image foetus fallopian tube
Teratoma
Kotsifou
Crete
Kotsifou Crete
Current local time Crete
Southern Crete
Rethymno Map
Kotsifou canyon
Kotsifou gorge
Why is there no street view in Crete
Why is there no street view in Greece
Images Kotsifou Crete

Restaurant Asomatos Crete Tripadvisor
Tony Death
Tony Death linkedin
Tony Death Cambridge
Tony Death Cambridge images
Merriam Webster
'Ambivalent'
Tiotropium
Ectopic
Non-tubal ectopic
Diethystilbestrol
'HCG' abbrev
'human chorionic gonadotrophin'
Gonadotrophin
'Time'
Merriam Webster
Adrienne Morrissey linkedin
why does a baby
cry?
cry when born?
get hiccups?
kick in the womb?
strange things happening baby
baby strange occurrences
baby telekinetic
strange things happening baby
can a baby call a dog?
capitalise ultrasound?
salpingotomy
salpingectomy
oophorectomy
ovariotomy

salpingo-oophorectomy
haematosalpinx
telescoping club attack self defence
ASP baton
Cheyne Stoking?
What is Cheyne–Stokes respiration?
'Abnormal patterns of respiration in the last days of life'
'Symptoms of active dying'
'Dying breaths'
Greek honey comb
Cretan honey
Cretan bees
John Mayer
John Mayer linkedin
John Mayer romford essex
John Mayer commando training
John Mayer commando training Clapham Common
ridgeback
Rhodesian ridgeback
Rhodesian ridgeback defence
Rhodesian ridgeback attack
Rhodesian ridgeback six month old baby
'Rhodesian ridgeback' AND 'six month old baby'
baby telekinesis kinesis
strange things happening baby
Rethymno
Rethymno holiday
Rethymno holiday summer
Greek honey comb
Cretan honey

Hilditch & Key

At the *Royal London Journal of Medicine*, we have a highly trained team of medical and healthcare professionals from all walks of life. Get to know Ibrahim al-Rayess, MD, on a professional and clinical level.

doctor photo jpg TK

Public health, trauma surgery, and English tailoring are Ibrahim's passions. He is a medical doctor and trauma surgeon with graduate degrees in public health and surgical medical science. Dr al-Rayess was born in Damascus, Syria where he practised medicine at Al Mouwasat and Damascus General Hospitals after taking his MBBChir at Cambridge and postgraduate study in public health and surgery at London's University College Hospital in the UK. He returned again to London last year to take on the role of visiting editor at the *Royal London*'s Bloomsbury offices. Dr al-Rayess's most recently edited paper is a long analysis of the development of the public healthcare system in Turkey, in the context of that country's bid for EU membership and of the Syrian conflict, where he was in close contact with the paper's Turkish authors and the experienced technical editor in-house at the *Royal*, James Ballard (who returned home from work last night to find Josephine, his neighbour's cat, decapitated, inexpertly disembowelled and crucified by paws wired to his cage door using supermarket twist ties). Dr al-Rayess is also currently working on a piece on ethical guidelines in medical publishing in an eastern context, and is second editor on a clinical review of cellulitis and primary editor on an analysis of the rise of opportunistic leishmaniasis in refugee camps in South Sudan. In the latter case he draws on his recent extensive experience working in Syrian refugee camps in southern Turkey. Dr al-Rayess is very tall and thin and is the father of two daughters, ages six and eleven, neither of whom he has seen in two years. One of his current projects is to find them on YouTube. He is paid very well at the *Royal London*, and he has an apartment—though with hardly any kitchen to speak of, Dr al-Rayess reports!—in the iconic Isokon Lawn Road Flats in London's Belsize Park, the same building where a refugee from a different kind of fascism, Walter Gropius, once lived and worked.

Today, Dr al-Rayess—Ibrahim, as he likes to be known—was taking the afternoon off. He was headed to Jermyn Street to buy some shirts, and possibly a pair of shoes, and later in the evening he was going to watch a horror movie—another of his passions. Tonight's film was to be a favourite (if that is quite the right word for the dull click of satisfaction, the sense of cruising hostility and blankness watching horror provides him): *The Cabin in the Woods*. He was going to drink, as he watched, as a bad Sunni Muslim, his first alcohol ever: an entire bottle of vodka, if possible, made by a popular manufacturer recommended to him today by a young woman in the Bloomsbury Oddbins, 42 Below. Because today, this morning, not long after the abandoned meeting for the *Royal*

London's ongoing process review, abandoned due to the riots-imposed absence of the process review's instigator and commander-in-chief, he found on YouTube the first video featuring his daughters, as well as his sister-in-law and her cousin, filmed at their country house in Al-Marah, northeast of Damascus. This video was two years old.

Ibrahim was 53 years old and he had seen a few things in his professional career. He had a rather hooked and sideways-tending nose with a notably twisted septum, a clearly Arab complexion of deep and patinaed chestnut, heavy eyebrows, a deeply wrinkled brow yet the palest blue eyes in that shade the English like to call grey. Those eyes got him in trouble a few times in the last few months in Syria.

Early this afternoon Ibrahim was on the Piccadilly line to Piccadilly station, heading towards the twin Meccas of English tailoring excellence, Savile Row and Jermyn Street. The cliché was not inaccurate given the extent to which both holy destinations were surrounded and diminished by venality and the tawdry market: bogus Zamzam, Abercrombie & Fitch. He was sitting still. Across the modestly crowded tube carriage was a middle-aged Sikh, a lawyer or doctor or banker, standing by the doors, and Ibrahim was making a very close yet quite subtle and unobtrusive study of the man's wardrobe. This was not one of those Frenchmen modelling the ghastly, garish and clichéd *le look Anglaise* with its virulent corduroys, clashing cashmere and loud tweeds stiff and still unbroken in. The professional Indian, Ibrahim had come to understand, appreciate and watch closely, was most often the best-dressed man in London.

The man wore the turban and kara bracelet of a Sikh. He had a ferocious beard. And he had such a suit. Clearly Huntsman, single-buttoned, single-breasted. A lay person would not notice it. This is its beauty. Ibrahim had one himself. One of the great pleasures, that: to stand in basted cloth on those floorboards emperors and presidents and princes have trod, and have the head Huntsman tailor emerge from the workshop, stand behind one in the mahogany mirror in a daze abstracted, his head bent just so, like a surgeon contemplating knife to skin, then reach with one hand around hips childbearing or skinny, jutting, like his—as in theatre, it did not matter here—to gently place his forefinger upon the precisely personal spot where the assistant tailor quickly pins a single paper button, thence to return to the workshop with neither greeting nor civility of any kind. Huntsman the acknowledged world authority on the perfectly balanced single-buttoned coat (please don't call it a jacket). Ibrahim automatically appraised, in a disassociation one would hesitate to call enjoyment, the deep Yorkshire cloth, 12oz or slightly heavier, the drape and fall, the wet of the weave, the horn buttons, the handsewn buttonhole at a sober angle by a sober 90-degree notched lapel of canvassed, horsehair-lined—and sober—width. Investment bankers and hedge fund managers who request their buttonholes on jaunty angles, even vertical: Ibrahim looks away.

This was a form of pleasure. The contemplation of the perfection of a craft, worn by a man who knew its worth, and his own. That at least was the illusion, the surface, some consolation. Please: no cuffs on the trouser.

A very restrained chalk stripe on a dark charcoal, simple, single-breasted suit made by Huntsman. A go-to suit for any occasion, anywhere in the world. Such was the tailoring that in it one could comfortably pole-vault. Starting at about £5000, depending on the cloth you chose. Certain types liked to have gold woven in, or to take a suit in cashmere, or vicuña. A beautiful suit but a fabric so fine your £10,000, your £20,000, would last just a single glorious season. The shirt beneath was anonymous enough to be high bespoke, either one of the Savile Row tailors or a shirt specialist like Emma Willis or Budd. Definitely not the proportions of a Turnbull & Asser or Harvie & Hudson. Dr al-Rayess could recognise Hilditch & Key stitching and collar rake from this distance. But with a closed jacket it would be a challenge for anyone. The tie looked like Drake's by its restraint—the Sikh had it in a slightly lighter burgundy Jacquard silk that did not lack for the dramatic with his dark skin. A pocket square puffed not folded in fine paisley golds and cobalt blues. The shoes were clearly a pair of Edward Greens, second only to Lobb, shoemakers to the future king, not impossibly bespoke, around £800 off the shelf for that pair of simple black Oxfords with light broguing to the toecap. The man was on his way to or from a business meeting or a lunch at which he was a recognised power and had no need to dominate, on an autumnal day not warranting a topcoat. His hand hung from the safety strap, shirt cuff extending precisely half an inch from suit cuff to the base of his thumb even with his arm thus raised and extended. A Patek Philippe glinting goldly there. Ibrahim made the inventory, and several more details besides, in a series of seconds in which his mind rather resembled his expression—calm, affectless, autopiloted, nearly peaceful. Empty, someone assisting might say. The same expression he would wear when catheterising a superior vena cava or picking the angle of IV attack for a patient with rolling or reticent veins. We never blame the patient for a blown vein, and we release the tourniquet at once to lessen bruising—they'll thank us for it later if not right away.

There were things to look at. Observe their behaviour: you are not really there with them.

Ibrahim emerged from Piccadilly station, exit Regent Street south, Piccadilly west side. A pleasant buzz on the street, a readily negotiable swarm of Spaniards. The circus's pedestrian traffic was self-regulating now, since they took the traffic barriers down—fear of death kept people still, while the lack of anything to do but hang around kept people moving, past the outlet stores, the trash on the ground. The only remaining chain store now was Boots—client for a series of *Royal London* EBM stories on their website. Health—private at least—was seemingly recession-proof. He headed south through sky-staring tourists, then west at the Tesco to Jermyn Street. It was one of London's smaller tragedies, perhaps, that Bates Hatters' store at 21A had closed. There was no frame to present the picture of the tweed cap, the felted bowler, the pristine panama, quite like the Victorian mahogany and dusty carpet of that little hole in the wall. The stud inside had been 20 feet high at least and rising either side of the narrow little shop mahogany shelving built into the walls held flatcaps in all the tweeds piled like pancakes. The shop was unenterably old and English when Ibrahim first visited the street as a young student. When he returned a year ago as a surgeon, sterilised father and man of exploded parts, it was gone.

Squeezed out by the rents, the brutal rates. The developers' developments. The whole east end of Piccadilly was going that way—hotels. Next door was Hawes & Curtis, who borrowed the shine of Jermyn Street and its history of royalty, rolled umbrellas, rentboys and the highest of shirtmaking artistry onto their made-in-China cotton shirts to make them silky on the shelves and unwearable cardboard two launderings later. Jones Bootmaker, and Emmett. Tesco. Babmaes Street, a dead end with Church's Shoes on the corner—an English classic eschewed since Prada bought them out—marked the pale beyond which, east, it was hopeless to find anything made in England. The next block west held some doubtful compromises: T.M.Lewin, Charles Tyrwhitt, another Hawes & Curtis, landbanking their business into prosperity. But then, at 97, the real business began: shirts by Harvie & Hudson. Opposite by the Princes Arcade: shirts by Hilditch & Key, shirtmakers since 1899.

Ibrahim's steps slow by Victorian facades, glossy black wrought iron, tile, and the window displays: Sea Island cotton shirts in butcher's apron stripes, braces in navy barathea with polished brass clasps and kid leather fasteners, socks in silk by Pantherella, crimson silk knots for cufflinks, classic navy blazers with great brass buttons—fully canvassed, though none of it bespoke, of course. But Ibrahim's steps slow. He absorbs the looks that the gentlemen of Harvie & Hudson, of Hilditch & Key, Turnbull & Asser have assembled for his pleasure and inspiration. A freshet of innocence; a game a man can play. Opposite was the church hall of St James's— in which they'd installed a Caffè Nero: cappuccino, panini, pasta. A peace was here, opposed to that: in the assemblage of elements, their very range and number, the depth of accrued taste: Ibrahim dips his fingers in the English aesthetic and savours it. He sees and recognises the hand of Richard Harvie in the particular combination of contrast collar and paisley tie. The large pattern and the small. He sees Alan from Hilditch & Key—an altogether different proposition from H&H, to the trained eye—sees Alan's playful hand in the stack of folded H&K shirts, grading by colour from a loud pink pinstripe at the bottom and through the rainbow, crowned by a plain poplin, button-cuffed classic collar in utterly simple, perfect white Egyptian cotton. Ibrahim knows the feel of that cotton, and that, like the 12oz wool of worsted cloths by Holland & Sherry—it is balm and armour.

Ibrahim's steps slow as he passes these storefronts. And the bottle of vodka sloshes softly in the poacher's pocket of his trench coat. His wallet—Swaine Adeney Brigg, pigskin and bridle—was in the other pocket but he'd forgotten his briefcase, left it under his desk when he'd risen and walked out of the gently buzzing, late morning, post-aborted-meeting offices of the *Royal London*. He'd closed his browser window and just left the office. Walked out. The YouTube video he'd just watched had been uploaded, with maybe 30 other videos seemingly completely unrelated other than by the Syrian civil war, none later than a year ago, by a SyrianSmurf19. When, presumably, SyrianSmurf19 was killed. WARNING: GRAPHIC. There were 40 seconds of Assad soldiers dancing to a flute in a barracks somewhere. There was phone footage of a blurred shape moving against a piece of concrete in the middle of a street that the caption revealed was 'Video: #Damascus #Syria l Woman Thrown in the St After #Assad Shabeeha Rape Her, and Then Snipers & Tanks Take Shots'. Another: '#Damascus #Syria #Assad Shabiha Round Up Males for Torture, Execution & Make Man Eat His Hair'. Uncaptioned, four men with guns turn another four men without guns into floppy meat and drop them into an oubliette in the middle of a dusty landscape. A bloody roomful of bound, naked men are pointlessly kicked in the smalls of their backs, rendered camouflage by the bruising, by the same dancing soldiers. A dusty severed foot posed in rubble. And then two thirds down there was a thumbnail of the familiar view from his sister-in-law's first floor bedroom balcony over the couple of dozen feet of tended garden, forget-me-nots and green beans, to the eight-foot security wall. It was her cousin's country house in Al-Marah where he'd hidden them. The upload date was two years ago. He could see his youngest daughter's topknotted ponytail at the bottom of the frame. He'd put on his headphones. He could hear his sister-in-law holding the camera saying oh, no, no, please don't let them. He could hear his elder daughter crying in confusion. No no no no no. He could see the video had been lifted from the camera Sharween had been given for Christmas and had been cut by someone to show only this: the truck full of soldiers and plainclothes *shabiha* (he'd translated that as 'apparitions' in one of his early guest editorial blogs) pulls up in the alley beyond the security wall and the lead *shabiha* jumps down from the tray and quickly shins up the wall, not even looking up to the women in the window filming him, as if he knows exactly what and who is up there where the linen curtain billows out and in, a bright blue sky beyond. The *shabiha* drops down into the garden and unlocks the big wooden door to the street, and in the squad of soldiers come to the garden, to the house. The video shakes and shivers. The caption is not to be remembered.

Ibrahim caught his own reflection in the window of Hilditch & Key. Their navy blue; the sublime font. The finest shirtmakers in the world. Beyond him the 1pm sun shone for an effervescent instant goldly down Jermyn Street on its afternoon decline, having barely, it seemed, breathed the day. He could see his dark outline formed by the sober navy Burberry trench. The rest of him was filled with bright yellow ties, formal wingtip shirts, cotton pyjamas too.

The homeless like Jermyn Street and its wealthy street traffic, and they don't seem to get moved along. Many years ago Princess Diana would visit Turnbull & Asser, and the staff would close the doors for her to shop. Dodi Fayed was a director of the company, and Jermyn Street rumour had it she first met him there when buying pyjamas for her young boys. Ibrahim had once asked Brian, the branch manager, about the princess—Brian was just an assistant, a young man of 20, lurking in the background then. 'Oh, we did look forward to it,' he said. 'A Diana day was a good day.' Ibrahim cannot quite help himself, usually—he prefers to deal with the English help when he shops. Too many stores were hiring presentable but semi-literate immigrants who didn't—couldn't—know the product; what it meant. Often knew far less than the doctor himself. About the Oxfords in the cross-hatched Russia reindeer leather at New & Lingwood, for example—how in 1974 bundles of the leather hides were found intact and perfectly preserved in the mud and ribs of the Danish two-master *Catharina von Flensburg*, sunk in Plymouth Sound in 1786. And subsequently sold off in tiny batches to the best shoemakers and leather workers in London. The Russia reindeer. Marvellously supple and idiosyncratic and overwhelmingly expensive. Why Cordings covert coats were never on sale. (Why would they be? They sell no matter what the price.) The limited shirtings and sizings in the slimfit Hilditch, and why they had no gussets.

Or who were flippant, rude, their English offensive to the ear. Or who were prematurely blank, brutalised by the money, the bastards they served, and the complexities of the class system of which they'd been incongruously placed at the bleeding edge with nothing to protect them but a pretty face. There'd been a post-Christmas sale at Crockett & Jones and Ibrahim had dropped in to look over the racks of exquisite English shoes. The small shop was uncomfortably packed, as was usual in the holiday sales. One of the staff was an Iranian named Henry, thoroughly assimilated, given—but frazzled and on some contact high after too many hours of too many customers from too many places, too many voices, too many spiels. He was pitching the shoes to a Saudi, who wasn't quite following him and nodding inscrutably: 'The Hand Grade range is our finest range of shoes, sir,' he said, 'and utilises the finest calf leather with channelled, oak bark tanned soles. The shoes are Goodyear welted in calf leather sourced from Italian cows who speak five languages handmade in our Northampton factory, the ancestral home of fine English shoemaking,' and Ibrahim looked up slowly at that and caught Henry's eye and the handsome young Iranian saw him and winked. Ibrahim nodded back—they all knew him there—but never again darkened their door when Henry was visible in the soft, expensive light within. At Tricker's the staff were all working-class men with East Midlands accents and frank, direct manners, and who seemed to have come straight from the factory and that was all right. Steer clear of the smart-arse South African at Cordings, the Chinese girl at Emma Willis. Emiko Matsuda at Foster & Son was a different proposition, as she was in bespoke and had the troubled eyes and underslept abstraction of a real apprentice—he recognised the look of the Foundation Year 1 doctor in her.

But Ibrahim liked to be served by an Englishman. He liked a bit of English irony, English fancy, the English fantasy. And here he was, after all, was he not? In England.

Past the homeless man squatting at the end of Princes Arcade he could see inside the smaller Hilditch & Key. The Spanish girl wasn't working today. There was no one immediately visible, and he climbed the old limestone steps and opened the shop door to its gentle tinkle of tingling bells.

'Speah some *chain*, sir,' the homeless man hissed, from his blanket. 'Ahm *ahngry*. Nahfink *teat*.'

There had once been a sudden and great calm as one wandered in through the carousels of Pantherella and the hanging handslipped Hilditch ties, coloured seasonally to the shirting. A great calm in the wooden aquarium. In the very artisanal, near-rusticity they managed to bring to even the plain plastic packaging of the new season's ready-to-wear shirts, stacked collar-to-tail in their mahogany cubbyholes. The shelving was made bespoke, for there was a sliding board that emerged at waist height for contending shirts to be laid out for the customer. Glass-fronted wooden cabinets of Hilditch handkerchiefs, scarves, boxer shorts, pocket squares.

There was Alan at the counter—not the anxious Alex Wong. Alan Thomas. His roundness, his rotundness elevated to a virtue by a double-cuffed Hilditch shirt in bold blue Bengal stripes and a solid pink silk tie, with a pair of Albert Thurston braces in Brigade of Guards wine-stripe boxcloth holding up a pair of plain grey flannels. A pale, giggly sort of man with a bobbing head anxious to please, thusly dressed he might have been an older banker or eccentric backbencher. He was in fact incredibly solicitous, and incredibly efficient and surprisingly witty, and Ibrahim was usually pleased to see him.

'Good afternoon, sir,' Alan said, and he nodded wobblingly. He seemed to both reach out to the customer and to simultaneously recoil in self-reflexive horror at having had to do so, and the possibility of intrusion or offence.

He was exceptionally good at what he did.

'Good afternoon, Alan,' Ibrahim said.

The anonymity, the English game, always forever shattered in that accent.

He went to the shelves of slimfits in his collar size.

Alan wobbled behind the counter slightly, consulting an invoice. Leaving wide the opening for Ibrahim to indicate his needs. Ibrahim stood in front of the cubbyholes of new season's shirtings, barely looking. He raised his chin and Alan, thus signalled, came silently from behind the gigantic ancient Victorian cash register made of brass and wood gone honey with age. Would he remember Ibrahim's name from the made-to-measure ledger? This had been an important thing to him, years and lives ago.

'Something for work, or something for the weekend, sir?' Alan said, and Ibrahim turned—Alan smiled at his little cliché and seemed so vulnerable that Ibrahim mechanically smiled back.

'Some shirts please, Alan,' Ibrahim said, as he might have normally when they both might have enjoyed the small moment.

'Certainly, sir. If you'll just allow me to check your measurements again—' That careful *again*: even if he'd forgotten him from his last bespoke order, he'd slipped away from the potential offence.

'Of course,' Ibrahim said, a touch too roughly.

Alan took his measurements in seconds: collar size, chest size, waist, and nape of the neck to base of the thumb down the arm bent at the elbow. 'Sir's lost weight,' he said with a faint, ironic edge of approval.

It was once a marvellous game, and a pleasure to be a player.

Taste like asphalt in his mouth.

'Give me,' Ibrahim said, almost croaking, 'one of each of the new fabrics in my size. I don't need them . . . adjusted. Socks, a selection of the Pantherellas, in 9. That tie'—he pointed—'five plain white pocket squares in the handrolled silk, a pair of—a pair of the navy gingham pyjamas in medium, and a gown in royal blue in medium, that—that'—he looked—'that scarf too.'

'Yes, sir,' Alan said immediately and unhesitatingly, 'if you'll just bear with me a moment—'

'How long will it take?' Ibrahim said, and he was sweating.

'Not too long at all, sir. If sir would like to take a seat—'

Alan was desperately trying to understand what was going on, indicating the wooden occasional chair by the stairs up to the workshop, trying very hard not to offend. But when he said *seat* a fat bubble of spittle flew from his mouth.

A cell of sputum, it lofted from him, large enough to heft a cargo of the salesman's spit but also to fly forth, describing a long, lazy, flat parabola, floating almost, in some uncanny and exquisite balance of glistening saliva and captured breath within rendering its flight in near slow-motion between them. Floating, flying slowly, languidly, to land and expire in spit and tiny spatter on the blue gabardine of the trench coat at Ibrahim's chest.

The men looked at each other for a very long moment. Alan's trembling smile had gone. His hand was still extended, indicating the chair—frozen, wavering slightly.

The doorbell tinkled. A young woman came in. She

looked at the carousel of socks. Then up at the frozen pair of well-dressed men by the shelves of shirts.

Ibrahim turned his face away. 'Will come back,' he croaked thickly. He cleared his throat. '*I will come back.*'

'Of course, sir,' said Alan. 'Of *course*, sir.'

It being far better not to acknowledge the thing had happened at all, of course.

Ibrahim had been in the room they used for debriefings at University College Hospital's Surgical Specialties wing with nine other male surgeons a year ago, when the announcement was made that by DoH fiat henceforth the wearing of neckties—which were, essentially, germ wicks—was to be barred in the NHS. In the interests of hygiene, and of hospital-related opportunistic infection control.

Geoffrey Boys, the head of section, made the announcement with some accompanying drolleries to a massive but undetectable sigh. The surgeons lay about the room in attitudes of high food-chain predators deeply intimate with their own particular and idiosyncratic experiences of thorough exhaustion. A surgeon lying near half-reclined in a desk chair. A surgeon seated directly upright but with his eyes closed. With the announcement, the atmosphere suddenly shifted to that of the constituent components of a sneer lying about waiting to be assembled.

'Following the so-called "deep clean" of the acute trusts, which cost the NHS upwards of £60 million,' said Geoffrey Boys, 'and the subsequent failure to address spiralling rates of hospital-acquired infection, I'm afraid, gentlemen, that this latest piece of DoH advice—'

There'd been a time when the stiffness and patina of the material deposits on a doctor's coat, the encrustations of blood and plasma and dried-up human jelly, were the very badge of his experience and prestige. The men around Ibrahim were wearing T-shirts, polos, jeans, even cargo pants. Laid about like big cats after the chase.

'Look Geoffrey, there isn't any evidence,' drawled Gordon Tearwhit.

'While it's true there's an apparent dearth of direct, robust evidence bearing on this particular piece of DoH guidance—'

'How many times has anyone in this room dry-cleaned a tie,' said Pashupati Ghosh. 'Dancer et al., 2008. Pants, policies, paranoia. Smith et al., 2009. "Tighten that tie, you horrible boy": effects of doctors' attire and impact of the presence of a stethoscope on trust and confidence in patients. Pais-Quigley et al., 2004. Equivalence of microflora in doctors' shirts and ties after laundering.'

He went on. 'The Royal College has published *extensively* in the *Bulletin* on the overuse of antibiotics in place of basic hygiene measures in younger doctors. The new regulations don't address the fundamental issues of a decline in awareness of the most simple principles of antiseptic prophylaxis and hit a lame duck. It's a simple thing. Wash your hands. We are members of a distinguished profession—'

Pashupati spoke as he wrote. He seemed to rely for his audience not on the natural responses and acknowledgement signals of his listeners and peers but on a sense of posterity or some future consultation of the record, the minutes of these meetings, or legal action of some awful kind, and was in large part tuned out by the entire group. He looked directly at Ibrahim for support.

'—and we should dress accordingly.'

There was a sense of a collective contemptuous exhalation without any detectable evidence of same or visible movement from the exhausted men.

Boys: '... indeed, indeed, and I thank you Pashupati for your thoughts. Though I rather think from briefly observing the attendees at today's meeting that this ruling will have little or no effect on your day-to-day.'

Brian Hairweatherer was slumped so low in front of Ibrahim his 30-year-old Evisu-jeaned bottom was not even in contact with the seat but suspended above the slipper-shined linoleum in front of it.

He rolled his head slowly back, to, from almost completely upside down, address Ibrahim's worsted, chalk-striped legs.

'Well now this is a pity, isn't it, *Abraham*,' he almost slurred. 'Perhaps a *bow tie* is the solution.'

Ibrahim al-Rayess took the Northern Line from Leicester Square around half past three with a new pair of Edward Green Oxfords in oxblood cordovan, packaged in individual shoe bags then wrapped in tissue, in a shoebox, in a carry bag; plus four New & Lingwood shirts, also in a carry bag and wrapped in tissue; a pair of Turnbull & Asser pyjamas made in England using Italian cloth woven from Egyptian cotton, in an embroidered cotton bag in yet another carry bag; and a £1000 Cordings mackintosh. In a carry bag.

Around Mornington Crescent he rose to stand by the tube doors, leaving the New & Lingwood bag on the seat. An obese and unshaven white man in a pilled and stained grey marle Adidas tracksuit across the aisle eyed the tall Syrian doctor in the dark coat. His lightless grey eyes; the other bags of shopping hanging from his hand. Camden Town. Good girls go to heaven, bad girls go to London. At Belsize Park the train deep underground. The train slowed, came to a halt. The doors opened. Ibrahim stepped off and the obese man, with an otherwise complete lack of movement, tensed his jowls and shouted, violently, '*Oi.*'

Several passengers flinched. Ibrahim, on the platform, turned around.

'*Shopping*, mate,' the man said. He leaned—only his head—exaggeratedly to indicate the bag left behind. Ibrahim just looked at him, his face empty.

'Your *shopping*, mate,' the man shouted, as if for the benefit of speakers of a second language. The train departure warning sounded. Ibrahim didn't move. The obese man leapt up, uncannily fast, snatched the bag handles, and with a wide swing of his arm threw the bag viciously fast out through the doors of the train. The bag slapped out on the platform and hissed across the tile in a flat spin. The doors closed.

'Wa-hey,' said a young man waiting for the next train.

The bag lay there. Ibrahim just turned away, towards the elevators, and as the train pulled away the grins of those who saw him go turned to headshakes and laughter.

What a loony, they seemed to say.

Into premature darkness down past the high brick Georgians of Downside Crescent, in a light rain falling. Points of brake lights bleeding lines of rippling red down the road at him, roving over his face. At the Isokon Dr al-Rayess laid the bags out on his neatly made bed. He lifted the bottle of vodka from his coat pocket and set it on the coffee table in front of his TV. He took a glass from his emaciated, bedsittish kitchen, shed his coat, loosened his tie. He cued up *The Cabin in the Woods* and set it playing, sat down on the sofa. Out through the curtained windows the streetlamp played through the dissembling leaves of the Isokon's streetside maple in the first breezes of the storm. He opened the bottle, poured a generous measure of the vodka neat, and left it on the table. He looked at the screen and there was the American star of the *West Wing* TV series Bradley Whitford talking to another older bureaucrat about Whitford's wife—she had child-proofed their home before they'd even managed to get pregnant. They are the artificers, the technicians, the arrangers of a narrative that plays out in the film's second strand: the slow torture and sacrifice of a clique of American teens in genre cliché, in order, the film asserts, to propitiate some blood-hungry gods of violence. The nuancing of the stereotypes of the American children being the refinement of the film *as* a genre piece.

Slam, a very loud musical sting, a smash cut and the title card read *The Cabin in the Woods*. Ibrahim held up the glass of his very first vodka. Turning it slightly. Held it to the light. The curve of the meniscus. The slow roll. He sniffed it. He drank down half. He did not react. Looking at the TV. The intro scenes of the five young Americans who were to die. He held his breath a while, then exhaled. The light of the streetlamp a pale camouflage rippling on his bare walls. He drank down the rest of the glass and poured another.

He opened his laptop. Killed Chrome. Opened Firefox. As the artificers' plans and role in the teenagers' demise were steadily made more and more apparent, the young

Americans drove out to the cabin in the woods. He opened up Quadrivium, and opened up a new *Royal London* visiting editor blog. Each editor has one, a semi-official blog, dedicated to the *obiter dicta* (Latin: 'said in passing'; pleasingly pronounced *oh, bitter*) of their primary work in Editorial. The offcuts of opinion and experience in the field, and their own business, largely—and published online in the *RLJM* directly via Quadrivium, and on trust. He drank another full glass, gasping slightly at the end of this one. On screen—the harbinger. The one who warns, to no avail, the doomed children, was being made fun of by the artificers, who had him on speakerphone. Ibrahim in the cold light of the TV and the streetlamp, his face a turning—the smudging and the dragging down one side of—is it pain? Or the taste of vodka, his first. Grey light on his grey eyes. He typed. Time passed. A zombie sawed the head off a young girl.

An hour later, with the guest editor blog on the conflicts of interest of the authors of the paper on Turkish healthcare written and irrevocably and irretrievably posted live to the *Royal London* site, Ibrahim had drunk five glasses of the good vodka. He was watching the last remaining American boy and girl descend by elevator into the fundament of the story, a labyrinth of monsters' cells where they wait beneath the world to be released. All those helpless to do the damage they do. The spider. The hellraiser. The ghost. The Valkyrie. The young ballerina with a face made of teeth. He'd first seen this film in London, six months out of Turkey, where he'd worked at the refugee camp just across the border, treating the freshly wounded as they arrived from Syrian territory, as well as dealing with the refugee camp's signature disease, leishmaniasis, and exposure, basic trauma, malnourishment, STDs from the rapes that were happening seemingly without cease. After he'd fled Damascus. Where he remembered the secretary of his department at Al Mouwasat Hospital coming to his office—crying—to tell him there were 'government officers' here for him. Telling her it was fine, soothing her, a gentle squeeze of her shoulder, hey it's all right, and managing to maintain some dignity and not make any futile protests or falters as he allowed himself to be taken by taxi to the Air Force Intelligence building where they had his wife in the cells and he was first beaten severely then forced to watch what they did to her. Knowing the girls were away and safe. The way Ibrahim al-Rayess had taken the punches, had cried, had told them to leave her, had told them that she was his crown, had not prevented anything that subsequently happened to her; to gut him and make him guilty and to film him all the while was enough to convince them he was harmless. And when he was released he went from there faithfully back to the hospital to treat those more needful than he until such time as they were no longer watching him as closely as before and he could flee Damascus for Al-Marah to see Sharween and Malia for the last time. Where he said goodbye and held them and told them—*told them*—they were safest here with his sister-in-law at her cousin's house and not to leave, and he travelled north, incognito, heading for the border. Was dragooned into a roaming brigade of Libyans and Iraqis and kept there to operate for a week on casualties out of the storm in Idlib, and stayed on another month till the retreat, when they all left, north. Crossed the border into Turkey on a wet November afternoon to offer his help in the refugee camp of flooded UN tents. Writing emails in the evenings to the UK and US universities, hospitals and royal colleges. Informed by the Syrian Observatory for Human Rights that his daughters had been abducted and killed in September, and that his life was in imminent danger. Took the offered short-term post at the *Royal London Journal of Medicine* a week later. Where each day in the mauve-carpeted offices he looked for his children on YouTube.

Monsters burst forth from the building's elevators, helpless to do anything but maim and kill in their particular and idiosyncratic ways anyone they could touch in a near complete abandon. The first time he saw the scene and the last time ever—not *saw* the scene; was simply *present*—he'd cried, on this couch. Scratching at his cheeks and eyes.

Ibrahim al-Rayess stood in the flicker-lit room, drinking his sixth glass of vodka, visibly swaying. His blog post had asserted that the authors of the just-published Turkish piece—among whom were high-level individuals at WHO and the IMF and the International Society for Infectious Diseases—were stone-cold liars elbow-deep in the pockets of their government and of several named large corporations, and had misled him, the journal, the peer reviewers and his tech editor James Ballard with crippled data and selective citations and outright lies about the ongoing privatisation of Turkish healthcare to further the country's EU bid, which was still hung up on immigration, infrastructure and basic human rights, and to line those corporate pockets now and for decades into the future. The blog was live. It was not retrievable, as per *Royal London* policy. We do not correct our texts once they are online. 42 Below. He waved the glass around gently, swinging the last inch of vodka in the foot of the glass. Watching the viscosity. The rise and hang.

How after the first few glasses it hardly tasted at all. Needle, syringe, IV bag and a 1000-milligram bottle of anaesthesia-grade propofol laid out upon the coffee table. *Royal London* policy is to post errata. We do not delete. Anything published under our banner is there forever.

What Dad does

The SIMPLY FOOD M&S at South End Green, just down from the florist dedicated to the families of patients of the Royal Free, had great glass windows shaded by plane trees, and at a particular distance and angle as you walked between the flowers and the bus stop it was almost impossible not to watch your reflection in them as you passed. You caught your eye. Some girls, James noticed, looked at themselves, then looked away in a second and hitched up their coats or adjusted a bag or boot. As if their reflections were local lads in a small town: barely eligible mates they near disdain but for whom appearances must nonetheless be maintained. Something schoolish, obligatory, angry. Some girls quickly and almost sneakily eyed their reflections as if they found its beauty perfectly intimidating. Some didn't. Boys pretended they didn't see themselves. It was something James noticed; he noticed more things, moving more slowly, with Fiona in the front pack. Moving more slowly for the weight of her. For the logistics of where things go, like little feet catching in belts. Or bumping the handle of the knife in its neoprene sleeve tucked down in his right jeans pocket. The potential pinch of soft thigh where the front pack's sling met his waist. And to be gentle, a gentle ride. To let her feel the calm, and be at rest, and but also because she was seeing these things, for the first time, too. That old feeling like the world was too wrong for her. Girls, sometimes, seemed less studious than boys about hiding the appearance of regarding their reflection. They looked themselves up and down. Like a frank and humourless, almost aggressive, flirt.

Some girls looked themselves right in the eye.

Text from Jane about 11:30:

Just checking you're coming in this pm still James? Claudia wants a meet about the Turkey analysis you edited with Ibrahim.

He barely remembered the piece; there'd been so many.

There's a shitstorm brewing . . .

He showed her the ponds of the dammed-up Fleet, and talked to her of the ducks. A soft wind soughed through the great trees and breathed a tremble across the water. He went down among the pigeons, and pointed out the swans to her. He said, 'Look at that one, he's just young isn't he. See his feathers are all dark.'

He'd front-packed a sleeping Fiona by the lower Hampstead ponds once, and a talkative owner of a Labrador had told him what happens when a dog chasing a stick swims too near the chicks. The swan climbs up on the dog, the man said, and pushes it under and holds it down until it drowns.

Fiona looked out quietly over the seam of the front pack, gumming the edge. A hemisphere there all gone dark from saliva. She was teething. Or was she? It helped to have things to say, didn't it. It helped to assert something and try to believe it. It wasn't very scientific: you said it and then you looked for supporting evidence. Bent the data to your hypothesis. To get in line behind your utterances.

'Down at the fire station,' he sang, 'early in the morning, see the little fire engines, all in a row.' He held her feet and squeezed them gently. She watched the swans, her eyes milky, closing, blinking slow and seeing everything he showed her. 'You are my sunshine,' he half sang, half murmured, 'my only sunshine. You make me happy, when skies are grey.'

Fiona's wriggling and kicking and heaves and moans verging on wails, part way back down the Fleet Road in the shadow of the hospital where she was born, gave way to a great and shuddery sigh. She crashed in his arms, a failing star. His arm wrapped around her in the front pack with the shopping bag held forward—he was always carrying a shopping bag now. He kept walking. Steam from the vents in the Georgian terraces fuming in the chill morning. Two burnt-out cars sat on their rims in rough pools of melted rubber opposite the Palgrave House estates. She laid her cheek on his chest and she stilled. The funny thing was the way she activated memories he'd not considered in decades. You spent a lot of time in early childcare remembering. You can't remember two weeks ago, but something utterly obliterated from two decades ago materialises like a lucid dream. Fond and terrifying. How he suddenly remembered what it was like to be almost only a physical, emotional thing. Some childless friend once said that being a baby was like being in love in Paris on four espressos. That great sigh, for instance: he'd forgotten the feeling of silvery, shivering giving up. To be just too tired to fight any longer and to give up where you lay. That wave of shiver, and then collapse. How it was total and totalitarian: the body was the brute fascist and the parent only some confused functionary of a secondary power—a bureaucracy; the world. It was different for everybody but it was the same for his daughter and him—he saw it, felt it, knew he was right. They felt the same. She gave up the fight then, and began to breathe hotly and moistly onto a patch of his shirted chest.

He walked faster. Not gently jolting her. Not trying to keep her up with conversation—the moment for that was clearly past—but to get home in time for her to elaborate the fall into her Moses basket. So he would have time for Tatia to arrive at 12, to dress for work and get to the bus. Elaborate the fall and gently extend it, seamlessly from his chest and his heart to her bed.

On to Mansfield beneath the great ash trees alongside Waxham.

She breathed into his chest, like *pfff pfff*. Her head began to sink forward inside the pack and the airlessness there, so he leaned sideways like a very pregnant woman reaching for dropped keys. Fiona fell upright. He held her there. Her cheek was already red and creased with the imprint of a shirt seam and a button. Tendrils of sweaty hair pasted to her temple like she'd been crying. Crisp and pointed little nose. The deep, deep concentration of her sleep. Forging forward bravely into something. She exhaled again then, lolled against his hand. Dreaming of what she'd seen, for the only things she'd seen were what he'd given her to see. He looked up the covered way opposite the Mansfield off-licence. Despite the curve he could see it was empty all the way to the cage of his door, where Tatia was waiting outside. Fiona's feet dangled and bumped at his thighs. He could smell the sweat in her hair. She was too hot and would wake fast if he didn't get her into bed. She was like him—she ran hot.

He couldn't wave to Tatia. She was standing close to the cage, her head slightly bowed. Talking on her phone or her hand to her face.

He held the shopping bag forward so it didn't catch the soft leather shoe, like a small velcroed bag, and wake her. With his other hand he held her head up and covered her ear. To shield her from the worst of the traffic and the malevolent Royal Free ambulances who fire up sirens right alongside at worst possible moments. He'll use the shopping bag hand to unlock the locks and take her weight with the other. About 20 metres from his door Tatia saw him and looked up. Something was wrong with her eye. She looked at him and then across the road, and he followed her look. There through the traffic, in the off-white light, was the GRAVIS boy with the ridgeback, and two of the original four, sitting on the fence of the terraces opposite the estate.

Watching him come.

He dropped the shopping and walked faster and reached up over his shoulder for the buckle that held together the back straps of the front pack. Tatia was looking at him, bent slightly from the waist. As if he had an answer to a desperate question. Her right eye was half closed up and colouring quickly and he checked over the road.

They were standing now, and the GRAVIS boy came

forward into the parking bays between a white van and a Volkswagen and looked down Mansfield for a gap in the oncoming cars. The other black boy was behind him, grinning up at James, and further down the street the white boy held on to the leash of the ridgeback and it was plunging and rearing around him.

'James,' said Tatia, sad and urgent. It sounded like *shame-is*.

He left off the front pack and pulled the keys from his pocket, and in one movement pincered the barrier door's barrel key and the Abloy for the padlock, let the front door key and the Yale hang free.

'Unlock the door and I'll give you her and then you get inside,' he said, and his voice was very distant from above him, not his own. She took the keys as they were offered and took up the padlock of the cage and worried the key at the hole, gasping slightly, almost crying.

'It's all right, it's all right,' he said uselessly, fumbling over his shoulder for the buckle high up his back, looking for the snaps to squeeze, and then he found them and released the buckle. Each movement became smoother and more deliberate. He unwrapped one strap and drew his arm from it. He held Fiona's dead weight upon his chest, leaned back, then released the other. He unbuckled the belt at the small of his back, let the front pack fall to the ground.

'It's all right, it's all right,' he said again and she looked back then past him, to where they were coming, and there was a thin tear of watery blood running from the punctum inside of her left eye. 'Just get that one undone now and then you take her inside.'

Tatia turned back to the padlock and he looked again and the GRAVIS boy and the other were halfway across the road now, waiting for a hole in the traffic heading to Hampstead. They were staring up at him, the GRAVIS boy grinning wide, and the white boy beyond them in the larger spot in the parking bay in front of the white van was dancing with the dog. It was rising and shying, its eyes and ears and muzzle dark, its face patient.

The padlock popped open but the Abloy key dragged and hung in the lock as she pulled at it and so he reached and grasped the lock to hold it steady and then she pulled it free. She put the barrel key to the main door lock, and he lifted the padlock free of the clasp as she did so, their hands moving close and carefully together. The boys were across the road now and at a run. They disappeared out of sight behind the window boxes as they went for the steps leading up to the covered way. Then the white boy and the dog came suddenly fast further down the road in the lull in the traffic, the dog low and its ears back, dragging the boy behind him by its leash.

The barrel lock sprang and the door squealed as Tatia pushed it in. She turned and came to him and took Fiona from him and into her arms and she was a drooped and sleeping girl in her sleepsuit still. The GRAVIS boy appeared at the top of the same brick steps he'd first risen from, head down. When he saw James was still there he slowed and raised his eyes and waved his head gently side to side as if dancing, easing out his neck muscles, he was grinning and he was flexing his fingers down at his sides and it was all exaggerated and the other boy came up the steps behind him and he was the one to watch, deliberate and slow and his face closed and eyeless.

It was too late. Tatia was inside the cage with Fiona. James was out. They could reach her there, through the bars. James pulled the cage door up closed behind him with a clang and he closed the padlock. Over his shoulder he said to Tatia in some weird grammar of the moment, 'Stand back in there as you do it.' She was holding Fiona close inside the cage and was working the Yale at the front door lock. The traffic on and on, breezeless, a temperatureless day, shadows in the covered way.

'All right blud, you fucking minge, you cunt, what,' said the GRAVIS boy reasonably, grinning, coming now.

'You like scaring babies,' James said, 'hitting girls, fucking round with people's cats.'

The faceless one behind him was just watching him and James made himself check the boy's hands but he wasn't carrying anything. Seeing they had him now, they slowed. It would be worse for him now the girls were gone and he considered throwing the knife out in the road. 'You got it? You got it?' James said as if to them but behind him the front door opened, to the arcane and familiar smell of his very own apartment rising out, the straw-like odour of the coir matting known so deeply, and Tatia slipped inside and turned, holding the sleeping baby, and he said loudly, 'Shut the door and call the cops,' and she shut the door.

The hard scrabble of the dog's claws on the slick brick came as it mounted the other steps and he turned quickly to that and the white boy came up too hauling back on the leash and the dog seemed huge even though it was flat on its chest and heaving forward, the collar rising up back on its shoulder blades and it was wheezing, open mouthed.

The door to the next apartment down opened. The Irishman appeared in a grey towelling dressing gown, his white hair standing up in bunches. The dog was right in front of him, clawing and slipping on the slick brick, and: '*Koff* cunt,' the white boy said whiningly, inclining towards him, and the Irishman backed inside without a sound and shut the door. James was looking left and right, left and right, his back to the bars of the cage.

'Keep that fucking dog off,' he said uselessly.

'Fucking dog off!' the GRAVIS boy said, and laughed, and he and the other boy moved like they knew each other well, he stepping out to the furthest edge of the covered way, and the faceless one stepping forward to take his place.

The white boy heaved back on the chain, causing the ridgeback to wheeze in its barking like something huge dying, and it leaped and froze and dived around in the extent of the leash.

'Can't keep him off mate. Can't do a thing with him,' the GRAVIS boy said reasonably. 'He'll fuckin' chew your face off like Butcher's Choice.'

'Keep that dog off,' James said again and he could feel his face work with the adrenaline, his lips and cheeks numb, twitching and spasming.

'What. What. *You* keep him off you cunt. Cunt. You're shit mate. We know who you are. Fucking laughing stock round here mate. What. What. Your gaff's shit, clothes are shit, your woman's a piece of shit mate.'

The eyeless one was completely calm and still and stepping closer along the wall and the GRAVIS was right in front and the dog rising and pawing and barking like *RO RO RO RO RO* and falling as if to bow with its forelegs splayed wide then rising up in its leash again to bark again, again. The white boy was heaving back on the leash two-handed and laughing at the effort required and the dog alternately barked and wheezed and drool fell from its tongue and teeth in flung spatters.

'Fucking chasing people round you fucking losers,' James sort of said, then corrected himself and said, 'All right, all right, easy, we're good, we're all good,' and then there was nothing more to say but his unplaceable accent was more clear and that gave them momentary pause. The GRAVIS boy looked at the white boy and said what sounded like '*Kim*' and the white boy let the leash go, just raised his hands in the air with a surprised grin, as if surrendering, absolving himself from all contention in who does what to whom and the dog came at him slipping and scrabbling on the bricks and then with sudden surety it leaped upon the eyeless boy, who made a noise like '*Gill*' and fell sideways with the dog all over him and James bolted away from the GRAVIS boy who was coming and the white boy who was staring unmanned and horrified at the ridgeback savaging the eyeless one and James ran past him, the weaker boy, heard him shouting high and in his breaths. James ran for the end of the covered way and he could hear the determined pats of the GRAVIS one's trainers coming after him without hesitation, too fast.

He ran past the next steps down to the road, then past the last steps down to the road, and then hard enough to smash into the fence at the end of the way at the top of the wheelchair ramp, and used the recoil to bounce off and keep going, down the narrow ramp to the next corner where it doubled back again towards the road and as he ducked round the hairpin he felt fingers tug at his shirted shoulder and miss. Halfway down the last half of the ramp the road was ahead and he knew he couldn't turn in time or cross and he'd be caught on the path and so he ducked sideways into the narrow passage by the caretaker's extension and the boy missed him and overshot. Just run, just run. Down the short accessway. Then he jumped the steps out onto the Oak

Village side street and turned right, heading back behind the estate. Looked behind his building to the lines of fences guarding gardens all the way to his own, but the first was draped in the great gilded frozen pompoms of the razor-wire barriers all the way across, so he kept going. Pounding down past the first back street of Oak Village, where Michael Palin once had a house—this last bastion of high middle class cheek by jowl with the Gospel Oak estates—not even looking, towards the Kiln Place low rises from where they'd come, not looking back, then hard right, back parallel with Mansfield Road, not looking back but holding the knife in his pocket and watching the terrain ahead because there were steep dropped kerbs for driveways, on Lamble Street towards the Lismore and he'd go on, on to South End Green and the pub and people or the Royal Free itself, and he was almost at the end of the shady street under the great Gospel oaks, with no one around in the middle of Lismore Circus but one Somali woman idly turning the pedals of an exercycle in the new outdoor gym of indestructible hi-vis green steel tube when he looked back to see the GRAVIS boy round the corner back behind him grinning and panting and enjoying himself and he hissed *go fuck yourself* and then, on the edge of a line of old Victorian cobblestones left behind in the pavement for whatever reason, the ankle went.

physician-assisted suicide
pI isoelectric point
pie UK: Pies can be meat, vegetable or fruit. Use 'pies' for plural. US: Use 'pie' for plural. Tend to be fruit.
PIF peak inspiratory flow
pinprick

The Acrobats

The cover of the last-ever print issue of the *Royal London* was to be a full print of Gustave Doré's *Les Saltimbanques*, 'The Acrobats', of 1874. It would break your heart. In its luminous orange and blood reds, golds and cornflower blues. The painting was of three circus performers, a father, mother and son. The mother, seated, clasps the boy to her breast like a pietà. He is wounded, and the blood on his rudely bandaged head, his pale face and closed eyelids, is the same red as his acrobat's sequinned pants, and that of his father's costume too—who sits beside him, slumped, in make-up, watching on hopelessly. The boy has fallen from a high wire visible in the background. The great mother who holds him is exquisitely draped and wears ballet slippers and a crown. The gypsies mourn their dying son.

But *is* he dying? His skin is so pale, his eyes are closed, his mother cries, and does it matter? The art assistant, Mancunian frightener Adrienne Morrissey, came around tech ed soliciting opinion on the find, and she said, 'The artist himself says so.' She emailed it to everybody: Doré reportedly claimed (Morrissey wrote), 'Yes, he is dying. To gain money they have killed their child and in killing him they have found out that they had hearts.'

No one in tech ed agreed with the artist.

The headline on the cover was 'Paediatric head trauma: to scan or not to scan?'

The last print issue of the *R Lond J Med*, ever. Before the journal went online only. With back-up servers in Berkshire and quakeproof LPG generators in the airconditioned basements. The title font is a restrained, little-known Times New Roman variant, narrow of serif and thin in the hairline, designed specifically for elegantly presenting large-point, highbrow headlines. It has not been altered in seven decades. You know it deeply; it's utterly familiar yet somehow weirdly invisible and for a typographical layman completely impossible to distinguish or adequately describe, because it is in the cultural DNA like Harris tweed. It's less a font than a feeling. A tambourine in red completes a quadrangle of the costumes of the father and child, and the tightrope's harness behind. A trumpet, three gold boules; the ephemera of circus performers lurk behind. The mother's tarot cards laid out. Circulation: in the tens of thousands worldwide, at implausible and unsustainable, frankly unnecessary and anachronistic distribution costs. High gloss; high GSM. Two small costumed dogs look up at their mourning masters, the mother and the father. The title, sober and authoritative, above the father's head, read:

Royal Lond

J Med

To his right, above the mother's gaudy crown:

PLUS: Big pharma junkets

The sick man of Europe: Turkish healthcare emerges from the shadow

A Patient's Tale: Fistula

Antibiotics in India

News, careers, more.

A chained owl, the one animal of the painting indifferent to the human pain, sits on the bench beside the mother and the boy. Its dead black eyes on the digital future. The boy is five or six and very petite, and he is so very collapsed on his mother's breast, as if sleeping. But for the bandage, the blood, the concentration in the face of pain in the very young. His feet are tiny, in soft and spangled slippers.

The cover story was an editorial, and part of a standard strategy in the journal whereby the Goddess pithily summarises and briefly inveighs upon a much longer and denser piece of research that might stretch to several pages of two-columned background, harms, methodology, results, stats and discussion, to run in later pages of the journal. The Goddess guides the journal's stand on the issues in a couple of paragraphs of very pointed, frank positioning: her writing is distilled, unambiguous, often quietly outraged, and strictly evidence based.

The point in this story was that, some of the finer distinctions of statistical significance aside, about 50% of US children with head trauma were being given CT scans. But of those sampled, only about 1% were being found to have a serious head injury. CT scanning exposes the brain to ionising radiation, particularly dangerous when the brain is young and developing. Stats cited in the research were that 1 in 1000 to 5000 CT scans cause a fatal brain cancer—ambiguous and contentious figures, vulnerable, as a companion analysis commissioned by Death points out, to multiple confounders, low n, free-ranging p-values, and confidence intervals that concertinaed in and out like an accordionist on crystal meth.

But the Goddess—Death's mitigating stats analysis

aside—was making the point, in this ultimate and final print issue, that scanning was being routinely ordered, unnecessarily, without proven benefit, at great cost, and was, in fact, delivering harms.

This was another of the *Royal*'s refreshing, iconoclastic and often fiercely unpopular stances that regularly caused pages and pages of comments, ripostes and flame wars, and subsequently less than scientific pieces in the tabloids cherry-picking and caveat-stripping for headlines. Sodium as a public health issue. Energy drinks. Alcohol. Midwifery versus hospital births. Another one was that uniform breast cancer screening, for example, was profligate and unnecessary, without statistically significant benefit, and caused more concern and anxiety than alleviated actual suffering. As was testicular screening. As was testicular *self-examination*.

Adrienne Morrissey found the cover image for the final print issue and worked on the design, and in the ongoing process review hers is the first of much blood to be spilled. The combined machinery of downsizing and office popular opinion was subtly, steadily aligning against her, and everyone knew it.

There are fashionable conditions that, for whatever reason and whatever period of time, gain a critical mass of awareness and popularity, with their concomitant foundations and lobby groups and celebrity endorsements, their Movembers and Septumbers ('Align your septum early for winter!') and Cocktobers ('Members get melanomas, too'), their Kate Moss-designed TopShop joint T-shirt and halter-top range for nipple cancer campaigns and their applied self-righteousness, their tacked-on anxiety-puncturing misdirected middle-class do-goodery-fests. There are third-world conditions the eradications of which have been made a focus of major world health bodies not because those conditions are a particularly severe blight or burden on those countries or economies but simply because certain very powerful personalities would quite like to have the eradication of a third-world disease on their CVs, please. The exposure of one such condition and its incredibly expensive and *unnecessary*—statistically, unfashionably, and on the evidence *unnecessary*—eradication campaign that named certain British names was the subject of another very, very unpopular *London* editorial that earned the Goddess a Whitehall audience (and, reportedly, 'a robust airing of views') with first the health secretary then the prime minister.

(She came back to the office that afternoon grinning and blushing as everyone stood up at the corners of their desks blushing and grinning as if waiting for the birthday cava to come out.)

The *Royal London*'s cover, its final cover, which, however briefly, would sit on the waiting room tables of doctors' surgeries from Cape Town to Alaska, with the first five or six pages of news and editorial and analysis thumbed until the cover and first and most readable and let's face it most illustrated fifth of the issue was an unreadable scroll of finger-oil and anxious sweat (the site's landing page now just a small, sober carousel of health-related photos connected to each article), was a thing of saturated beauty, high-res colour and profound melancholy. Everyone said that although in the last 120 years of illustrated covers it might be a bit rich to say it was the best ever or something like that, the find and design and layout was Morrissey's best work, no doubt about that, and it made them proud.

Which made things awkward, because she was being fired.

From out of a soft and sad and blurry reverie, anger called.

Kristian Shattuck had become aware that there was a fight going on not 10 feet away from him. Adrienne Morrissey was standing at Julia's desk. Adrienne was leaning over her. Kristian slipped on the new spectacles—£300 Cutler and Gross frames, a gift to himself after his diagnosis—and entered the lurid super-reality of 20/20.

'I *asked* you,' he heard Adrienne hiss. She was bent from the hip, not tall but a big woman, rangy and wide in the shoulders and a tense rigour to her way. Julia was small and swivelled in her chair, hands in her lap, looking up at her. They were hissing small statements to each other. Kristian couldn't hear or bear any particulars. He was typing an email, pausing at plausible moments that might not seem to punctuate what they said. The argument was accelerating quickly. Their voices were growing quieter and quieter, all treble, their stares unwavering.

'Only *five people* turn up—' he heard Adrienne say. He hit enter three times, then delete three times. Woolly haired and woolly dressed Harriet, in the desk unit alongside Julia, was right behind Adrienne and seemed frozen in shock or disbelief. She was staring at her screen, not typing or mousing or even attempting to seem otherwise than eavesdropping in appal. Nothing else could be heard from only 10 feet but the occasional stressed word from the series of speeches Adrienne was making. Her head shaking slightly side to side. Bending to emphasise, to be close when she couldn't be loud. It was horrible to watch. Julia was listening closely, it seemed, and in fact leaning in to Adrienne's fury as if she couldn't not. Kristian could read her screen but couldn't hear anything but Adrienne's hisses, her sharp Mancunian t's and d's. Adrienne jammed her glasses back up the bridge of her nose with one erect forefinger as if stabbing herself between the eyes. The office all about was near silent. Their argument was so quiet and controlled it was really not like anything was happening at all. Julia looked very small. Her hands in the skirt of her lap. Adrienne's speech settled into the rhythm of someone who had vented the initial urgency and was now certain that what they were saying was being heard.

Which was when Julia stood up. Still so much smaller and slighter than Adrienne. Her precise auburn ponytail bobbing. Kristian watched her interrupt: three small gestures punctuating her retort, three wags of a forefinger downward, the balls of her palm upward, an utterly unconscious gesture of defiance in defeat, her eyes up to Adrienne—questioning but not yet pleading.

'You're—' Kristian heard Julia whisper-hiss. 'You're—you're—'

Then she walked off.

Down the office, past Emily Pheromone and the news desks, towards the bathrooms and kitchen. Adrienne stared after her like someone who'd missed their ferry. Then she snorted violently, stalked past James to the lifts for a cigarette, in her thick, thick glasses, the rage swollen in her oversized eyes.

Kristian had been typing the email throughout. He figured by the ambient rhythms of typing that no one behind him in tech ed had actually noticed the altercation. The office's eternal low white noise flowed back to quickly drown the small eruption. Typing. The printer came to life for three pages, falling back to sleep before the last page hummed out. There was a subject-lineless all-*Royal London* email from unknown@rlondjmed.com that appeared in everybody's inbox earlier that day and read simply in its entirety, 'Hlör u fang axaxaxas mlö.' There was another five minutes later that read, 'Get out of London early tonight.' There was the idle clank of the blind half-down bumping against the wall above Birgit's always half-inch-open window. The blind always half down. The window always open half an inch.

Kristian watched Harriet, the closest bysitter. She hadn't resumed her work. From behind, her gestures were sporadic and hesitant. She at last stood up from her cubicle and he saw her face then, that she was distressed and unsure, and she walked after Julia to the bathrooms.

No one in tech ed had noticed.

D1 was standing, talking on the phone, thumbweb in his braces, saying, 'It was overnight. No, no, she's in Norway. Finland. The Arctic Circle. God knows. Ultima Thule.' There were 10 feet, a width of desk, whispers, a bank of computers (three), and some agreement between them all not to reach out. You just knew Julia was crying in there. On Harriet's screen, a Google image search of video projectors.

Kristian typed. He tagged. He edited. He chose pull quotes. He reduced the article in front of him from 500 to 250 words in about a minute. Reading something several times and refining it down is ultimately an exercise in calm and care, and brings—or can bring—an enormous peace. The precision of the text when he wore glasses was alarming and nearly unbearable, and the white page behind swam and eddied like filthy water. But when he looked he could not find the filth. They were rather large and square and feminine glasses in a sort of elaborate hipster Edna Everage mode and suited him while comprehensively outing him. He was the kind of gay man whose body language otherwise read 'I am none of your business' and who might be simply thin and neat. These particular lenses would become increasingly vital as the vision went, but for a brief window only, the doctor had said, before the prescription would have to be upped, in the first of probably five stages before it was hopeless, the doctor didn't quite say but directly and horribly implied with the words he carefully chose, like 'resolved' and 'completed'—in the context of an unspeakable decline—and Kristian ought to be using the glasses for everything right now, but the headaches were unbearable by about 2pm, and he'd had to go home once. Which he couldn't afford. Kristian had about a year at most of editing left in him and he was 46 and he had a degree in art history and no other qualifications. When he deliberately panned up and refocused from the screen, down the office Harriet was talking to Emily Pheromone. Telling her what happened? So she hadn't gone after Julia after all. Harriet returned to her desk and sat down. Sitting thoughtfully at her Mac, the screen of which had gone dim. Then she turned and looked at Julia's swivelled and empty chair. Sat and looked at it. Quietly, without a fidget. It was a very actorly, filmic gesture, though it seemed unconscious. A semaphore of doubt.

Kristian typed, then removed the glasses and eased the pads of his forefinger and thumb over the lids of his old eyeballs in the fine soft oil of his good clean skin. That ache, and that fine and dusty feeling. Putting glasses on for the first time felt like some tiny sadist stood astride each eye, holding the pupil open with two fierce hands to lean down and shout something final and awful in there. Then Julia was back at her desk with a cup of tea, and then David 1 was coming down the aisle and Kristian tensed, froze, stared at his screen.

He edited; he laid out text.

'*Jyilliuh*!' David 1 said quite loudly indeed. She looked up, sudden, in what looked like, for the first time, really, shock. 'I'll be at conference in Liverpool for the rest of the week,' he said, 'so I need someone to cover the guest editor blogs and that someone might be you. Just till next Monday! Is that all right for you?'

Her eyes were quite red. D1 was standing where Adrienne had been five minutes ago, and that was about right for a cigarette, wasn't it.

'Yes,' she said.

'Okay, thanks!' David 1 said loudly and was gone.

Julia turned back to her screen.

She bobbed up and down to adjust her skirt beneath her.

Then she sipped her cup of tea.

Kristian watched.

After a while she retied her ponytail into a tight bun.

She took a long sip of tea.

She began to nod, fightingly, as if reliving the conversation.

Gingham-shirted David 2 had been typing over there throughout the incident, squinting into his screen like it was a cold wind as he did. He abruptly sighed and rose and came round the computers, all smiles and bounces, problem surmounted, and materialised leaning over her screen.

'D'you want a cup of tea?' he said brightly.

'No . . .'

'You're not looking very well!' he said, and smiled. 'You got a cold too?'

'No, I'm okay,' Julia said.

He laughed. 'Okay!' And wheeled away in his own private success and was gone.

Harriet, listening, got up and came over to Julia.

Julia had started to cry and she got up and headed out the door to the stairwell, wiping her eyes and cheeks as fast as the tears were coming, and Harriet followed.

Ten minutes later? They were both back at their desks. Harriet had her headphones on. Julia was working, in conversation, even laughing at something Birgit had said.

Ten more minutes. Paraic, the handsome Irish harasser, rose from his slump and came over to her. He crouched down for a full hug—as was his wont with seated women at the *Royal London*, especially, in the recent past, Annabel Pitti— his hand to the back of Julia's necklaced neck, touching her hair, and left. The timing, sort of quite right; but the act: not quite. Julia wiped her eyes again. She had to get up and get tissues.

Periodically thereafter she blew her nose. It was now 11am, and this to and fro had gone on for an hour. The scars on that relationship near permanent. *You made me feel this way*.

Kristian removed his glasses, turned up the view zoom per cent and let it all go soft and fuzzy again.

The Acrobats II

James was editing two news stories, one of which was Annabel's and needed heavy work, plus an op-ed and a research article, at the same time as working on the stylebook conversion, and it was exhausting. A specialist in alteration, in shifting the tone, shifting the focus, he shifted the aching ankle from the ground to the footrest and back again. Move this paragraph to the top and see what you have. Cut the first half and start there. Disassociate from, say, the intimate first-person of a comment into a more scholarly tone and suddenly you have an analysis. Eliminate the passive voice. Between editorial and tech ed you can change the whole subject of a piece. You can rewrite it all and tell a different story and if only you make sure track changes is disabled who can know or detect or tease out from the hairless patch and suture scars and blood-browned linens the other narrative concealed beneath? A good editor might. But there's this thing you do, and it's called in CV-speak something bland like time management, but in this job it really is quite the art: you intricately stagger your responsibilities such that any waiting time—for CMS conversion, for XML processing, for proofing, the old editorial yay or nay—cascades in to be spent on other projects. The goal being perpetual motion. Planes landing on the tarmac one after the other, regardless of their origin. Ducks in a row and stars aligned, &c., &c. Working hard tactically but never letting the strategy slip from mind. 'Nimble'—*sigh*—was the Goddess's buzzword du jour. The anti-Parkinson's law. But despite your best efforts, now and again you can find yourself abruptly bereft of work to do: everything winds up at once, waiting on an XML issue or a bottleneck somewhere and here you are, head full of stuff and nothing to do and staring at a blank 10-pt Verdana page.

Just death and waiting in cold rooms on the other side.

So he looked up, out, and around himself.

Adrienne Morrissey, wallet of tobacco in one hand, final print issue of the *Royal London* in the other, was stomping back down the aisle towards James and tech ed with Annabel Pitti in tow. Adrienne stopped off at Birgit's desk, opposite Julia's still-empty chair, and whispered several rapid things in the split seconds it took before Birgit began to make exaggerated and elaborate hand-shuffling gestures and from here audibly cry out, 'Go *away*. I want to *work*.'

Morrissey had just today discovered James was smoking again and was dragging him out with her every time she indulged.

The Morrissey lectures, delivered over roll-your-owns under the long late afternoon shade of Tavistock Square's great plane trees, looking out enviously towards BMA House, home of the *BMJ*, and towards the lonely red neon of the sign for the Cunty Hotel were what, he'd claimed, had led Benjamin Subramaniam to give up five years of smoking.

Morrissey clomped on, stopped at James's desk. She leaned down, breath reeking of late morning, stale Drum and solitude, her big eyes crinkling in what appeared a generous mirth, and said very loudly for everyone in tech ed to hear, 'Irony of ironies. Private health insurance is advertising in the *Royal*'—she held up the last print *Royal London* and gave it a shake; the Cigna pamphlet dropped out and fell in the recycling bin—'yet *we're* not allowed to have it.' She cackled throatily, turned back to Annabel, tagging along behind sore-eyed-looking and fingering a fresh new pack of Bensons, then back to James. 'Coming out? C'mon you. I want a word with you.'

Over at the edge of tech ed, one of the lieutenant editors had brought in her son. This was allowed, tolerated, not much commented upon. Simon Smyther-Jones was about six years old and bespectacled like his mother, and drew or played games peering up at Trish's PC all day when he was in. Quietly enough, apart from the occasional outburst when he forgot himself and shouted out his results to his mum. But just now Lisa Pratchett, diagnosed with chronic endometrial scarring 20 years before and given certain final advice when not much was or could be done about the condition, was caught, paused, frozen, rising from her desk, turned, her hair all mussed with work, just staring at him. Staring at him turning over some pages.

Outside through the great glass doors and gathered tight in the strip of veranda sheltered by the Regency terrace above were Benjamin Subramaniam and his replacement as student ed, Oliver Reed, smoking and giggling and subsiding with slight uneasiness at the approach of Morrissey. Slight hope at the sight of Pitti. Slight ambivalence at the sight of limping Ballard, who nobody, if anybody knew anybody, seemed to know very well.

'All right?'

'All right.'

'All right.'

'What's up with the ankle there?'

'Oh, I sprained it running.'

'Oh dear!'

'Mmm.'

The square hovered in a cold mist as the taxis muttered past.

'Mwot diz quistian doo, 'en, in teg-ed?' said Morrissey, a filter tip in her lips, over her rolling.

'He works on news and obituaries,' said Annabel quickly. 'Very well too! Or at least he did when I was working with him. Does he—?' She looked up at Ballard then back down at her Bensons she was struggling to efficiently unwrap. The pull tab had peeled away in a minute strip, leaving the end of the plastic sleeve still occlusively sealed to the now unopenable lid, and she couldn't get it off.

Kristian had made another rather drastic and unprecedented error today. He had, in a published headline of a news story built live to the homepage at about half past nine, substituted 'H2N1' for 'H5N1'. Unprecedented only because all Kristian's other recent errors have been caught in time by the *London*'s multifarious mechanisms, various cool eyes and sharp heads. Not to mention his discreet friends. This big error might just have tipped the scales of tolerance and forgiveness, though, and its correction, alongside and as synecdoche and microcosmic example and potential precedent for Ibrahim al-Rayess's moment of catastrophic indiscretion, was apparently the emergency behind the current and ongoing extremely high-level exec meeting going on upstairs in the Heatherington. The emergency had gone up the chain and James's meeting with the Goddess cancelled. The high-level exec meeting now involved all seven members of the executive advisory board, the Goddess, Death, the three Trishes, Barbara Jones, and a lawyer named Jarndyce from Jarndyce Balls George, the *London*'s on-retainer firm, and they were, people supposed, discussing whether for the first time in the *London*'s modern history to make a retraction as opposed to posting an erratum. One was a news item, a headline, and on an online news feed. One was a blog post.

Some journals publish just the fact of their corrections and correct the original. So while the publication keeps to the windy side of the law the error does not itself stay on the record for enemies to consult, collate and disseminate in evidence. As the *Guardian* was wont to write: 'This article was amended on [date] to comply with our editorial guidelines.' It was slippery yet effective. Why keep a record of your own crimes?

So people wondered: did the *London* have to now stand by Ibrahim's piece, even though it was a blog post, bitter obiter, and explicitly represented only those bitter views of the individual concerned? Fact-check it, and defend it, maybe, in an op-ed? What if it were true? What could the *Royal* expect then, lining up against the Turkish government? And their supporters in the EU and those they would muster for a fight? Can a country bring a libel suit in another country, and what kinds of overwhelming resources could they then bring to bear? The *London* was vulnerable—possibly even a tempting target for ironically minded lawyers given the Goddess's extensive editorialising on the chilling effect of the UK's elastic libel laws on British science publication. Or can we say these are only al-Rayess's views, in a blog post, and that's that. Those views, though: expressed under the aegis of the *London*, in its employ and beneath its masthead.

Would a deletion be simpler and more modern? Just pull the blog post—a disgruntled employee, a very troubled employee in fact, a moment's indiscretion, a moment's madness, private stresses, personal lives, tragedies and irrevocable losses—who can imagine or mediate his suffering?—system failure, good faith, goodwill, firm hand on the tiller, and etc. What was the status of a blog in the journal? Was it the same as a comment? We don't 'pull' those. But we 'moderate' them, don't we—we delete spam and 'offensive' material and select from them to recast and edit and publish as letters to the editor in print. But would a deletion—in an open access, fully cached world—then become the story? A story in which the *Royal London* became not a villain but a dupe and hypocrite, some kind of early fail-exemplar, morally and ethically, losing the high ground in a campaign who knows how long and bloody?

On this day of all days do the old ways apply?

And what if the writer were right?

'Freelancers get it in the neck,' Adrienne said, and she lit up and took a huge and rapacious drag on her Drum. She clutched her smoking elbow with her other hand, her smoking hand twitching up and down to bump the ash. James observed a thumbnail of it fall and instantly roll down the back of that hand and disappear inside her sleeve. 'He'll be all right. But freelancers get it in the neck.' She looked significantly but not without humour at James. 'Just be scared, okay? I'm not into *scare*mongering . . . but *be scared.*'

Benjamin Subramaniam stared at Morrissey as if terrified, then laughed helplessly, and the new student ed laughed heartily, not having any idea.

Annabel turned to him then, Oliver Reed. She said loudly, 'I'm doing this article . . .' then she edited herself and turned down the volume a bit, '. . . on "Semengate".'

A sort of silence rose around them.

The muttered conversation of the sound of traffic went on. Adrienne leaned her head to one side rather further than looked comfortable, took a gigantic puff, nodded once, and looked at Annabel encouragingly.

The blush on Annabel rose then, uncontrollably, in feverish rashes and prickled patches, her entire neck crimsoning, asymmetric lilypads of raspberry red forming frighteningly fast on her cheeks and forehead.

Oliver, the new student ed, was instantly relaxed, and James found himself liking him intensely.

'Oh really?' Oliver said, and the politeness was unimpeachable.

Annabel glanced at each in the group.

The gentle push was enough.

'Yes, so, well, now, I'm writing an article on political correctness in medical school and as part of the research huh-hah hah hah I uncovered this piece about Lazar Greenfield, president of the American College of Surgeons, who ages ago wrote a piece on Valentine's Day for *Surgery News* which drew on actual research from *Arch Sexual Behave*—'

Moving faster now, Annabel, and in the pronunciations of

the journals and the colleges and the journals' ISO 4 standard abbreviations she knew she was on safe and professional ground and her safe and professional mode and voice seemed to compete with the urge—and who knew? Maybe it was her real nature, deep down, and an urge that only the accidents and doubt engendered by a life any one of us might have accidentally lived had thwarted—to seek to successfully tell a funny, naughty story to near strangers. Who knew? Her ringtone was the opening riff to 'Sweet Child o' Mine'. Perhaps even a terrible, big drive to *live* one.

'—and he, Greenfield, in this informal Valentine's Day piece in *Surgery News* asserted, using a large number of examples that, uh, the attraction between the genders was only—'

She paused and looked around. Her blush was now a particularly deep and plummy hue. The initial bloom had settled in determinedly for the breadth of the anecdote—of one paid attention to. The group was listening.

'Or'—then realising she had got that a bit wrong—'between partners, of animals attracted to each other, anyway, of any gender, or really, sex, I mean, biological sex, because'—she laughed as if she were laughing knowingly—'gender's a social construct, isn't it, and what he means is between the partners, sexual partners who are attracted to each other, anyway—'

She attempted to bear down. Oliver took a drag. Benjamin was grinning a bit too wildly. It was possible, James thought, that Annabel was an actual virgin, and given the dating and men's advice websites it was possible Benjamin was not far off it. Oliver, though—very far from there indeed. He momentarily felt like getting or giving a blowjob. Doing something dirty that involved straddling and effort and disappearance. Unlike other more technical parts of the journal, this work world's sexuality was well tamped down. There would be no Geoff at pub table freely confiding how he 'whacked one out' mid-afternoon in the journal toilets. There would be no Jennie concurring and saying sometimes you simply had to. Half the editors' eyes as wide as their mouths were closed. (Apart from one, that one; that sad star, the new editor, Mandy, unconfessed sufferer, if that were the word, of *objectum sexualia*, and secretly, guiltily in love with a decommissioned, wingless, rusting RAF English Electric Lightning in a field in Northumberland—*she* was suddenly listening closely.)

James suddenly felt very old, as if the marrow of his limbs had gained sudden weight and malignance. Tired of living without her.

'. . . *and* that the romantic feeling, romance, the thing you supposedly feel in your stomach or in your heart, that there is evidence of chemicals that raise the feelings of wellbeing in the other partner that have an evolutionary basis, such as the, it's really very good, he uses the example of the drosophila fruit fly that feeds on starch being more likely to mate with another starch-eating fly, and asexual rotifers.'

And then she just stopped.

A bus went by with a billboard advertising the magician-acrobat who would levitate over St Pancras that afternoon.

Annabel was almost panting, ready to laugh, if only those around her, her audience, would commence for her.

Adrienne Morrissey had been watching the whole performance with an increasingly visible bitter glee, and she looked around the waiting faces once it was clear Annabel had come to the apparent end of her story, before bursting into wheezing, clearly choreographed, sarcastic laughter.

Benjamin laughed too, at something, then, unimpeachably sincere.

In the slow steady flow of students and guests of the clusters of Bloomsbury hotels all around, a black hoodie on the pavement opposite caught James's attention, and the gait and shape was familiar. His heart started up hard and fast before he was fully cognisant of the fact that he was making the recognition. His heart started knocking—small and hard and fast in there, pounding like someone trapped in a room down the hall, like *oompah oompah oompah*—and he felt himself come up in his skin, prickling and tingling. Afraid. Then the black hoodie turned and it did not read GRAVIS. It was not serious. It was University of London. And not even close to his muscle mass—some skinny, pubescent white kid, a welter of scars on his face, not even close. He breathed out and watched the kid walk on. The surrealism of the adrenaline: like some boy had attacked him out of nowhere in the street, then metamorphosed just as uncannily as if he'd erupted into a bird.

There were all kinds of bitterness.

James drew on his cigarette.

'I'm not sure we quite follow what happened,' he said gently to Annabel. He breathed out smoke.

'Yes. Yes, you're almost there,' said Oliver amiably. He was going to be somebody at the journal. And after. You could feel it even now.

Annabel backtracked. She thought. She was silent as she reviewed her speech in the small warm allowance Oliver and James had offered her.

'Oh and but what I meant is that he was *fired*,' she said, suddenly full and sure of herself. 'Greenfield was *fired* for the publication of this piece they'd done for fun about there being no such thing as romance on Valentine's Day.' She looked about. She knew she had shied away from the material, from the anecdotal to the professional. Perhaps she didn't quite understand why this hurt her standing, friendship-wise, at work. Or perhaps she did, but she was willing to pay that price for the future. For her career. Some of us can't do charm. Not all of us can be charming.

'Is this about Ibrahim then?' said Oliver. 'Not much fun about that blog.'

'I'm using the whole Greenfield scandal as a stepping board for talking about political correctness in the deaneries and how it affects students and that's why I wanted to ask.'

Having shied comprehensively away from her first and truest urge, she did her questioning journalist's face, her cheek half raised, her eyes utterly hidden. So things were back to normal and she'd stopped smiling and the blush bled out.

Adrienne was looking out over the square, overtly ignoring them. Performing her disgust. There were no longer any rules for her, social or otherwise. Adrienne had separated from a drunk man, now unemployed, who was being prescribed anti-psychotics on the NHS that were very powerful indeed and rendered him less than able to complete most tasks short of preparing a pot of tea. She had a five-year-old child to raise and was facing, in the coming weeks of her day job, a series of meetings where the executive, HR and her co-workers were, in intent and effect, conspiring to put her out of work and send her away from them forever, like a medieval expulsion.

A bored silence fell.

'I'm not quite sure I understand the title "Semengate" though,' said Oliver.

Annabel looked at him with an odd ferocity. This was it—she was wild, she was electric to watch.

'It's because he says in the piece, and he quotes it from *Arch Sexual Behave*, that only 5% is sperm and actually 95% of men's ejaculate'—she wasn't blushing at all anymore—'is a seminal plasma that is in fact a rich soup of mood-enhancing chemicals.'

'Oh, I already knew *that*,' said Oliver, and looked fairly comfortable.

The Acrobats III

Work expands so as to fill the time available for its completion, states Parkinson's law, so when the fire alarm rang at 4:29pm there were loud and angry groans over the ringing. With assembly and headcount and return and finishing off tasks and emails, that meant a sharp 5pm exit done for. A lot of griping on the stairs down was usual; silence meant people were very pissed off indeed.

Adrienne Morrissey was a fire marshal and had a hi-vis vest on the back of her desk chair all the time anyway—she donned it with verve—'C'mon you,' she said to John Mayer (who always stood at his desk when talking on the phone, and who as her direct superior was being forced to work, in his spare time also, with pleasureless grim resolve, on Editorial's response to Morrissey's case against dismissal). 'Nope,' she said. 'Put—that—*down*. Out.' And she whipped the phone right out of his hand, and he stood there, blinking—at Martin, at Jane, at Susan—to show them, look, here he was, nonplussed, blinking. Benjamin Subramaniam laughed uproariously, then the complexity and seriousness of it all subdued him as fast as if he'd been gently pushed underwater.

The staff filed downstairs, silent in the din of the old steel firebells.

It was out in Tavistock Square that Oliver remembered the magician-acrobat levitating over St Pancras that afternoon. They all stood about in the approaching uncertainty of a Monday night, waiting on the all-clear, watching the interrupted board meeting's members farewell the Goddess at the steps to the building. Her calm grey eyes, her bobbing head, towering over Jarndyce in his sleek black suit. The board members, just metres away, surgeons, lords, presidents of Royal Colleges, editors in chief, likewise discombobulated, likewise briskly moved along, away from the building, by a gleeful Morrissey in hi-vis and with nothing in particular to lose. Oliver and Benjamin were up for it, and John Mayer and Martin, then Jane too, and Susan had grabbed her stuff and was heading to King's Cross anyway.

To divert themselves from the emergency they went to see the acrobat.

Standing under the trees, as the sky clouded and darkened unseasonally, as the lit aquaria of buses passed by above them, the glazed misery of post-work Monday looking down upon the spontaneous cluster of *RLJM* workers' faces bent penitently to their phones, the tame dogs running by in pursuit of feral pigeons, the high dark plane trees like giants from some forgotten pantheon and Jeremy from IT's phone rang with its recording of some reasonable upper-middle-class English voice saying, with a very long, breathy, drawn-out 'to', both muted and small, yet piercing, high treble, carrying over the murmur, 'I want to . . . rub the human face in its own'—and it's here that those who don't know Jeremy's phone always start to pay attention—'*vomit* . . . and force it to look in the *mirror* . . .' and Gandhi sits there still, in silence, bent.

The pavement opposite the St Pancras Hotel. Traffic on Euston Road back to back. Everyone half-left already, panning the gathering crowds, half regretting agreeing to come now that it was five o'clock and, Susan apart, all of them would have to go back to the office to shut down their Dells and phones and retrieve their bags.

The acrobat was there, picked out standing in space up on the gently sloping St Pancras Hotel forecourt. He was a young man and bearded and unprepossessing; dressed casually in skinny chinos, T-shirt and a pea coat. He held an iPhone in one hand and wore glasses. The only sign of anything to happen was the strange space around him. Behind, St Pancras doormen, big and bemused eastern Europeans, gathered in an overcoated gang. The crowds were that awkward mixture of those who'd come for the event, those passing through, and those torn and listless and diverted by the promise of something they didn't know what. Spilling onto the road in dangerous hernias. The cries of car horns. A crew of boys like young crows balancing on the railing of the narrow traffic island.

'Is he going to do it then?' Oliver said, up on tippy toes to see.

'Better bloody do it,' Jane said.

'Do it soon or I'm off,' said Susan.

And the crowd roared half ironically and everyone turned, as the magician raised his arms to cruciform and levitated. The faces rose with him as he floated up in a brief and soft acceleration, slowing to bob 15 feet above the crowd.

'Oh,' went the crowd.

'Oh, that's quite good, isn't it,' Oliver said, holding up his iPhone to get the shot. The acrobat looked up to the sky and levitated again, rising a further gentle, uncanny 20 feet. He was now one third up the massive brick Gothic of St Pancras, and the traffic had all but halted. The acrobat then executed a somersault, then another, then a double somersault; he finished halfway through the third and rotated gently to face Euston Road, arms out wide and quite upside down. Then he began to shoot the crowd with his own iPhone, upside down. There was a moment then when everything was paused, the acrobat's face above a field of faces looking back and holding up their phones to him. Then the first stone was thrown. This stone silently hit his leg, and the boys on the traffic island called out their laughter. The acrobat reached up to his thigh and half turned away, then he dropped his phone. Another object flew by. The doormen outside the St Pancras Hotel doors turned quickly and quietly and went inside. The acrobat somersaulted upright, holding his leg. Then what was clearly a bottle flew past him.

'Oh no,' said Jane.

The next object missed the acrobat too but hit a hotel window. The sound was inaudible. Flickering glass fell like a dropped sheet. A man near them shouted, '*Who's throwing fucking stones.*' The boys on the traffic island turned idly to see who said that, then back again. They seemed relaxed by the turn of events, calmed. No one could move anywhere. The lights had changed and the traffic was trickling again. James felt his heart knocking, and he looked to Jane and Susan and he said, 'It's time to go. Time to go home.'

And Jane, his boss, turned with him, quick and mild as if she were under his care, and Susan seemed momentarily torn—King's Cross was in her muscle memory, all things escape were the other way. 'Come on, just for now,' James said, and her face was swimming and uncertain.

He reached to take her arm and she came too, and he shouted to Oliver, 'Time to *go*, mate,' and John Mayer heard him and nodded sharply and moved quickly through the crowd and Oliver looked over from his iPhone but was already separated from them, and he waved his phone as if to say all right, yes, no problem! Benjamin beyond grinning wildly, and above them all, hovering in the air above the car roofs glittering and the tight packed crowds, the acrobat was crumpled and silent and unmoving as stones and bottles came from different directions, materialising for brief and soundless seconds to silently touch him, pause and fall to the ground and out of sight.

'Mistake he made was staying still,' said a man.

'Can't ix-*scape*, canny,' said another man.

'Where are the *poliss*,' said a northern woman.

As they pushed through to the back of the watchers there was a rivulet of passersby heading west, hard up against the buildings of Camden Council, and James looked back as they joined the exodus at the revolving acrobat crumpled up, the phones catching it all.

The Boot

'I like a pub with an air of threat,' said John, and grimaced like he wanted it to be understood: I'm only mostly being ironic.

'Well there's the Flyer,' James said—meaning the Euston Road tourist/commuter hell that was often still quite worrying, and London Pride on tap—'but there's somewhere better off the beaten.'

Limping ahead of the three remaining (Martin, John Mayer and Benjamin Subramaniam: all who fancied a pint after pain and fear), James led them this way and that through trash and sprays of milky sugarcubes of smashed windscreen glass into the King's Cross back lanes and alleys—shortly to the Boot in Cromer Street.

Dinner menu: gammon steaks and egg, fish and chips with mushy peas and a small paper cup of, went the laminated page, like a rumour: 'tartar sauce'. Only one customer and only one ale on tap, plus Guinness, Carling and Magners. A proper English pool table, St George's cross flags on the walls, an actual fruit machine. And above the bar, inexplicably, a pair of skis. Across the way was the brick red Bramber estate, and the 123-year-old stone of the Holy Cross Church. Sleepy, tree-dreamy, isolated corners for discreet kickings. A proper pub then, with an air of threat, and all this only a couple of minutes from St Pancras station. They drank pints and talked about anything but stonings and fallings. ''Ere comes the doctor,' John was wont to tell his first pint, both meaning the accent he was using, and not. The other two didn't last long and headed for the Russell Square tube, and then it was just James and John, who seemed to understand there was something up, over the pool table with whiskies and Guinness chasers, both quite absorbed in the game.

He'd drunk more than he meant to and they hadn't eaten, as they rarely did at *Royal* pub nights, but he was sober enough when the moment presented itself. And it was actually quite easy after all.

'So,' said James, 'I've actually run into a bit of trouble too.' He took his shot and sank it.

John never, in James's experience, appeared drunk. The drunker he got, the more still and anchored and delighted he became. He would find a place to stand and his face would redden a little and he would grin crazily and sometimes even begin to mix up words—this was as bad as he ever got before one's memory of everything dimmed and faded away and he redly presided over your fall as if a ghost.

John stood off the quarter of the table with his legs slightly splayed, the pool cue across his body like a big decision lightly made. 'Not this ongoing thing with David 2, then, is it,' he said at the table.

'No, no, ha ha. Did that not go down well then?'

'But he's a proud one.' Mayer shrugged, smirked at the table. Then he did an odd little gesture: he bent one leg, pursed his lips, let his hand go limp at the wrist, just slightly.

So there was that—something he would never have allowed himself sober.

'No,' said James. 'Might be serious, actually.'

'Sort of serious?'

James could hear his accent changing. It felt quite natural. 'Bit of trouble with some boys in our neighbourhood.' He shot and missed.

'Sort of boys.'

'Teenagers. Estate boys.'

'Well, best nipped in the bud if you can,' Mayer said as he moved around the table. How amazing. He'd stopped smiling. 'Soon as you can, nip that in the bud.'

'Few of them, though.'

'Did note the plural.'

This compounding of vernacular and how they really talked at work—who were they now?

'Four at least.'

'Four.'

John took his shot and sank a ball and straightened and looked at James directly. In the 18 months they'd worked together this was the first time, James suddenly saw, he'd ever looked at him this way. Directly and deeply. With a kind of contempt: that of alliance. Or responsibility? Of a man who saw another man unable to defend himself. John had visibly relaxed. Moving differently; an ease. A whole new life and register of Mayer assembling itself before him.

'What's going on then.'

James told him. He found a voice and ran with it. The night, the last run on the Heath, the chase, the club the boy carried. How he'd grabbed the boy in the covered way. John played shot after shot, gradually slowing down, sinking every ball. Then the dogshit in the cage, the note. It didn't take long. The only question he asked was what the boy was carrying on the Heath. James described the telescoping club he'd googled, and said, 'Ay ess pee batten,' and Mayer corrected him: 'Asp ba-*ton*.'

And nodded to himself.

James told him about the cat cut up and tied to the cage. Mayer listened and listened. James left out the flooded floor and the dog inside. Left out Fiona home alone. Told him about the boys waiting across the road, how they'd come, and the dog, how it had jumped one of them. An odd bit of choreography asserted itself: as James wound up the body of his story with how he'd run, and the pair of community constables coming out the door of the Somali Community Centre at the Lismore (beside a hairdressers' called Goddess) when his ankle went, the GRAVIS boy peeling away into the alleys behind the high rise, Mayer potted the black then stood up straight and looked directly at him as—so measured, so *literate*—he entered the coda.

'I have a babysitter, a Lithuanian girl named Tatia. She's about 23. She came in that day with a black eye. They'd used her like a kind of bait. I'm letting her go so she doesn't have to come round but she needs the money and it's a pity.'

He watched him.

'Lithuanian?' He pronounced it correctly.

'Yes.'

'She got a family?'

'She's alone in London so far as I know.'

'And they give her a black eye.'

'Yeah.'

'Why are you coming to me?'

'I don't have anyone else. I thought you might know someone.'

'Know who?'

'Someone capable.'

'Capable of what?'

'To warn them off or threaten them. It's gotten serious.'

'What you're saying is you want me and some *pals* to *pop round the gaff* and hurt some boys who messed with you and your babysitter?'

'No. No. I'm asking for advice. For help.'

'. . .'

'. . .'

'You've been to the police.'

'They say they've spoken to them and they've got a different story.'

'Because they have.'

'Because they have.'

James looked down at the pool table. Mayer's eyes were moving around the pub. Skis above the bar. St George's flags hung high in the corners. Fruit machine blinking like there's no tomorrow.

'If you set a thing in motion like this, you'll be left to walk in the path it leaves behind. The thing itself is gone,' Mayer said. 'Gone like you'd never even known it was there.'

'. . .'

'You're all right. Decent bloke. Can you walk round your bit of street with everyone knowing how this got settled? You going to change and get a big head about that? What about the next tool who wants a crack? You ready for that? Everyone's got relations.'

'I'm out of options. What would you do? If it was your wife? I've got a little girl. I'm all she has. There's no one at home for her. I can't get on a plane. I can't *put her on a plane.*'

There wouldn't be any more sweetie darling. He'd traded feeling afraid for feeling cheap—*a Lithuanian girl*, indeed—and it was a bad trade. Mayer just looked at him for a long,

long time, until the question receded.

'You're asking me to suit up and meet some people I don't know, is it. Want me to walk round and knock on a door and see who I find.' He said it fairly cheerfully and was no longer looking at him.

'What would *you* do?' James said. 'It's an honest question. I want to know what to do.'

'What would *I* do.' Mayer said and he sighed then as if it was all old and weary-making. A rut of blood and mud he had to wade back through to find some laggard.

'Okay. Look, forget it,' said James. 'No, it's been good to actually talk about it anyway. Fuck it. Don't worry.'

'You talk about threatening.'

'Yeah.'

'You see what this is like.' He waved a hand at the whole scenario. 'The only option you have when threatened is to remove yourself or remove the source of the threat. It's your gaff. I would remove the source of the threat.'

'And how would you do that.'

'No messages, no warnings, no tit for tat. No instalments.'

'What does that mean?'

'Crystallise a new reality. In this new reality your antagonist's role is irrevocably transformed into a function benign or insignificant. In this new reality you are no longer at risk or under threat.'

'What does that *mean*, John?'

'You want a for example?'

'A for example.'

'Hospital. Eyes or tongue.'

'Hospital.'

'Send them to the Royal Free. You've got to make them afraid of what's through the door.'

'What, eyes or tongue—what does that mean?'

Mayer was looking at him and there was a kind of glow of kindness, or a more abstract energy.

'Look James, I can see you're all right and you're in a jam. I'll look into it. I've got a wife too and I'm a bloke who's got to make his way.'

'Okay.'

'And 'cos fuck 'em, that's why,' he said, but he wasn't seeing him anymore. He stared at him as if he'd seen all he needed to see and was looking through him to the future. Then he turned away. Lines of his pint's head down the glass. 'You want me and some pals to pop round the gaff,' he said cheerfully to the pool table's baize, and laughed. Pals sounded like *pulse*. He laughed again. 'All right then. Who are these wee cunts.' And he jammed a £2 coin in the table and the balls crashed into the ball return and James physically jumped.

The mediation of suffering

Quotes A direct quote needs quotation marks. Should be used sparingly and in exceptional circumstances.

Sometime anaesthetist, medical journal editor and later prolific novelist Tom McNeill claimed he learned to write fiction while working on *Royal London* obituaries.

Anastomosis the union of parts or branches (as of streams, blood vessels, or leaf veins) so as to intercommunicate or interconnect

Paraprosdokian a figure of speech in which the latter part of a sentence or phrase is surprising or unexpected in a way that causes the reader or listener to

The Goddess in her navy blue overcoat. The Goddess takes five minutes with everybody.
'This is it,' she says.
Frowning at screens, beaming at one another.
A retinue of tech eds.
Beaming up at the Goddess now, Jane, touching her hair.
How swanlike her neck.

Choo.
Bless you.
Thank you.
. . .
. . .
Why do people always sneeze in threes? Always in threes.
I really hate sneezing that's one of the things I hate.
Hmm?
It's always so violent.
Ha ha.
You never know what's going to happen.

Jeanie, Jeanie, full of hopes,
Read a book by Marie Stopes,
But, to judge from her condition,
She must have read the wrong edition.

Dear James,
One change: from
'died from pneumonia following a fall on 28 September.'
to
'died from pneumonia after a fall on 28 September.'
(You're right; it wasn't worth it.)
T. D'Ath
(btw/ noticed the creative misspelling of my rather uncommon family name here and elsewhere, James—because of the apostrophe on the shift+2 key on these old keyboards and not intentional I trust?)

David 2
LinkedIn.

David 1
On what, David?

David 2
Linked, in.

David 1
What then?

David 2
Linked. In, David.
[Then, doing D1's voice]
'Digital *watch*! What's a *digital watch*?'
[Surrounding tech eds hold collective breath for daring]

David 1
[Long, considered pause]
Waste of time. Read a book.
[Collective phew]

'Essentially, we are all motivated, dedicated, decent people.'

'Ere come the doctor, but there int no fuckin nurse.

Sing-song, out of nowhere: 'Bore-dom!'

Swan drowns dog.

Dear friends. May I. Open the window.
    Oooh, yes please.
    Yes, please.
    In winter, it's like white sun, isn't it.

I love chocolate digestives. They're definitely . . . [embarrassment seeping in] my favourite . . . [turns and GONE]

You're cheerful, Jane said.

Oliver said, But in relation to the thing about, you know. What I was thinking was all our lives are to a large extent fictions we've assembled, anyway, aren't they, but though most don't get so thoroughgoingly debunked by someone. What we remember, what we want, what we report upon what we were told and taught, why we now do all these things the way we do, goals, plans, ambitions, our pasts. That's all essentially fiction.

What we fear is getting reviewed maliciously. The hostile read. Being really found out. *Plumbed*, as it were.

Leave my plumbing out of it, et cetera.

Hoping for the grand and generous exegesis of love over time, ha ha. The close, sympathetic read and the lengthy, benevolent review. Oh you're just young.

Or a good, brisk copy edit.

dilatation (not **dilation**) It comes from the Latin dilatare; the verb form should be dilatate but is dilate.
—To **dilate** is what happens when something (e.g. an artery) becomes larger (intransitive; no object).
—To **dilatate** is to perform the procedure (transitive; it takes an object).

Spot of tea? Spot of tea?

D1: Do you ever wonder about for example the *Encyclopaedia Britannica*? How are they doing these days? The site hasn't been updated in a while.

D2: 'Traffic is down year on year', ha ha.

D1: The last blog post announcing suspension of the blog itself made for strangely moving reading.

D2: Gives the word 'Help' in the menu bar a whole different feel, doesn't it.

D1: Those purple pebbled leather spines waiting faithfully for the rainy Sunday afternoon. You know, the sadness of failing businesses.

D2: In your Alan Bennett voice. 'Light from the two-bar fire rippling softly over the faded images of the, of the crustaceans of C gently rutting in their, on their C-bed, I'd, I'd, with flushed cheek I'd gently, reverently turn the fine onionskin pages of my beloved *Britannica* and, and.'

D1: Oh, ha ha! Oh.

Adrienne: I always feel sorry for the dogs of paedophiles and child killers. Completely innocent. Mark Bridger had that lovely collie, didn't he.

D2, D1: [. . .]

I'll fucking boxcutter you right now, you cunt, look at me again.

'Singular.'
'Nope.'
'When—when I write my novel I'm going to use the singular.'
'When—and when I'm your copy editor I'll change it. Eh heh heh heh.'
'And if I'm the author I'll sack you.'
'Eh heh heh.'
'Heh heh heh.'
'. . .'
'. . .'

WILL A DELICIOUS DELI BUFFET LUNCH BE PROVIDED FREE OF CHARGE?
Yes!*

*No.

All you've got to ask yourself is if they'd gone to Eton would we have this trouble.

'Hello Jane!'
'Hello, Charles.'

Dear all, as you will know, Adrienne Morrissey's post of senior art worker was put at risk of redundancy a few months ago. The redundancy has now been confirmed, and John is arranging a time for drinks to say goodbye to Adrienne in the next week or so. With best wishes, Claudia

B did you write the obit of Laurie and MacKinnon?
    Yes. They died within days of each other. Well months. Of the same thing.
    Was it contagious?
    They weren't even in the same place as each other.
    How did they die?
    Pneumonia. The old man's friend.

The Glasgow Coma Scale.

The general rule is that 'only' should go before the word it refers to. But note: It only made things worse.

Eye me like that again I'll rasp it up. File into it measured like take my time till it pops open and runs down your cheek like you're crying and I'll fucking lick that up. That's me.

'James!—second language alert. Can you fix?'
Using a computer for long hours is linked to dry eye disease, according to a study conducted among Japanese office workers, and decreased concentrations of mucin 5AC (MUC5AC) in tears. The tears of workers and normal subjects were collected using . . .
[This is a free preview. Please log in for the entire article.]

We modelled this fear to a cohort of 10,000 women.

I'd love a tea.
   Hold still.

Ooh, Susan you've laddered your stocking.

[very slowly and quietly and smilingly] I know, David, and I haven't got any others and do you know what? I don't care.

I've got a brown felt tip.

Ah ha ha!

. . .

. . .

Is it *gravy* brown?

[in a sort of hurt defeated way]

HA HA HA. HA HA HA HA HA HA

'Richmal Oates-Whitehead,' said David 2.

'Hmm?' said James.

'Know her?'

Medical Association

Caught at the kitchen door on the way out back to the style guide, James with his full mug, by D2 with his empty teacup and his attitude.

'Did you know her? Richmal Oates-Whitehead? *She* was a New Zealander.'

On guard in an instant. Waiting for D2 to show his stripes and make his move. Waiting for it.

'I haven't heard of her,' James said, and waited. 'Is that a person's name, David?'

James politely pivoted and reversed slightly to let him in, eyes down on the swaying coffee. 'Whoops!' he said pleasantly. The first time they'd been together since the process review and covert limerick—was it the right thing to do to let him in?

Your move.

'You haven't heard of her? But she's a New *Zeal*ander.'

'Oh really!'

'Well, anyway—'

D2 was at the counter gathering his teabag and his spoon. James was in the doorway looking out. Out there was the Pheromone sitting with her back to him and directly opposite was Annabel Pitti who appeared to be actually physically hiding from her behind her Dell. Would he get away?

'—*she* was something of a chronic fabulist, wasn't she!'

James was stopped in his tracks. All right, this was it. He turned and stood in the doorway. Let's see what you've got, then.

'Is that so?'

'You really don't know her!'

'This is a person? Who is this person you're so interested in?'

'Richmal Oates-Whitehead. You really don't know her? But I gather she was all over your newspaper. I mean, they were the rag who outed her. The *Auckland Graun* or whatever you like to call it.'

'Again . . .' James shook his head slowly, half grinning, no. 'Again, I have no idea . . .'

But again he'd been snared.

'Richmal Oates-Whitehead. What a name.' D2 smiled slightly and gently scrubbed the inside of his cup and turned and leaned back, his butt against the sink, and the brush and cup in hand. 'Quite the belletrist, that one! The fictioneer!'

Oliver Reed came in then with his own teacup, sidling past James.

'—*lo*!' murmured Oliver, followed by an inward hiss over his teeth, eyeing them both, so as not to interrupt. James widened his eyes to Oliver in both warning and greeting. David 2 smiled like someone getting ready to lift something.

'So, this fabulist. Now, this was after the 7/7 bombings. The whole sorry saga. A goodly time ago. I was at our competitors' across the park then.'

'Wow, a *long* time ago,' said James innocently and looked at Oliver.

David 2 blinked slowly. 'So, after the bus bomb went off—'

'What's that?' said Oliver. 'What's a belletrist?'

'What's *what*,' said David 2 and audibly breathed through his nose.

'What now? A bomb? Who said a bomb on top of all this?'

'*No*—pay attention.' D2 made a half-ironic *moue* to try to hide the irritation. 'We're talking about 7/7.'

'David was at the *BMJ* then. You were barely out of primary school,' James said to Oliver, free of culpability. 'When the bus was blown up over the way.'

And at that D2 looked at him with a pleased smile. All right then, he seemed to say. Come on then.

'Yes. Yes, I was there,' D2 said. 'Yes, it was a long time ago, wasn't it.'

'Wow,' said Oliver. 'You were there when the bomb went off.'

The dish rack was made of rusted wire caught bravely in a struggle to shuck off its skin of pale blue enamel.

Something had equalised between the two men, at a slightly higher plane than before.

'So anyway,' David 2 said, and breathed, 'this Oates-Whitehead woman, one of yours. The New Zealander. I worked with her. She worked on *Clinical Evidence* for the *BMJ*. That's their version of our, you know, *EBM*. Well, *EBM*'s our version of the *BMJ*'s *CE*. We tried to rip it off, unsuccessfully. ETA TBD. Anyway.'

Oliver chortled, but David looked slightly disgusted.

'On the day of the bombings she went down there from the offices, as we all did, all into the road where the bombed bus was. Into the street where it was. A lot of us took part in the resuscitations and triage and stabilising and other work. Allegedly she was invited by rescue personnel to board the bus itself to assist with medical support in moving some of the victims off. Because there were rumours of a second device. It was rather brave, you know.'

'Oh!' said James, and waited.

Oliver said, 'I've seen that shot of the blood sprayed up over the BMA sign. Powerful image.'

D2 ignored him.

'Anyway a lot of people were brave that day and there was a lot of chaos and it was more or less expected.' He was staring at James's chest, as if thinking through the layers of what he was doing. 'But someone took it upon themselves to send an email to your newspaper, the *New Zealand Mail* or whatever you call it, with information about this lone New Zealander among the people who did that work.'

It was hard to know whether to rise to this particular bait about the newspapers or if there were bigger outrages to come.

'Because newspapers like that, don't they. The local lead. *Nordic Day* reports that amongst the four million dead were two Swedish newlyweds on their honeymoon, et cetera. So but anyway. They tracked this woman down and she gave this rag an interview wherein she told the story I've just told you. And made mention of the secondary device the emergency staff knew about when they asked her to help. You know—there's another bomb that might go off. Will you board? Will you help get these injured people off? The clock might be ticking. *Die Hard* stuff. Of course she went.

'They publish the story of this heroic work in the ensuing article. But the mention of a second device gets tongues wagging. No one else had heard about a second device at the Tavistock Square explosion. It was supposed to be one chap with a backpack. So the good civic journalists of the world turn up to start teasing out the holes in her story.'

They were looking at each other right in the eye now. Oliver had gone quiet.

'Very eccentric woman. I remember her. Dressed oddly—big dresses, lots of colours, lots of material. Looked like a pile of secondhand curtains for sale. Just one of those editors you know. Reeked of spinst and telly and baked beans on toast, but a decent brain on her. Solid background in epi and public health. Good writer. Like you, James! Not disrespectful. She'd got the job at *Clinical Evidence* via the Cochrane Collaboration and JH, where he is now. Who'd worked under James Breath at the *BMJ*. He's now head of Cochrane London. Got the job claiming she was a medical doctor. She wasn't a doctor. But that wasn't all.

'Because of course it turned out she'd written the email about her exploits to your *Herald* herself. Had a history. Sending communications home about her magical life. Emailing all her friends in New Zealand about gaining professor, about a *chair* in epidemiology. Ludicrous stuff. I mean the gullibility. But worse stuff too. A husband who was a physician, in obstetrics. Name of "Michael Fitzgerald" of all things. Stories about giving birth to premature twins who'd died after an emergency C. This person posted actual death notices in your paper for two invented children and an invented husband. Other emotional postings to online forums about their deaths. Invented middle names for them. Complete fantasist. She'd fudged her CV from a concatenation of facts and imaginings involving degrees and but actual real competence. That's the sad part: she was competent. But out of nowhere this family and even a stepdaughter too, and then she killed them off. I remember her actually. A bit wobbly and uptight but basically well-meaning and hard-working.

Intense. Smiled too much. Sometimes like she was incredibly relieved to be feeling an emotion she could smile about. That surprised quality that goes on a bit too long. Lovely smile, though. Just a bit unnerving. Richmal Oates-Whitehead. There's no proof she got on that bus. The BMA investigated internally after these things came to light and she was quickly and quietly let go soon after. Quick talk on the terrace. The journal was all she had. Thirty-something. Within a month she was dead of a pulmonary embolism in this dismal and otherwise empty little bedsit in Shepherd's Bush. Now there's a cliché.'

'Christ,' said Oliver.

'I've never heard of her,' James said, honestly. He sipped his coffee and waited for it.

'Is that so,' said David 2. 'You can't really know anyone you work with, can you. The funny thing was the rumour about the second device turned out to be true. There was a controlled explosion of a John Lewis microwave in a cardboard box. She was possibly quite heroic that day and no one will ever know.'

He looked at James.

'But then a lot of people were.'

Fiona

He's all right, my dad. He isn't afraid of anything. Even the big bad wolf. He has a certain twist to his face when he's reading aloud to me, like he doesn't quite believe. He wants to teach me how to say 'pyjamas'. Because he says it's his favourite word. That he'd forgotten that till right this minute. He says that happens all the time, and, Jesus.

    He's all right my dad. He doesn't want me to turn into him. He said that once to me out loud, looking into my eyes. Don't turn into me. He's very afraid. And although one of the things he is afraid of is me, the others are what will befall me and who will protect me but still he is not afraid to burst out laughing in a mean kind of way when I topple gently over from this sitting thing I'm recently almost able to do. He fears I am a terrible anchor and anchored so he cannot ride out safely the storm to come that will plumb and scour each harbour. He fears money. And violence. He's all right my dad. He can wrestle with giants. He doesn't want me to turn into him. He'd hoped things were a different way. He has a song of sighs he doesn't know he sings. I am his only audience. I can grasp his thumbs. He doesn't know his fingers move my heart; for some reason he cannot allow himself to believe this might be so. Things have moved too fast for him, and he doesn't remember the beeping room, the splashes and the registrar, the urgent nurse who ordered him shirtless and laid me grey upon his chest which was my only home thenceforth.

My dad can eat like a horse, and he can swim like a fish and he can imagine a house on a sunny hill with five clean bedrooms and clean high spaces and a life in every room all quick and light with cash and love and summer coming.

He is thwarted, thwarted at every turn, by me and what he would wish for me; he is my nursemaid: I am immovable, unleavable and utterly unfamiliar. He fears his thinking: that I am the worst kind of vampire, one that doesn't know its nature and anaesthetises its bite with a love it doesn't know it in turn demands by right. Formula falling from my fangs. He fears his failings are reified and magnified by me: the money, the paternity he didn't know as a child and doesn't know now. What difficulties there are in debt for a man alone are surmountable always: through contempt and gin and a turning of the other cheek. His thoughts are as seen through broken, milky glass from lack of sleep and drinking late at night. (Though he makes plans for anything that happens then, to me, if he's been drinking—a bleary watchful paranoia over the Angelcare, a leap from the bed, a taxi number on his phone, a run with the buggy to the Royal Free.) He's all right, my dad. He volunteers for more work all the time and feels guilty for not wanting to come home to me. He cannot stand the ghosts of old pornography who roam the rooms and spread their legs where he changes me. Yet he says he will allow himself an entire evening masturbating if it brings him the equilibrium and calm sufficient to carry on. A taste enough of an old life, but his face takes a certain cast as he is forced to some internal agreement between those videos and the sight of me, unclothed in all the fire of my light. He's all right my dad.

He's inarticulate and earns the money for my milk through rescue of the words of others from ruin, yet he knows the formality of failure and that I will not recognise that the only mother I have known, a kind Lithuanian economics student of 24, is gone, bruised and poorer, looking for other work, other daughters. That I will not complain about that loss except through the bleatings of a heart reduced. On a half life scale. Reduced, he knows, and pale already, for a hemisphere in sunlight forever lost and irretrievable. And a diminishment increasing. He's all right my dad. He's as wise as an owl, except when he tries to help. For he remembers those moments we lie side by side on our backs, me on the woollen blanket he inherited from his mad mother long gone in a far-off land I have not known—family—and he on the coir matting bathed in and staring out at the flickering gold coin of London light in the leaves of the honey locust where the pigeons have returned to coo now Josephine is gone, past Oak Village, past the Barrington Court tower block to the stained and sadless English skies, and when the decision he has made and forces he has called upon remembered send his cold heart a-beating and there is no one real to call him cock-a-roach or weak or even all right and in a jam he freezes further beside me and he drops my hand and shrinks an inch all over, but he does not remember that no matter the duration of the terror and the will he takes it up again eventually, his cheeks hardened, frowning deeper, more intently, and goes on. And doesn't know that in time through the repetitions of those moments decided upon to retake my hand he will form a new person around the wreckage and start to feel me uncanny as a phantom necklace light and strong and warm about his shirtless chest, a rising up within him, another heart beating forward in time.

In the south

Descending the Kotsifou Gorge, down to the southern coast of Crete, the history makes sense. It's hard; the canyon steep and the stone loose and dry and useless. It is a place for monsters and monasteries, changeless and austere. The road winds like a river along the very pitch of the floor of this inverted church. The act of driving becomes akin to paddling a canoe: stroke left, stroke right, down the winding road to the south. As if the very ocean here were lower, colder, the shelf fallen off faster than the northern resorts of Panormos, Rethymno.

In a hired Peugeot, sun flashing through the dust and clear entrails of the insects snatched from flight upon their windscreen, they drove south.

She: she in a black skirt and black singlet like a Greek girl, arms gone tan for the first time in so many London summers. In the passenger seat, everything in the car in a fine dust pulsing in the sun as if suspended underwater. Freckles came up in her sunblessed skin. He had forgotten she transformed that way. Leaning dreamily against the door, in sunglasses, hand on her bump, seven months gone. The sun picked up blonde streaks in her chestnut hair. Strands waving in the sun, in the light breeze, the dust. They drove for an hour without talking. 'Pegasus,' she suddenly said. And she turned and grinned at him, her eyes invisible behind those €5 sunglasses she'd bought from a German-speaking street vendor in Rethymno. There was a market Simon had told them about that sold cheap clothes, two-packs of T-shirts and singlets in black or white. Good Egyptian cotton, next to nothing, possibly really old, because on the packaging was a very tan, very muscled Greek from an oily 80s, singlet-smug. James, Simon and Tom—New Zealand friends they'd rented the Cretan villa with—had invented a joke and found it funny while high on the long drive and the nicotine gum he was chewing all the time now he'd given up smoking for the baby.

It was a possible scenario for a TV commercial: they'd imagined a buff Greek in his tight Pegasus singlet on a beach against Mediterranean azure. A football lands at his feet. A boy enters the shot to retrieve it, looks up to the man and hopefully, plaintively, says, 'Daddy?'

'I'm not your daddy,' the Greek says, smiling, and the *PEGASUS* brand flashes up and the music rises and the Greek saunters down the beach into freedom as the boy with the football looks after him, admiring, longing.

I'm not your daddy, he'd say now and again, and it was good. But she never would, never even to allude to the joke, which she had no problem with. She just wouldn't let herself say that.

She was trying to keep him entertained on a long drive. She never drove. She had only a restricted licence when they got to London and never sat the test for her full. Flat rocks were strewn across the road sometimes, some fallen hundreds of metres out of the crystalline void above to shatter and spray over the tarmac. She lay back, sun sweeping in and out the mottled windscreen in the turns, this way and that down through the canyons. He was just scared. That was all right. There were debts. What if she were hurt when she gave birth? What if the baby were damaged? A low Apgar score? There were debts. He talked too much when he was nervous. She'd sometimes remind him of the joke, though maybe it wasn't to her taste. She was the kind of person who seemed to think—well, what of that? Her womb full under the fine black cotton and her hand gently upon it. That look of ingenuous surprise and she'd seize upon his wrist to make him feel it: the stretches, the pushes, risings, soundings from another country. He didn't know that after Fiona was born he would see and recognise the rhythm and reach of those stretches of her long little legs folded in good fat—didn't know he already knew all about them.

The big story going round was about a Cretan girl who threw a brandy on some predatory British boy who'd groped her in a club, and set fire to him with a cigarette lighter. His third-degree burns. Everyone liked that story in Crete. British boys in Heraklion Airport, heading home with hangovers and frightened looks and bandaged heads and armcasts.

They swept left, and right. The stone of the south was grey and flinty, different from the north where it was sandy, taupe, dusty. In the canyons no plants grew; just rusty shotgun cartridges, sun and wind and stone.

Until they emerged to a small village poured down a hillside in terraced orchards and inflamed angles. They found a restaurant there with an outdoor veranda arboured in flowers. Black feathers from the chicken coop below the terrace rose in the thermals. Floating over the valley where from the foot a great triangle of turf rose, kilometres wide, fenced and pastured to its very peak, to a cliff over the southern Mediterranean like a calved iceberg midway fallen, some vast tearing half accomplished, a great wound—avulsion, it was called—that in its abrupt and improbable violation, though the flesh beneath was visible, the skin of its surface unknowing of its fate was healthy still, flush with sun and life.

They ordered orange juices and sat half in shade, watching it. She made daisy chains from the arbour, and the taverna's owner brought them complimentary goat's cheese and honey in the comb and spoke to her in the gentle lisp of Greek and smiled down upon them and this was how it was for a time. Sunny, dusty, downy, news of a cold wind to the south, but that great fold of land, its pitch, its improbability, gave them shelter for this quiet.

The destination of this bus has changed

London. Annabel Pitti—whose suffering is so relaxing, cathartic, purgative, so essentially entertaining to witness—lit out for work one Thursday morning in road tights, hi-vis jacket and gloves, backpack on, bike shoes changed for trainers. She headed for the bus stop on the corner of Agincourt and Mansfield Road because that morning her bike—a Pinarello carbon-fibre frame that cost £1000—had been stolen right out of the shed behind her father's terraced house. Padlock, hasp and latch on the door ripped right off: bike just gone. It would have been a job to do, getting in there—over four or five walls from the street, knowing exactly which of four or five more or less identical sheds in identical backyards to do. It was someone in the neighbourhood, then, who knew her and knew about the bike. What a big effort—what a contrivance. All for the purpose of torturing her.

She'd greeted the busted door with that familiar sigh because she should have known. Should have known to chain the frame to the workbench as well as lock the door. Should have known that this was going to happen to her, at the worst, latest, most-consequences-lined-up-for-lateness-possible moment. She should not have left it alone. Her dad stood in the kitchen doorway across their blighted little backyard and shook his head. 'Oh, I'm sorry love.' And she fumed, furious, said nothing, and stamped past him as if it were his fault, upstairs to change her shoes and stash her helmet and grab her Oyster: pay as you go, which is what you do if you love to ride.

James Ballard didn't know that sometimes Annabel took the same bus as him. When a tyre was flat or it was just too miserable and foul, or if she was ill. She had an Oyster in her wallet for spontaneous stuff in the city (so it was hardly ever used) and she had a spare Oyster upstairs in a papier-mâchéd silver-painted trinket box she'd had since she was 12, and she had a proven and uncanny instinct for the level of funds on each. It's not like she knew how much was on there, but the minute she left the house through her dad's neat front garden she knew whether the Oyster she had on her would fail, and whether the spare would work, or neither and she'd have to head east to the Turks to put money on it and be badly, badly late. She could put on an automatic debit but that would seem like a betrayal of the bike somehow—seem weak.

She had soft, greyish skin. A pale gold in her pale auburn hair, cut in a pageboy. Tidy, reserved, freckled eyes. She was 27.

She was now going to be late. Cycling in, from the house in NW3 where her father had lived since he was a little immigrant boy, to the *Royal London* in WC1H, took her between seven and nine minutes. The bus took at least half an hour. At the *very* least and requiring all kinds of optimal conditions. So with the delay in getting organised to leave, changing her shoes, etc., etc., getting to the GA stop and waiting for the next 24, *with luck* she'd be in the 9:10 sweet spot for post-rush-hour commute with the hijabed mummies late for Rhyl Primary and have clear and quiet roads through

Camden and only be maybe half an hour late. Emily wouldn't even say anything and that would be the worst. The *Royal* silence. No, so she wouldn't have time to print out her notes for the Clinch, and so when she spoke she would blush. *That* was going to be the worst.

The walls of Fleet Primary School were papered with the new Camden Council 'Age at Disappearance' portraits—right now they were spookily similar to the South Bank University posters they were posting north of the river since the visa restrictions closed down their cash-cow foreign students. It was an unfortunate coincidence of design, and because the portraits of the missing kids in the posters were usually taken at happy moments, the mood was oddly similar too. Like recruitment.

Annabel made a mental note to make a physical note of that in the ideas file in her Filofax once she was seated in the bus, for an article or a blog or just a tweet, or for an anecdote to use at the pub. That might be a useful comment for awkward silences. That might smooth an exit or make an entrance.

Annabel hated writing. Which was tough, for a writer. She struggled with her stories. They opened horrifically, her first drafts, like a drunken actor moaning themselves out of a nightmare, barely even English. They would shout about the stage a bit, gesturing here and there, trying to hit their marks. Then abruptly, as if in injury, they would end. Trip over the scenery. Step off into the orchestra pit. Metaphors mixed. Similes would burst and leak like hernias. Sentences wriggling on the page, metastatic, non-homogeneous, like fast tumours. They mutated horribly when she tried to fix them, hold them down, apply the chemotherapy of her concentration. Writing felt to her like trying to wrestle an enraged and alien centreless thing made only of limbs. Half-made metaphors pushed in and proliferated and writhed about. First person secretly morphed to second and she couldn't allow herself the 'one'. She had in fact taken to cut-and-pasting more generic Pheromone-authored pieces and find-and-replacing the nouns and proper names, just to get a head start on building a piece. These things, these *sentences* slipped from her intent and understanding, her *meaning*, just like people did.

Constant unpleasant surprises.

She made another note to write a note to herself on the bus: How can I express myself coolly, professionally, with a genuine passion and competence, in the Clinch? Without over-egging the pudding? One strategy was to turn her face slightly away after saying what she had to say, after saying what she meant. Not making eye contact or looking for the reaction. *That* was the way. It would both look and feel like confidence. I am complete; I am sure of myself. I do not need to say '. . . *I* think' at the ends of my sentences, stressing the 'I' as if saying but hey, that's just me, like Emily does. Because Emily's got the chops and time in the saddle and the impatience and authority to do that. Her 'just me' is in fact an awful lot. *I* know well enough not to make the mistake of imitating *that*. I, however, no longer need to append or qualify or modify. I can simply stop speaking after I have made my point. Leave it at that. I am open to response and rebuttal. Argument makes me strong. I am open to all and anything that helps me learn.

Cultivate the tech eds. Talk to James Ballard more. *Talk* to him. Perhaps tell him you've seen him on the bus, now and again, but don't be creepy. Don't be creepy, especially with him. He with his guarded, furrowed brow and the unknowable blank eyes he lives behind. Say something like, I'm usually at the back, is why I don't come and say hello, and emphasise it's only occasionally that you see him, as you usually ride the bike. Or that he looked busy and you didn't want to interrupt him, or something that seems like a slight compliment, or like that kind of winning modesty that Emily does. Don't say I know where you live and you live behind your eyes like I do, and I am even further back than there, behind my own eyes in my head in the back of that bus behind your eyes in your own head, and happy to be there. And I didn't want to have to interact. And try to stand with Jane at birthday drinks more. *Cultivate* that potential friendship. There might even be an invite home or out shopping there, one day. There might be friends. In Angel, in Hackney. Be open but respectful with the senior eds, and to the tech eds who will help you with your prose. Stop being so flippant with Death, because you're just halfway starting to treat him like you treat your dad, i.e. making fun and being slightly contemptuous, which is your default way of being familiar and friendly with men, and it's dangerous. Let Paraic be friendly but no more hugs or touching. Let him be funny or feel he's funny without any more touching.

She'd seen James's rewrites of her stuff, and it hurt. Especially the rewrites of her first paras, which she compared with her first drafts and which in comparison with his edits were airdrowned octopuses, those horrible first paras with their tacked-on speech tags in super-repetitious sequence, she *said*, then she *reported*, *replied*, *remarked* and later, obviously, *added*, and their unmanageable explicatory clause multiplyings, those twitching tentacles branching off, introducing horrible ambiguities she couldn't seem to fend off without stamping each clause completely dead and pinning it to the page with a period.

Tom Winnicott, an psychoanalyst and paediatrition at London's Whittington NHS Trust's Whittington Hospital of the Whittington NHS Trust, in Islington, London, said this week that the new NHS bill amendments were a 'substantial move towards the privatisation and thus dismantling of the NHS as we know it,' reported columnist at the *Independent* columnist Isabelle Wintermere, a freelance health writer and columnist at the *Independent,* at the NHS Futures Conference last Friday, reported, and remarked, 'we can't yet know the consequences of that,' he added.

Hate it hate it *hate it*.

Yet when James touched these pieces they grew simple, perfect, anonymous. They bloomed. Relaxed as if caressed, as if he were releasing them from the horrible steel traps she throws over their sense. The dead octopus resolved into a poised and purposeful—and rather straightforward—snake. How did he do it? The pieces left her with all her flaws—goodwill, falsity and weakness, clumsiness—writ large. They returned othered and calm. The pieces went out for quiet dinners with journalist friends in Old Street, unfrantic, looking fine. In Angel, in Hackney. She shouldn't have to rely on tech ed for this. And she knew Emily was reading her drafts in the pre-edit folder. Taking notes; appraising. *Reviewing* her *process*. Terrifying. She'd gone, once, to open up an old draft, because she'd remembered a possible error she had to make sure to right—not appending 'Sir' to a knight's name—and double-clicked on the doc only to receive the horrible rebuff:

This file is locked for editing by emilyf. Do you want to open a read-only file?

God, no. Stop reacting to the word *emilyf* or any word of a certain poise with l's and f's and m's and n's and y's, like *milf* or *film*, *family* or sometimes on a puncture repair kit, *emulsify*, or even just *read-only file* with such stupid, stomach-drop fear and dread. Don't be read-only. Don't be dread-only.

Write.

Allow yourself to be scrutinised, calmly. *Produce*. Give yourself *permissions*. You are perfectly fit, able and up to this or they wouldn't have given you the job. (Though she'd clicked out of that file as fast as if she'd opened something radically NSFW, and did a little behind-the-shoulder glance, one of those useless over-the-shoulder head dips, like when she once did a totally innocent and credulous search for 'penile degloving' with the resultant page of horrific image results, half thinking—in hindsight, obviously stupidly, but *still*—it was a boxing metaphor, something to do with getting tough on prison sentencing.) Emily was sitting directly opposite her when she'd clicked on that file; beautiful, erect, old and unflappable. Reading her stuff right in front of her. Annabel had had to hunch slightly, bend slightly behind the Dell 19" to avoid eye contact, then go and get a glass of water.

Why did they have to steal the bike.

This bucking, overcrowded, hopelessly delayed and utterly suffocating train of thought had carried her all the way to the GA bus stop on Agincourt Road to join the line waiting there, to stand with her back to the wall beside the Methodist church and its billboard of self-satisfied Methodist lambs. Annabel was entirely unaware she was moving from foot to foot in agitation, there by the wall, and that she was audibly sighing—one tiny sigh for each of her multiple, graven follies.

To be swanlike, sunlike: at speed down Malden, Ferdinand, Chalk Farm Road. Surfing the wake of this very bus arriving now, gaining 30% more power from the slipstream, then slingshotting him, sailing right by the bus, surprising the driver as she overtook him, a metre from his seat, right by him; at one with the cobbling rippling in her calves on the right-hand lane down the one-way past the Hawley Arms, at great speed, yes, and so fast down Hawley Road to jump the lights and find Camden Street empty and shining in the morning, all the way to Oakley Square in the sun, if you please.

To be that.

She should not have left the bike alone.

But the queue for the bus was 20 strong. Annabel was beginning to realise something was different. A small, barely owned irritation giving way to the need to pay attention. She'd risen in increments from self-exhortation mode to a quick, at-Dad-like anger that she hates in herself—why are we shuffling forward at this unfamiliar pace; it's someone else's fault—to a series of rapid, almost unconscious connections: there were 20 or more people waiting in this queue, only two stops from the bus's origin at South End Green, and at five past nine. Which meant they'd been waiting a long time and thus some of these people were late for work. Which meant something was up.

A nice old lady with a little trolley and a toaster oven tied on the top with its own power cord. A well-dressed middle-aged man with his prepubescent son. All at leisure; all un-late. Annabel felt her hackles rise a little—a blonde white woman in her mid-twenties, tallish, pretty, half glamorous, foreign, Polish-looking in a leopard-print jacket, on her phone with a black eye and her roots showing. Then a teenage black boy, who loudly hoiked and then wiped his nose with the back of his hand and in the same gesture jammed his hand in his jeans pocket at a certain angle with a certain force—clearly scraping off what he'd got on his hand with the hem of his jeans pocket like teenage boys who feel they are invisible do. A tough-looking white woman, clearly from Waxham or the Lismore, smoking the last, stinkiest drags of a revolting rag of a cigarette while her daughter—13, 14—stood beside her blankly and watched, guarded, very, very closely, that cigarette. As the queue shuffled forward everyone dipped their eyes to mind the gap, and the impression was of penitents passing before the Christ. Annabel saw the woman drop her fag, her face lifted as if for a greeting or a fight, and her daughter watched with evident vast experience the cigarette fall to spark on the concrete kerb and stepped carefully around it. A man in a suit with a pinkie ring and a pink-paged *Financial Times*. An old lady with a girl of four or five, a granddaughter.

And then she saw the limping, ravaged wreck with bricked-up eyes coming down the street. An apparent man in camouflage pants, hands buried deep in the pockets of a reeking oilskin. He was watching the eastern European woman. Staring at this woman. Openly. Daring her to notice him. Until suddenly, under the pressure of that waiting and watching, she *did* notice and looked up from her conversation to meet his eyes, and then the damaged man could do what he was waiting to do: he shook his head, no, quickly, no, at her, and smirked, I'm not for you, he was saying, oh no, and limped on down the shuffling queue.

The woman with the black eye barely registered this, or the data existed and was noted but it was better to do nothing with it. Just as London does with a black-eyed woman.

'E9? God forbid. Wouldn't even know where it was,' a posh-ish, older-looking woman said to her phone.

Annabel had to muster some good tweets today. She was thinking of a joke about the recent NHS posters that read *Don't be a dummy. Go to your GP if something feels funny.* But the punchline wouldn't take. It was funny, the slogan; it was funny and dumb, wasn't it, or at least you could imagine someone saying something, someone like John Mayer, that would make it funny. But then again it was just true, and right, wasn't it, and important too. Annabel knew enough about herself to know that what she found funny she couldn't often communicate easily and so it was better not to risk humour that might not cross over to other consciousnesses, and might undermine her, professionally. So she usually kept it to herself, this letting on of what her sense of humour might actually be. She moved her backpack to her other shoulder. The teenage boy with the runny nose stepped on the bus with half a glance at the lady with the toaster oven. The smoker watched him with wide eyes then she turned to the lady and said decorously, with a laugh, 'Oh, after *you*.'

'Fank you.'

'Nah.'

'Tsa shame,' said the older lady, loudly for the boy, 'Uvvah paypul don do va saym fing innit? Dya see that?'

'Yeahp.'

The daughter kept her eyes on the concrete, a silent appendage to her mother.

Annabel's mother had died when she was five, and Annabel thought, in the horrible glassy coherency it seemed her fate to be experiencing this morning: My problem is I am not learning about the individuals behind the work persona but simply and lazily treating other women with exaggerated respect; with respect, like colleagues, but very distant, untested and over-acted respect. (Like at book club, which is all women—everyone just wants to have fun, but I act too seriously and do too much research and I ruin it slightly for everyone. I make them feel tired.) And, to be familiar, or when I relax too much, I seem to have to either denigrate and make fun of men or pretend I'm better than them, because I do the same thing to my father and I have done that for a long time, a very long time, with him, and now I have to stop before it hurts my prospects more than it already has. And maybe then I can stop it with my father too.

She moved from foot to foot.

'Justept in, dinny?'

'Yeahp.'

Then the Polish-looking woman, having managed to step just inside the bus while still on her phone, said something loudly and clearly.

'I have a commitment to the work. I have an experience across the world. I am stable and dedicated. I *know* you have to hide my emotions.'

She had only a hint of an accent now for this work call. She was staring past her phone at the great raw rubber tyre of the bus.

The oilskinned danger was behind her somewhere in the queue now. The smoker was at the head of the queue and engaging, at length, it seemed, with the bus driver, and Annabel was close enough to see something was going on. The driver was pointing at the tray in the hole in his cubicle. On the Plexiglas read a sign: *Treat our staff with RESPECT!* The Polish woman was looking around inside her purse, but the cyan blue of her Oyster card was pinched between her two be-ringed knuckles like a cigarette. She wasn't using it.

Was it out of funds, like Annabel's just might be? It didn't *feel* out.

There was another hole between the dashboard and the change tray. The whole Oyster reader and ticket dispenser and fare calculator mechanism had been ripped right out. It was sitting inside the driver's cubicle in a mess of wires and dangling screws jammed between his dashboard and the windscreen.

The bus driver was only taking cash, and he was hoisting up his pelvis and putting it in his pockets.

It seemed at first a minor glitch. Annabel came to the head of the queue. She gave him £3. He had on a woollen skullcap over wild eyes, and he put the money in his pocket and then shook his head once, checked his mirror and said, 'No change.'

This was simply too much. The stresses had compounded. Annabel made her scoffing noise, which, she knew, was an admission of defeat to service people, like waiters who brought her the wrong thing or ushers who gave her the terrible seat. Scoff, then laugh, and look around for sanction, for somebody else to notice the outrage just foisted upon her, again. And yes, for someone to take over the horrible, excruciating possibility of having to publicly get angry and seek redress. She scoffed. She looked behind her, then down the bus. The faces looked back at her, waiting. Had the same thing happened to them? Blank. No solidarity. A wall of waiting. They looked away.

She looked back at the driver, and laughed, and the defeat was total.

The bus driver turned in his little seat to face her squarely, and he opened his eyes wide and tilted his head to one side in a dare. And it was just like, and a horrible parody of, her

I'm-extraordinarily-professionally-interested-in-what-you-have-to-tell-me face.

She turned quickly away and went up the stairs.

Upstairs the little girl and her grandma sat on the left-hand side fourth from the front and she swept the London paper and some crumbs from the empty pair of seats in front of them and sat by the window. In front of her was the Polish woman, and right at the front was the posh-ish older woman reading a book. Annabel glimpsed shades of lavender and khaki on the cover: a novel set in Provence. Front right was the father and son.

'Ooh, these seats are rock hard, Grandma!' the little girl said. 'These seats aren't soft. They're rock hard!'

'What a wicked man,' the grandmother said, as if in answer, in her little-girl voice. 'What a horrible man, that driver. I hope he gets bitten by fleas on his bottom.'

They were talkers. Annabel looked around for another seat but there were too many free and it was too awkward to immediately move after they had spoken.

A filthy white van pulled to a halt in front of them. In fingertip in the grime: ALSO IN WHITE. Annabel was tensed and clutching her backpack. What a wicked man. Done out of 70p, and what had she done about it? And the rest of them on the bus, had they argued or had they paid too? How long was it since she'd taken a bus? A month? What was going on? They waited for the rest of the queue to board. She could hear the father and son talking in Russian. A Middle Eastern man in a robe materialised beside her at the top of the stairs, talking on his phone, and stared piercingly at her a second too long. She held her backpack tighter, looked out the window. He went down the aisle. The Polish woman was still on her phone, bent over it like she was looking for something in her navel. 'If anything,' she suddenly said, 'I am treated more like a slave.'

It was 9:10. The bus chugging gently and still not moving. Annabel looked out her window to see the last of the queue disappear inside the doors beneath her. A girl in headphones came decisively up the stairs, leaned over the posh woman to shut the window, and sat down beside her. The posh woman looked up, eyes bulging, tracking this way and that around the girl. 'Sorry! I'd rather have it open!' she said loudly. Her accent was really somewhere between here and lower Hampstead, and then she made no further move. The girl didn't even notice.

Oh God to be on a bike.

'You know, when I get a feedback I expect I am told what I'm doing wrong and how to do it better. So—'

The mist-burning sun grew nebulous and golden as the number of passengers hit critical mass and the windows quickly marbled. As if in balance. Annabel looked back down the street to see the bus stop disappear into the clouds. The novel the woman was reading was called, absurdly, *Safe Passage*, and the outraged, impotent woman only now opened it again. Many people live lives of quiet desperation, don't they, didn't some writer write. That was right and true. Was that health-related? Enough to tweet something about? You could use that as an opening line of something bigger on telehealth and staying in touch with people trapped in their own homes, with major chronic conditions, or those who care for demented relations. Or about choosing to die at home and getting the right kind of care for that. She could link to that Patient's Tale by the daughter of the woman with cancer who wanted to die at home and how her wishes were respected and honoured inasmuch as was possible but the reality of that, the suffering and the drawn-out pain of that death, without a proper range of options for medication to ease the suffering, and with the impacts on jobs and the emotional lives of the children, drawn out over months, and the simple impossible practicalities, like the incontinence, like getting a proper bed with elevation for Fowler's position through the door and up to the second storey of the daughter's old house, were so completely unexpected and terrible. A very good piece. You could tweet, then headline or pull quote, that some people *die* lives of quiet desperation. Or was that glib? What was that other quote that spoke to her, from book club: the one Emily brought in when they did *Anna Karenina* and only two people had finished it and they hardly talked about the book at all. It was a quote from a Scottish writer about the 19th-century novel. He said that sometimes it seemed like the purpose of the entire narrative was just the elaborated torture of the heroine, ending only with her murder. Annabel sat as close to the window as she could, praying for someone nice or someone professional or just a woman to be the one who took the seat beside her. Or, who knew, maybe even today, in recompense for the theft of the Pinarello, a £1000 bike—it had taken her a year to pay it off and an hour on the weekend to melt the paraffin wax in a bain-marie on the stove and to dip and dry the chain; an old lubrication technique that meant the chain wouldn't pick up dust and that her father taught her, and it was that long job and effort that seemed to focus and sharpen the pain of this theft—maybe today she'd be the one, the miraculous one, with two seats to herself all the way to Euston station.

'Yeah, I know, I know, I know, I *kno-ow*!' Came a bright posh voice, too loud, and a girl in Wayfarers presented herself in a final leap into the top saloon, and Annabel just knew she'd be the one. The one who'd sit down and shout in her ear all the way. 'I'm just running really late in and the fucking bus driver just took all my change!'

Annabel sighed and turned the backpack around and around in her lap.

But: 'Awe-right! Bye! Byee!' the girl said and she carried on down the aisle.

'It's just the way it is, you know. Not don't turn up because of *reliability*.'

Annabel then took a huge and decisive step. She swivelled her backpack round once more, then she pushed its butt off her lap and firmly right to completely occupy the seat beside her, unzipped a pocket and acted professional absorption in investigating its contents.

'I've done the shitty work my entire life. But I have a life outside of the work I do for him.'

'Granny, why doesn't the bus go?'

'*Hate* when that happens.'

'Hate.'

'Eez pocketing it innit.'

'The amount of trouble this.'

'Twenny people in that one there that's 60 quid inna bag.'

'[Arabic Arabic] Euston station [Arabic Arabic].'

'[Russian Russian].'

'[Russian].'

'The amount of trouble.'

Someone whistling down at the fire station early in the morning, see the little fire engines . . .

Then the oilskinned man appeared at the top of the stairs.

He was hanging from the rail, grinning down the packed saloon. Underneath the oilskin he seemed to be wearing a bin bag like a petticoat. The bus shuddered to life and moved out into the traffic of Agincourt Road. The man had to hang on with two hands, and, as if in spite of the challenge, grinned wider. The smell even from where she sat was violent: ancient canvas wrapped round old broiled meat, deep brown sweat, layers of brassy, vintage urine, and petrol. Under it all, something she couldn't identify, something sickly and goatish.

'Well maybe she does think that, but there is other people dealing with that, as such.'

At this comment, the woman with the Provence novel turned to stare, furious. The Polish woman was bent 90 degrees at the neck. The seat beside her was empty too. For the damaged oilskinned man there were two prime empty seats right in front of him from which he was at liberty to choose.

'Rosie does 90%. If anything she's the one must go,' the woman said.

The Provence woman glanced at the damaged man, then back at the woman, and sighed loudly, looking straight at her.

'It's not easy to let someone *go*.'

Something changed slightly on the Provence woman's face.

'Because there's lots of *things*.'

Dogged, doomed. Each sentence paused in falling like the second-spanned failure of flight in a hunt-shot partridge.

'Of *course*. There is lots of different factors—and I had a very normal conversation with Janine and then I hear back "What's been wrong with *you* today." And it's like—'

'. . .'

'There's lots of *things*—'

The woman turned back to the front and closed her novel.

'—come into *play*.'

Nine-twelve, misty Thursday morning turning fine. The bus come to a halt at the lights. The oilskinned man took two steps down the aisle, grinning here and there. Odours growing. Paused beside Annabel and the Polish woman. Four blacked-out Range Rovers crept around and past them onto the wrong side of the road and onto the intersection against the red light, and when the Mansfield Road traffic was forced to wait for them, accelerated away in a feeble blast of horns.

The Polish woman looked up then, noticing, at last, with a blank and pale and hunted look of unrecognition, her eye gone quite black, the oilskinned man.

Annabel, expressionless, leaned down, zipped up the pocket of her pack and pulled the pack onto her lap.

The man looked down at the two empty seats and actually simpered. The odours electric, coming off him in waves.

And crunched softly down beside her.

He was big and filled up the whole seat. He touched her body completely from deltoid to calf. She looked down hard out the steamed-up window, hugging the backpack tight. She shrank in every dimension. *Don't be a dummy. Go to your GP if something feels funny.* They lumbered on down Southampton Road. Annabel was now turned almost 90 degrees left in her seat and staring outside with sudden massive fascination and breathing through her mouth in shallow and controlled breaths that were further fogging the window and her view. The bus must have been full up because they didn't even slow for the Wendling stop. With her elbows jammed into her sides she had only enough room to wipe a tiny easement with the back of her one available hand to see the queues of people at the Wendling stop across the road from the barbers who were waving, furious, as the bus sailed past.

'I bet that was the highlight of his day,' said the grandmother brightly behind her.

'I would never put myself in front of camera,' said the Polish girl, 'and I know I'm not best person with other *people*, and that's why we hire . . . I just feel now that I'm expected to sudden be—'

Then the roads were open. The bus sailed down Malden, the sun burning off the mist and lighting up the road paint in silver sigils. The driver ran the lights at the Fiddler's Elbow on Prince of Wales Road. The passengers barely noticed. Tyre squeals and horns beeping behind them. Past the Harmood Children's Centre. Past the shirtless man always sitting in his deckchair in the lowest balcony of Rugmere. Annabel not noticing either, breathing slow, controlled breaths, and concentrating hard. If you can't take notes you have to remember. Be at peace. Focus on the *issue*. Eye contact can be doled out in token amounts, like a check for those who are or aren't paying attention. The way Death makes eye contact. Not to ingratiate or make you feel involved, but to check that you're paying attention to him. As if he'll single you out, strike you down, send you from the room. Every single person is either asset or enemy. And that you're not Death is not a problem, because she's observed that it's okay to actually openly appear as if you're using a public speaking technique, however much you might not be using it 100% effectively or effortlessly. That the art and the effort become part of the charm of the speaker—I am working hard for you, my audience. You may be noticing how open I am about my being less than perfect and wonderful at this. Look at me: I know I'm consciously and openly using this technique that more powerful and experienced figures use incredibly effectively but that I am using only perhaps half as well but you can please see I'm also using it, or my attempt at it, and working at it, only for *you*, all just for *you*, here I am for you, and yes, as a kind of act, a performance; one with no attempt to beguile or mislead or put one over you, though, but merely to let you know that here I am learning in front of you, *you*, working hard, young, enthusiastic, full of sprouting beans, trying to be this person who uses this technique and who might one day perfect it and whom you might one day recognise as competent for that. You can at least appreciate this. That I'm both working very hard to perform for you and that I'm getting better. That I'm working very hard. You can forgive me. You can't fire me for that.

Might that work in writing?

'—no it's just *not*. That's what I planned to do today. I'm in my way in now and sorry I'm late. I plan to sit in the meeting'—her voice rising, strengthening, a new authority—'and discuss what—'

Past Leverton & Sons funeral directors and onto Chalk Farm Road. The driver seemed to see what she could not, for he took the traffic-lighted corner without pausing, into Camden. They passed her local, Cycle Surgery. And she looked down then with the most intensest and desiringest longing to be imaginatively lost for just a while, just a small collection of seconds, in contemplation of one beautiful carbon frame in the window, one new gearset, or a whole new bike she hadn't seen before and which surprised her—

'Just doesn't—'

Two cyclists outside with their bikes and gear, one a courier, smoking. The window of the shop was smashed. Too fast. His thin wide shoulders over a body like a serifed I.

'Doesn't really—'

How cyclists grow to resemble their bikes.

The thing beside her heaved side to side and was actually leaning on her now when they appeared to run over something, because the bus rose and fell in a long rocking motion like water in a bath.

'I know I'm not the hero. Well there's really only three of us—'

'Jesus Christ!' said someone downstairs.

The Russian man and his son were pointing at four British Transport Police trucks as big as fire appliances, heavily armoured, cruising north past them on the sun-gold Camden Road. 'Bawby!' said the father, and then something else in Russian.

'I don't see it's professional that I'm banned from the office and not to turn up to the office now. I don't find that criticism *helpful*. That doesn't *help* me.'

'Bawby!' said the son, and laughed.

'—I . . . *need* that visa.'

Bobby, he was saying.

'Dahty fawin bahstids,' at last the wreckage next to her loudly croaked. He breathed against her cheek. '*Dir-eeh fawrinse laaags.*'

Everyone heard it.

A small silence from the granny and the little girl rippled quickly back the entire upper saloon. Nobody moved. Nothing else changed.

'Fahkeen *minge*. Can'ts. Calm over ear-neck in orla nashnil elf. Dahty fawrin *slags*.'

Opposite the Sainsbury's there was a crowd of dozens by the bus stop. There were hooded figures out in the road by the World's End. By the stop was a man in indigo jeans, a white Kangol windbreaker, bent over with his legs straight and his Pumas wide as if stretching for a run. He was briskly vomiting onto the pavement beside his Big Can of White Lightning cider, at a quarter past nine in the morning. When the bus sped up and sailed past that stop too he stood up straight again and ironically or just opportunistically joined in with the cries of the crowd under the shelter and gave it merry fingers. But then, as if inspired, he bent back down and picked up his can and staring apparently straight at Annabel he reared back and hurled it. As other objects flew wildly from the crowd only approximately towards the bus, like cans and bottles and the bump of a brick, and other unidentifiable stuff, the can of White Lightning flew true. Leaving a trail of colourless above-average-strength cider, it parabola-ed through the air towards the upper deck of the bus and with an improbably loud bang smashed on the window inches from Annabel's cheek. Having watched it come, transfixed, she nevertheless actually squealed and leapt and recoiled violently from the spattered dripping window and into the aura of the reeking damaged man, where she rested for a stunned moment, huddled into him and his oilskin, where she'd placed her hand like a proprietorial lover on what purported to be a thigh, and she stared at the window with the disbelief of a Neanderthal first encountering the properties of glass until she became aware that what she was experiencing under her hand had a texture, a texture combining both the yielding qualities of soft, rotting, furry peach and the sticky stiffness of old leather long unloved and subjected to who knew what liquid indignities and she came then into sudden cognisance of her situation and its odours, textures and proximity and she whiplashed sideways from the reeking hideousness, turning back as she did so to say sorry for *bumping him*, and in flinching and apologising so vigorously she then smacked the back of her head on the Plexiglas window high up on the left parietal and bobbed sideways back into the reeking man's orbit again while dropping her bag and her Filofax of ideas between her legs and it was like fucking hell and the man turned with some glowering interest to see what was all the sudden physical attention about then and she recoiled to the dripping window again and said, sorry, sorry, to the back of the seat in front of her and then remembered her dropped bag and Filofax and when she leant down to get the bag and all her ideas she hit her forehead on the hard plastic handle of the back of the seat in front where the incised and inked graffito read ragged WILSON YOU NUT and when she finally, after rocking minutely and repetitively in place for a while, was somewhat combobulated and still enough to sit back with her pack in her lap and start to quietly cry, really outraged more than anything, she found that all this wasn't even the worst of it.

It was 9:16 in the morning.

Pigeons asleep on the suicide nets of the Gillfoot estate.

The auto-announcement over the Tannoy came then, to an aria of groans of those who hadn't been paying attention to what was going on, to what the driver had been doing, or rather what he hadn't been doing, to date:

'The destination of this bus has changed. Please listen for further announcements.'

John Mayer opened the door and James looked up from the style guide. John went by him as if he were not there. At Helen Jackson's desk Mayer stopped, and she swung round in her chair and leaned back and looked up at him and they chatted. The easy intimacy of those who exercise hard together, who know each other at a deep and wordless and unbarriered level. She said something, made some unparsable gesture, and he held up his right hand swathed in a bandage, and they laughed.

Ten minutes later, Annabel, sighing with the terror and futility of it all, with vast relief stepped from the doors of the prematurely halted 24 bus on Eversholt Street directly into the path of the filthy van on which was written ALSO IN WHITE.

She was taken from the road and placed in an ambulance at a more or less crucial period of time thereafter, a foam collar on her neck against brain or spinal injury for which they had no time to check (they were in such a hurry to get away from the kids throwing bricks).

The pulses of work in an office. The thrumming of coming and going. The constancy of language always, in the rising of voices and the smiles and the leaned back chairs, in the falling of voices and the brutal clatter of keys. In the early morning the sense of a long quiet sigh being gone about collectively. Motivated, dedicated, decent. Beeps and clatters like a thousand plastic somethings sucked down a vacuum cleaner tube. This was another morning of greetings at their most minimal. There was no Clinch today, as the

Goddess was still absent and unable to make it to a phone. On Goddessless days in digiprod when the workload wasn't so bad (there were few) the vibe could go low and slow. So it wasn't really a noticeable thing that Annabel was as yet absent too. Mist outside. Moving down Euston Road. Wet trees above like mothers waiting in the rain for lost sons. The Clinch is often where language starts, where it gets greased and moving again. Clinch-less days it's onscreen, where interactions are more manageable—the slow triage and pre-op of email hygiene. John Mayer, for instance, has 15,466 unread emails yet never misses a reply on something current. That takes work.

The sun over Gordon Square, coming in the windows in rare golden oblongs and bleeding down the walls over the lieutenant editors. Thirty seconds of sun a summer, on Death's desk. The constant clatter of keys—here rising the sound of language, the cups of tea accelerating it, managed, manipulated language accumulating, in the service of more managed, manipulated language. What process is like it? It was like they were technicians hard at work resalinating the entire world's seawater to slightly different parts per thousand. Diligent, focused, self-reflective. Bagged of eye, foul of breath, hungover, underslept—did Death ever feel like death in the morning? He gave the impression of a drill sergeant who drinks a gallon of bourbon in celebration of some dark emotion, wakes on time, sits bolt upright, shits, showers and shaves to schedule, steps into his clothes to run to work without breaking so much as a sweat. Press releasing a story about a study. No one in tech ed knew where he lived because no one in tech ed had ever seen him go home. No one had ever even seen him on the street. *Ever*. He would never die. Was he an angel? When Vivien had joined digiprod at the *Royal London* at the tail end of a viciously stressful period of linked articles on rare leukaemias she'd been scared, she'd said, because nobody talked. Nobody ever talked. Not to her, not to each other. They seemed to know what to do and did it, headphones on, in utter silence. So she sat there, insecure, new, alone, at a hotdesk cruelly allocated to face away from the main cluster. And she had no idea whether or how to break ice so transparent and complete that nobody on this frozen world could see it or sense it but her, this new warm body, so iced up and unfeeling and monomaniacal had they all become. Only she could see it, and how long before she lost feeling too? She said she'd seriously considered quitting several times that first week, and the following Monday and every Monday after for months. Had called home in her lunch hour for a cry; had wandered off into Bloomsbury hoping to get lost and not find her way back again. But it was she who couldn't sense it; it was she who was not attuned to the new rhythms. The Junoesque six-foot-two IT spec, Sophie, for instance, occasionally passed the digiprod unit in its refurbished area, causing minor tremors in the new flooring. Close attention would reveal that after each of these passages with their minor tremors the typing of Stuart and Geoff would seem to suddenly rise in intensity and tempo like seismic recorders at the source of their frenzy filling up with data, falling off slowly and slightly, only to rise to improbable speeds again, accompanied by occasional coughing fits to hide the laughter, when the IT spec returned from whatever had brought her to Editorial. To Vivien's and the outsider's eye nothing had happened but a slight rise in workload, perhaps. But there was in fact a five-way IM going on as Stuart and Geoff competed to out-dirty each other in exchanges of what Stuart cheerfully referred to as 'filf', the other three dropping off, usually, as the filf attained awful and job-endangering intensities. Incredibly detailed, unrestrained, 9:30am, highly caffeinated, psychologically unhidden, ingenuous and linguistically ingenious schoolboy filf involving a seemingly limitless series of scenarios featuring the IT spec, elaborated upon with massive adolescent energy: cheerful buttock asphyxiations and thigh throttlings and digital proddings and squashings and crushings and sittings-upon both naked and clothed, with and without audiences and musical accompaniments in varying exotic and banal locations and extremes of weather and historical eras and costume. (They were nearly middle-aged men who had never once spoken a word to Sophie and she didn't even know their names.) Alongside equally detailed commentary on the Ashes, intricate onomatopoeic representations of the laughter of Kevin 'sleesh-who' Perkins, alarming reports of an editor named Toby farting in situ at his desk and just not stopping, dissection of this and that strand of TV show, links to guitars, to gigs, to sales, to bars. Brief and seemingly harmless queries that dropped into holes of horrific and alienating inappropriateness with alarming abruptness and a weird, doomed fin-de-siècle finality that soon became a lurching inevitability: Payday lunch tomorrow? Meh. I shan't be here, I have a debauched hen weekend to attend. I bet there'll be lezzing in the showers, I can't see how that wouldn't happen. Pretty sure they don't have showers at hen weekends. 'Baby showers'. That's the one you're thinking of. Definitely lezzing. Pregnant lezzing. Nice. All this kind of thing. All the female voices dropping off the thread. What Vivien didn't know. A whole black market of conversation and community was out of her reach. She didn't yet have MSN Messenger installed.

But everyone did it. The rhythms were the same no matter what the subject or the medium. And the more experienced and more appropriately matched in talent and employment knew how to channel it better, to manage their time and energy, to make the shift from downtime smut and skirts and shirts and singles and nostalgio tourism and to start a real-life conversation, talk to someone, get back on the team, get back to work and feel the yoke of responsibility to the *Royal Lond J Med* settle on them not as burden but as ballast to prevent them careening off into the lightless void of linkbait and their own worst tendencies, shoulders sinking, eyes reddening, closer, closer to the screen as the IMs reduce down to just cut-and-pasted URLs dense with reference to the foregoing conversation. This happened in the short term of a hungover morning and in the long term of a business restructuring, too. They get back to work and think of their paypacket and for the lucky ones even the promise of a pension.

They even think of the sick.

The paramedics gave up on the A&E at UCH because Euston Road was blocked off with armoured police vans attempting to kettle the rioters back east to King's Cross. So the ambulance was bombing it north up Eversholt Street towards the Royal Free, sirens silent to stay off radar, only the occasional bang of a brick or a can against the side of the vehicle.

Somewhat confused by her cycling gear in the rapid loading, the paramedic leaned over Annabel on the stretcher.

'Were you wearing a helmet, darling?'

Annabel's left ankle, otherwise quite normal, at a terrible wrong angle. Worse, right femur broken. Possible pelvic injuries. Classic fractures for cyclists hit by car, usually accompanied by secondary head and neck injuries when they subsequently hit the windscreen and/or the road. Hence the foam collar. Her right leg enveloped in a bright orange vacuum splint, after they had assessed for bone breakthrough, straightened the fracture to terrible screams, a second pivot point, a second knee. Distal pulse intact and no apparent blood loss, no time for IV morphine because there were groups of kids in balaclavas and grey marle Nike fleece behind police lines pulling up concrete tiles from the very pavements and stoning anyone in the street.

Annabel sucking on Entonox, pale, and points of vague light in her eyes gone black from pain dilatation, panting. She said something inaudible into the mask.

'What was that darling?' said the paramedic warmly, a woman not much older than Annabel herself.

Annabel moved the mask an inch and said, 'Bike was stolen,' in small and huffing breaths.

The paramedic smiled down upon her.

'That's okay Annabel. Don't you worry about your bike now. Do you remember if you were wearing a helmet?'

The paramedic leaned this way and that, as the ambulance veered onto the wrong side of the road to clear a crowd across the road from Koko at the foot of Camden High Street. She wasn't trying to keep her balance, she was looking for blood in Annabel's hair. Then she caressed Annabel's head gently with both hands, her fingertips, an abstracted look in her eye. Checking for obvious deformity, blood, brain or bone. She leaned down and looked right into Annabel's ear, for watery cerebrospinal fluid pooling, running lost into her pale auburn hair. Then she pulled the pen torch from her breast pocket and shone it in her dilated eyes.

The driver floored it in sudden space by the Camden Head. Annabel sucked hard on the Entonox to gather her strength; the ambulance veered into the left-hand single lane again, hit the sirens and slowed only gently to get through amber flashing lights at the Camden Road intersection by the tube station.

'My . . . bike . . . got *stolen*,' Annabel said and then she made some awful sounds and arched her back as the Entonox failed to rise to the occasion, the ambulance veered again, there was the hollow smash of a bottle against the steel, the paramedic braced herself against the stretcher, and the ambulance more or less came to a halt.

'We'll get you a new bike, even better than before,' the paramedic said brightly, watching Annabel's eyes. Now was the moment to get the IV in before A&E cursed her for an amateur. Another bang on the side of the van. She turned to look forward out the small interior window to the driver and the windscreen for what they were coming into. That grand asymmetry of carer and cared for, that total market failure. 'Were you wearing a helmet, though, can you remember, Annabel?' she said, sounding a little worried now.

Seen it all before, though not quite like this, not under fire.

London nurses call London cyclists 'organ donors'.

The same ambulance, as it happens, as Annabel's, a Mercedes-Benz Sprinter, but six months ago with a mother-to-be on board, was driven fast, so fast. To make those eight-minute targets laid down as NHS quality measures from on high.

It started off briskly to the Royal Free—but the traffic that day slowed things down irretrievably.

Fires on the horizon, fires to the north. Tottenham Court Road empty from the Warren Street station to the Freddie Mercury statue perched astride the awning of the Dominion Theatre. Mounted police emerging from the stables off Great Scotland Yard, limbed shadows loud in the echoing, rainsilked streets, joining the column of loose lines of riot squad, none of whom more than 20 years of age, suited up and filing out of Whitehall Place and up to Trafalgar Square. Where the armoured buses in their legions waited, to take them to the front. Smoke glowing in the rain, perfused and smudgy with stoplight like blood entrained to the weave of hospital linen. A man throwing filing cabinets from the sixth-floor window of a Tottenham Court Road office building built in 1832. Dies of congestive heart failure 500 metres from UCH A&E. The Amazon warehouse just outside London ablaze for nearly 72 hours straight. A historian in a loft apartment straight out of a Hammershøi in a street near the British Museum, watching the eclipse through the smoke in a pair of 3D glasses with a glass of sherry in his hand. Crowds gathered on Parliament Hill to watch the smoke and fires, like they used to do for the New Year's lanterns set adrift over London, until the first rains, a stabbing, the first rape in the treeline. Homeless sleeping in the copse where Boadicea's corpse was supposed to lie interred. Pregnant women held in holding wards till fistulas form like those that third-world women bear. So the rumours go, and are cited. P-values as low as 0.0001. Clouds yellow as sucked sour sweets and the mists chill, so chill. Men riding the trains endlessly, choosing certain women to ask for money. Trains avoiding certain stations; just run right through them now. 'Al Pacino's' off-licence on Hornsey High Street ('European food' it says) burgled three times then just left open by the heartbroken owners till burned down to a black stone skeleton recognisable only to that first architect who drew it up from nothing. Plate glass windows of a pub on Euston Road smashed in by the son of a man who was once charged a premium on an orange juice in the immediate aftermath of the 7/7 bombings when all transport stopped and people hid out in the pubs to wait and who did not stint on remembrances of that tariff to his family. The Royal Colleges closed. The Wellcome Trust closed. Euston station closed. Two boys on a moped looking for an unclosed clinic, riding the empty Streatham streets like the silent days of snowed-in Christmas; one quite collapsed upon the other in hypoglycaemic shock.

And the lights on up the towers.

(Six months ago: she called strange words with no sequitur to speak of and spoke them into the microphone of the gas. She went from all fours to flat on her back. And there it began.)

For Kristian, no matter how bad the news on Twitter the deadlines don't change. The maw, great and dark and obscure, of the CMS waits. You may not look upon it or even picture it. You are permitted only to know you owe it copy-edited content and it lives and over all of us it reigns. Death its gatekeeper; the Goddess dam and check to its holy foal. James Ballard its odist and archivist of record. Lightless, a transformer of work into words. Just as when, as freelancer, you invoice Bethany in HR via email, to nary a reply or acknowledgement of any kind, trusting the pay will arrive two weeks later: send your hours into the hole.

Kristian, in his new glasses, watched on the Twitter feed the riots spread to within two stops of his tube station, and found distance enough to find it incredible in himself that he was experiencing it like a story. Like the best and most involving novel. It was simply just very good—so big, pacy, always a leap ahead and to one side of the foreseeable development. Constantly blindsided, as it were, by new occasions for the designer's genius. The street razed where he was raised: a line behind a hashtag. There and gone. Not even the liveblogging BBC had it yet. In sunlit 1080 HD, his Twitter desktop was a desert, easy on eyes. He had kept the first referral letter from his optometrist six months ago. He'd gone in about a blurriness in one eye and about a possible prescription for reading glasses to help at work. *This PX, read the referral letter in wild cursive, is 1/0 poor vision to his left eye which has worsened over the last few weeks. There are changes to left macula which need urgent HES examination.*

There are changes indeed.

Kristian now had approximately a year to see and no plan to provide for his partner or himself thereafter. So why shouldn't he enjoy it, nearly slackmouthed and apparently disengaged, but in fact lost in the crisp kerning, the beauty of the image of the words holding together the things that are falling apart. Even the errors were beautiful now—the way his sight had changed. The condition, you see: the first casualty was irony, a tone of voice.

It was only 10:30, and Kristian had sent an email to Rob, cc'ing D1, spot on 9, warning them of his latest appointments, which were staggered awkwardly, and asking for yet more time off that week. Wednesday pm and Friday am, at the Western Eye Hospital in Marylebone. Not far from here, so he could be there and back in about 60 minutes, but the drops they used to artificially dilatate his eyes left them fully dilated and unable to process and react to light for up to eight hours. More or less like having your eyelids taken off. (Good practice too, one supposes, for later in the condition, having to, at a trim and neat age 46, ask strangers at bus stops to tell him the number of the big red blur approaching.) Being of course unable to tell anybody at work about this situation, he told Rob and D1 a well-researched lie in a very convincing two-tiered structure. First he told them about the symptoms, and after that the fairly benign diagnosis he'd researched and applied, as if mimicking the usual structure of a Patient's Tale, suckling its readers on a pulse of suspense and revelation, fear and disclosure, the natural narrative of easy disease, or as if finding some plausible scenario for a character in a fiction: 'Dear Rob, David, I'm afraid I have to go to an eye apointment for blurry vision in one eye brought on apparently, ha ha, by stress,' he wrote. 'They think it is most likly a mild CSR or central serious retinopathy that needs confirming by optical coherence tomography (OCT). That's just an efflorescence of fluid under the retina (on OCT it looks like an old Amiga rendering a far-off volcano—quite pretty!) which spontaneously resolves upon easing, ha ha, of the "causative pressures upon the patent".' (There were three spelling errors in the email, and an uncomma-ed 'which' for a 'that', and he'd used the term 'efflorescence' wrongly.)

The causative pressures jokily mentioned being those routinely applied on him by Rob and D1 to get his (Kristian's) you know, *work done*, so with that pair of matesy, comradely and collegial yet restrained ha ha's—restrained, 'cos you know, we've all got problems, mate—he'd sent off this email requesting yet more half days off. Eight hours of dilated pupils . . . if he squinted hard but not too obtrusively he could work Friday pm after he'd been given the treatment, when a lot of people were WAH anyway. Black-eyed and wide-eyed on a Friday afternoon, he'd need tissue for the tears, trying to read like a frightened animal staring at his screen in terror, because they always do both eyes.

And so here now in that quietening time down the aisle came Rob and—why?—David 1, to *talk to him*. Down the aisle they were coming, smiling too gently. That quietening time after the morning's self-indulgence before the conversations start up and the real work starts to get done.

He didn't ever think of himself as a brave person, or that he was being brave.

It happens in a sunny haze, low and twilit and silent.

Kristian suddenly realising *he* was *their* real work today.

It was only 10:30, no Clinch, and still no word from Annabel.

Her face had changed from a species of agony to one of transport and a terrible calm and the midwife, pale, looked up and hissed to the nurse, 'Call her in *now*.'

Susan watched James type. Typing, typing, typing, always typing, into the stylebook document he was converting. Intense bursts, followed by gazes up to the far-off corners of the office. Staring down to the clanking blind. From where she was sitting she'd see the words become image: a trim line of bolded terms lined up down the left-hand side of the page, and the ragged edge of the right: terms and their definitions, elaborations, guidance, the collected method and wisdom of 160 years—then see it all turn blue as he selected it, and, in gigantic chunks with a quick, distracted thunk of the delete key, disappear. As presumably he finished converting that section. Again and again. And then he'd type.

She watched him, intrigued, and at the same time 100% prepared to abruptly kill that interest at any given moment should it prove too involving.

When Susan returned to work after the birth of her son she had made several new arrangements. She had aggressively pursued this particular desk, with its view outside over the atrium and the terrace, and inside over the tech eds' heads and screens through Editorial all the way to Death in the corner. Her good seat with its back to the wall. She had aggressively pursued a part-time contract that had an actual contract with specified hours—she knew freelancers got it in the neck. She had aggressively pursued one of Editorial's rubber plants to ornament her desk. And HR to send over the ergonomics expert to tailor her keyboard and workstation to prevent RSI and minimise eye strain. She had aggressively pursued a footrest. She hunkered down and put out her spines. This was her hole in the rock in the storm to come and she meant to stay there.

And from this spot, gently fingering the hole in her stocking, alongside Jane but at such an angle that Jane couldn't see her screen, she watched over her team without judgement or anything more than a love she could forgo. As her son grew, other people became to her a kind of attractive, fondly thought-of but unpredictable furniture one might just have to abandon. A rickety chair, the dowel reglued one too many times. Or more or less complex pieces of software—vital to her job for now but inevitably to be updated. To be loved and known quite intimately, but to also be handled and managed and ultimately discarded. Her kindness, what she gave of herself, was now simply mathematically useful to her cause. Susan intended to become so much a part of the machinery here it would be unthinkable to take her out on the atrium's windy terrace, to talk about her future here at the *Royal*.

Here came Death down the aisle, following D1 and Rob, who turned off at Kristian's desk. She'd covered for Kristian countless times. He was having troubles at home and was underslept and stressed. He was arguing with or splitting with his partner, and Susan had been there. It was not difficult to inconspicuously review his pieces in XML and make a few adjustments before rebuilding them to the CMS. 'Media' for 'medical'. 'H2N1' for 'H5N1', which he did more than once. Missing US and OED spellings for -ise/-ize words, which: amateur hour. But sometimes she was busy. Didn't have time to cover for him.

She hit print on her article; she'd surprise Death with the

proof early and while he was down here in tech ed on some other errand. The thing with Death she knew, perhaps the only thing: he liked to be surprised. Be unsettled, kept on edge. He thrived on negative things: hatred in the comments, vitriol in the broadsheets, public Fiskings, outraged professors emeriti. He loved it, loved to respond with inflamed authority, goad them on to a peak of indignation with hard stats and remorseless refusal to compromise, then—leave them up there, exposed and wide open and shaking with fury, as he slipped away to some other topic. And he was always right.

Down the aisle he came towards them all, and everybody slightly tensing. Everybody but James. Typing, typing what seemed like large and detailed email-worthy amounts of text for a stylebook entry. (The largest of which, incidentally, and horribly, is #**References**.) Where was James's wife? She'd never met her. He was one of those who never mentioned their partners. Death paused at his shoulder, by the printer there, and examined the bookshelf above him. Laden and improbably bowed with all the *Royal*'s dusty reference texts, stylebooks, encyclopaedias, dictionaries, and two 20-foot shelves of the leatherbound archival bindings of every issue going back to 1842 and the retreat from Kabul after the First Anglo–Afghan War, when there'd been a guidance on treatment of frostbite by a military surgeon. (Who was, indeed, *that* William Brydon, the lone bedraggled rider of Lady Butler's gigantic oil on canvas *Remnants of an Army*: sole survivor of the horrific withdrawal through the wintered passes of the Hindu Kush, and his subsequent sober, restrained and helpful piece on digital amputation in the field the only mention of the subsequent massacre of 16,000 soldiers and civilians, more or less, made in the *London* that issue.) Susan had worked on some of those books—the illustrated

Dorlands, 10th edition; a Dorling Kindersley illustrated encyclopaedia. Her life, his blood, the food on their table was etched invisibly in the margins, corrections and deletions of the extant text. There is her work, her boy's pilled pyjamas. In that pulp. Death looked distracted. Typical of him to look for the printed reference book, miles from his desk, rather than search the massive number of online reference resources to which the *Royal* is subscribed. Just coming down to get the scent in his nose. To ream someone, get a victim, sharpen his claws. 'Get out of London early tonight' the mass email had read. She wasn't going anywhere. Here and home, that was all. She wasn't going anywhere.

'Mind if I just come over the top of you there?' Death murmured distractedly.

James sat bolt upright and very, very quickly minimised the document he was typing into. Behind: a blameless browser full of the front page of the *London*.

'Yes,' he said politely, 'I mean no,' and leaned sideways.

Death reached over him for the book—what book was it?

As Susan watched, James looked past Death's taut stomach to catch her eye. He probably knew she knew something of what he was doing, but did he care? Did she? Only as much as she had to. He grinned at Susan, past Death's crotch, his motherly hips. Sounded a bit naughty, that, didn't it.

Margaret caught it too, widened her eyes in faux alarm. Loves that kind of thing.

The registrar, the registrar. Oh she came and seemed so big and competent, and yet nothing to be done.

Rob considered himself, when he considered himself, basically a nice guy, a good person who had been wronged, once, badly, in the far-off past, and that was that about that. And those wrongs done to him—by his parents and his sister, in cutting him off, disowning him when he told them he was a gay man; wrongs done in telling him that that was not something they were ever prepared to be a part of or to support or understand or countenance or even ever speak specifically about—he understood those wrongs were done to him out of a nexus of inbred ignorance and nurtured not natural disgust rising out of the very stones of the Herefordshire village he hailed from and from which he couldn't imagine any ordinary person easily extricating themselves. And his family were ordinary people. So he forgave them.

(As he came down the sunny aisle towards Kristian, about the same moment Annabel Pitti was formally consented for emergency orthopaedic surgery, not quite aware he was a half step in front of David 1, his superior, and that David 1 was, as well, half smiling.)

So he had forgiven his family and he took pleasure in that forgiveness and the well-earned peace it brought him. And he took pleasure in knowing their various movements and life concerns and, in their sporadic meetings on his returns home after many years had elapsed, despite his family's apparent inability to be curious about or know or ask after him or his progress on his difficult path, with its usual struggles and hardships and hard choices and things of moment lost and striven for, he was unfailingly informed about and pleasant and bubbly in his enquiries into their own troubles and triumphs. And he had had, in the far, far-off past, too, his meltdown, and had dropped out of Oxford and his promising career as an academic physicist after two years of the DPhil. And he'd done his years of London's chems and clubs of cambered floors and drains. He'd been fisted publicly and he'd fisted back. He'd been up to his elbows in ass. And had come out of that time at well-earned peace and now he was Boring Gay Couple, mostly monogamous, all but married to the right man and looking for a house in Hackney, somewhere with space for their greyhounds—a doer-upper. He was in line for heading up content commissioning for a whole section of the *London*.

(Down the aisle he came, the orphan, sun on his chinos, as he'd come some months before with a proposal for tech ed, for Kristian et al., that perhaps editors could do their own tech editing on a lot of articles, absolutely, couldn't they, to save us serious money on freelancers, you know? It got turned down, that proposal, and that night he'd dreamed badly.)

He liked a pint or five on Thursdays and Fridays and the occasional Sunday afternoon. He liked beer gardens in the sun and faded denim shirts and woven leather belts on ripped old khaki shorts and Greek beaches and in-jokes and naughty stories with a bit of an edge. He liked it when people pushed it a bit too far.

Down the sun-glazed aisle he came, with pretty bad news for Kristian, the first part of which, after the pleasantries, was to be a very soft-voiced and delicate dressing-down commencing with a list of his less-significant errors collated over the past six months, never mentioning the big one, the H2N1/H5N1 thing, out of delicacy and comradeship, and not mentioning the errors in Kristian's email requesting more time off (having just clicked on 'include original email in reply' when he replied and turning on the spellchecker so that when re-sent they were red-lined, those spelling errors, just FYI, for Kristian, so he knows, for the future). The second part of the bad news being the on-paper Formal Warning, of course, which, behind him, David 1 was carrying.

(Down the sun-glazed aisle came Rob, a veritable spring in his step, and there was Kristian, red-eyed, red-rising from beyond his screen in recognition, and even relief, it looked like, maybe, was it perhaps even relief that here it was at last: the appearance of the executioner. But he, Rob, was only the herald; that wasn't something he would like to do. It was for David 1 to wield the blade, not him, wasn't it? Was it not?)

'All healthcare professional groups said they did not know what to say to partners or fathers during prolonged resuscitation.'

Death in stockinged feet, otherwise naked, padding through his darkened apartment that night. At leisure. He'd cycled, he'd run the Heath, he'd swum the ponds for an hour and now he was home: the Eldridge Smerin house in high

Highgate up between the two halves of the cemetery. Nearing midnight on a Thursday with the promise of a slow morning before he headed to the country. He padded through the dark kitchen, lights of the oven's LEDs a blurred traffic in the hanging scanpans. All worked out. Death ran barefoot. When he walked there was a trace of that rolling gait through the Kenwood trees. He was hairy on the thighs, a patch beneath his bellybutton. Those maternal hips. His nipples hard. Down the long corridor to the front of the apartment overlooking the west cemetery. The few jobs that needed doing tonight all but done: a phone call to the Royal Navy admiral from whom he'd solicited a thinkpiece on the implications of climate change for national defence after hearing him speak, quite literally, at Chatham House. But once outside Chatham House rules the admiral had for print and public consumption tamed the frightening speech right down to some fairly predictable bromides on Bangladeshi migration waves, and vulnerabilities for international shipping in bodies of water like the Malacca Strait. Death had been talking to him for weeks about it but tonight put it to the Goddess in a quick email thus: 'Like his aircraft carrier I suspect he's not for turning.' They were going to press with the piece anyway, all toned down. To have that voice between the covers (as they still put it). An admiral, speaking almost frankly.

Molesworth's contract had been torn up by phone tonight, too—the business had gone into some fairly severe form of Chinese receivership following a revenue downturn attributable not only to routine incompetence with the editing side of things but also to revelations surrounding apparently manufactured citations of the journal papers for which they provided a translation service on the side—

publish or perish being a near-literal imperative in small-centre Chinese academia and citations of those papers thus being a form of life insurance. But Molesworth were manufacturing not just citations and not just settling for whole faked journal articles that extensively cited the papers written by their clients but were also inventing *ab ovo* entire online journals that charged small 'publication fees' to authors; journals with appropriate-sounding names and online presences and back issues and supplements and impact factors and honorary editorial boards. To publish their clients' articles therein. But not just invented journals, also *conferences*; invented conferences related to those journals' fields; conferences with real corporate sponsors and printed programmes and affiliate hotels and rental car companies and *stationery*, held in verifiable locations in verifiable hotels in Marbella, the Algarve and the south of France, where pre-paying 'invited' delegates met perhaps somewhat uncertainly at first in garishly undecorated ballrooms wearing their unevenly printed *First Annual Conference of the Journal of South East Asian Applied Gastrointestinal Biostatistics Hello My Name is* . . . badges before doing exactly what people do at conferences—sharing their knowledge and research—so who was to say the conference was a fiction anyway? The flights there were verifiably real, the room was real, the food was awful but technically real, the people, as in any profession, more or less real. The next step obviously was to invent an entire field of research, but meanwhile the breadth and gall of it all was already amazing, and all dependent on the ambition of authors and contingent on the sacredness of peer review.

Plus, Death had taken Charles Boddington out on the terrace tonight by phone too—having brought him in to stir things up, it was time now for him to go. Boddington had taken the news rather too well, like a dog used to being whipped. 'More time for my fiction!' he'd said, and laughed hissingly with his tongue and his teeth, for the phone. 'Yes, yes,' said Death and quickly got off the call. Gently padding, soft sucking sounds of his feet on the cool marble of the darkened corridor. Luggage lined up there: suitcases, suit bags, a leather Gladstone. Along the concrete walls, his art: Jamie Wyeth's *Monhegan's Schoolteacher*. A private commission from Alan Magee: a photorealist anatomy made of stones. The frontispiece to Blake's *Song of Los*. No text anywhere. From the living room, audible now, the soft bone chords of Keith Jarrett's *Köln Concert* gently played. Wandering over the cityscape, a disinterested ghost. The seasons all awry. He opened the bathroom door to utter darkness, lifted a silk robe from behind the door and slipped it on.

The phone rang again.

He lifted the receiver in the hall and stepped to the blacked-out window a floor above the almost anonymous entrance on Swain's Lane: a single handle-less door in the same black steel as the street walls, like it had been sealed up. He looked through his reflection into the dark out there in the narrow lane under the mighty ashes of the cemeteries.

It was the Goddess.

'Doctor,' she said.

'Doctor,' said Death pleasantly. 'How are you, then?'

'Fine, thank you. And you?'

'So, Ibrahim al-Rayess. Let's not keep anyone in suspense,' said Death. 'I mean, as I think probably we now know, none of what he wrote is untrue.'

Claudia was silent.

Death grinned out in the dark and said, 'It's the way he

went about it that must needs trouble us, from the point of view of the journal.'

'But it's too late for that.'

'So what, then, is the journal's point of view?' said Death.

'This is going to be a faff, Tony. Are we up for it?'

'Are *you* up for it, Claudia? You are the editor-in-chief of the *Royal London*.'

'Oh, I'm up for it. But the question is, is it worth it? Given who he is and who he was.'

'Do you want my advice?'

'I'm asking you to advise, yes, in your role, Tony.'

'If it's true, then in for a penny, in for a pound. Doesn't matter whose penny in the end game.'

'That's my thinking. We defend it. At length. Two thousand words. The battleship's for turning.'

'An editorial?'

'Something more nonchalant. A feature co-authored by senior leadership. We get the facts straight. We now know his personal situation and we are sorry for it. As far as we may extend our sympathies we do, by our saying so. We otherwise don't and cannot care. The journal is bigger than him. The journal is bigger than us. Bigger than that measure of unfairness handed any of us no matter how severe. The journal's bigger than an EU bid. Bigger than Syria. *Turkey*. Bigger than whichever governments or civil wars affect events and stances in this particular slip of time. You think this. Two thousand words. We will publish and be damned. Doesn't merit an editorial. Doesn't merit real language.'

'No?'

'I mean it's not as if it's a changed guidance. It's not some kind of *revelation*. In how we care for *patients*.'

'It might be to the Turks.'

'Let's get to it.'

'If you think so, Claudia.'

He stood staring out down the lane between Highgate Cemetery east and west, as if choosing a side. The journal: ever-bright, everchanging, ever-fascinating. Death woke happy to this every morning. He smiled into the darkness, his reflection.

'Well,' said Claudia.

'Well, I'll start the draft on my trip away and circulate.'

'Get it lawyered sooner rather than later. And stay safe, Tony.'

'You too. Goodnight, then.'

'Goodnight.'

He replaced the phone and padded down the hall. In his great empty concrete living room a long flat sofa looked out over London. The fires in the city—Holloway, Islington, Holborn, Shoreditch, Camden—lit the room golden-grey and he looked down at his body: grey-gold flickers and shapes moved over him like water; he held out his palms and looked down at himself as if he'd assumed new form. Helen Jackson, naked, sat up from the couch and looked at him and breathed through her nose in imitation of a slightly irritated sigh.

'Do hurry up.'

Death looked up and grinned mightily. 'I've a man's memory to consecrate,' he said.

'Well, I've got *work* to do.'

He came across the room to her as the record's needle slipped into the run-out groove with a gentle crunch and crackle.

A few hundred feet from where a daughter's mamma died and left her, Annabel slept.

The T&O registrar slid a malleable retractor into the long incision in her thigh. He bent it gently under the broken bone. He laid the bone plate over the fracture line and the scrub nurse reached in and held the pieces of Annabel's femur in place, roughly straight. Fracture line and fracture gap: no more than a single-millimetre gap.

The T&O took up his surgical drill, tested it backward and forward, then commenced to drill the screw holes through the bone using the bone plate as a jig. A little give, when he broke through into the marrow, another resistance, a whining sound, then another little give as the drill bit came out the other side.

He picked up his screwdriver and the first screw, then to the bone plate, to the bone and to the nurse, he murmured, 'Tight's tight, and too tight's broken.'

There was very little general orthopaedics in the *Royal London Journal of Medicine*. There were plenty of specialist journals for that.

Annabel slept on.

Only you now, grey and warm and heavy, sleeping on my heart.

'Fox without fox. Fox without fox. Fox *without* fox. Fox without fox without fox.'

You and only you, and he. Sleeping on his heart. Heavy round his neck.

Dong. Patter patter patter.

The phrase was going round and round repeating and repeating, like those voices do for the depressed. With the complete authority those damning voices have.

Fox without fox, it said. Fox without fox. Fox *without* fox. Without fox.

Dong. Patter patter patter. It was looping sometimes, rolling and slowing and speeding up again, like something swinging and fast and then steep and relentless that someone big and grown-up had put you on and you couldn't get off on your own. Fox without fox without fox. Without fox without fox. It would stop and then just say it again. Without fox. *Patter patter, patter.* That voice: it was actually his own, but rich with experience, power, paternity, deep and toneless as a grade on a paper. That's depression. Talking shit back with better equipment. Without fox. Without fox. *Dong.* Fox without fox without fox *patter patter patter* and *sss* the Angelcare was saying and had been saying for how long and there were footsteps above and he woke into it, the semi-sanguine light-hearted half waking that it was happening again something awful *you should not have left her alone* and he jumped out of the bed and ran across the room and headfirst hard into the edge of the open bedroom door.

It hit him high on the forehead, on the right frontal eminence, just below the spot a quality headbutt ought to use and it floored him. The one and a half inches of the edge of the door invisible in the dim and facing him backed by 66 inches of medium density fibreboard hit him right in the head.

He went straight down and the door then swung slightly open for him, having done its job.

He climbed up again in the dark, from the floor, freezing cold—and walked into a wall. But there was light playing down the stairs, flickering and coloured. He found his bearings, switched on the stairway lights. Up the stairs two at a time to the middle floor of the apartment. The temperature was rising, and a gassy, steely stink. Lights flickering red and blue playing on the leaves of the honey locust out the balcony windows and *pitter patter pitter patter* went the footsteps on the covered way above.

Fire in the estate.

Seeing this and sensing this and smelling this James turned and ran down the hall but her door—FIO and the N beginning to peel away—was wide open to pitch black and the slush of soaked coir matting underfoot.

It had flooded again.

He suddenly knew what he was going to find.

And flicked on the light.

The room was full of water and leaves and twigs and debris and her Moses basket was empty of she, the swaddle, all. Its veneered wooden legs were footed in six inches of river water, gently rocking. He stood there in his pyjamas, staring at the empty basket. Then he fell to all fours and began dredging his hands through the floodwater. Sweeping this way and that. Pulling up handfuls, handfuls of ash and plane tree leaves as big as sunflowers, throwing them across the tiny room and sweeping through and across and grasping toys and twigs and swathes of muslin, leaves and nappies, tiny sleepsuits, and saying out loud to no one, *oh no, no, no* and then he felt the sudden heft.

The heavy swaddled weight down under the Moses basket.

He made a high moaning, a keening sound back up in his throat and raised from the water wrapped in swaddling clothes the heavy sodden burden—the dripping, staring teddy bear.

Hurled it out the door and to his feet and full of rage he turned back down the hallway.

And stopped.

Past the drowned bear, darkness dripped all along the narrow hall. He turned on the hallway light. He touched his forehead and examined his hand for blood from the collision. Nothing. Dripped evidence, a spattered line, of someone passing from the flooded room. He ran down the hallway and up the stairs to the front door. Into rising heat and steely stink, red and blue light playing through the front door's eye slit and across the darkened walls. Moving doubtless, economically. Stopping only to from behind the front door pull on his yellow raincoat and from behind that grasp the Husqvarna axe and he opened the front door wide.

The cage was wide open, the lock simply gone, and police and fire service lights were flashing blinding everywhere. Sinusoid grind and roar of a helicopter above and smoke. People passing, everywhere out there. Running. Voices. Under it all a deep and far-off rushing sound.

The smoke was two doors down, pouring from the Irishman's front door and pooling under the corridor's ceiling and rolling out and falling up into the sky. He bent to the brick of the entranceway, looking for traces of the dripping water. Left or right. Right—here; the spatter and fall. Backing out the door and following the sign definitively towards the Old Oak, and towards the Heath.

He set off running down the covered way, holding the axe tight to his side. His neighbours in pyjamas stood in the corridor by the Irishman's door and out on the road were people come out to the orbits of their front doors and hooded boys were out on the road and by the off-licence the recycling bins were burning again and cordoned off further down at the informal border to Hampstead proper the police support units reflected back the smoke and lights in the clouded lenses of their shields and James ran, ducking through the scalding smoke to the wheelchair ramp at the end of the covered way towards the Heath.

'James. Are you all right?' came the voice from 51B as he passed and it was Marcella who was an architect and James retched 'They've taken the baby' and that was all and he ran on into the street.

Which was carless, Mansfield Road, like never, and a kind of roadblock of average people had filled the other end of the street, by the Old Oak. Between them and the police were maybe 30 boys in hoods and scarves and someone male yelled 'C'mon it's your fuckin' neighbourhood you dicks' and like oxygen called by the flames people walked forward to the burning, looked back and walked back, all apart and holding up their phones in landscape view.

And he couldn't see any trail anymore, any trail was gone but he carried on in that direction, on until the ragged edge of the crowd where people held their hands over their mouths and someone female said, 'You know how sad this is, seriously,' and over them the smoke rose and rolled turning endlessly in on itself and north-east towards the Lido and Highgate and he was going on there and he pushed through the people, growling, who had come from Oak Village and Kiln Place and Brentwood Towers to see and to protect their neighbourhood and then he saw the GRAVIS boy standing with his mum.

The boy was grey and sick and a bright white puckered bandage covered half his face. He saw James and his visible eye widened and he stepped back and there was nowhere to run—60 people in the road and he was just a boy. His mum looked at him and saw his face. She turned and saw James and then she saw the axe.

She stepped immediately between them.

'You fuck off, right off out of here, you go,' she said. She made a sweeping movement with her hand.

The boy stared with his remaining eye and there was no one else, just people, and behind him Marcella said, 'His baby's missing.'

'You fuck off, right off out of here,' the mother said again. And James made the keening sound and around him people didn't even notice and then people did.

'Fuckin' hell,' said somebody and they saw the way he stared and they saw the axe and behind him flashover in the Irishman's apartment came and flame burst out the door and 'Fuckin' hell' voices shouted and a laughing voice called back, 'We're gonna rob Hampstead,' and the smoke rolled and rippled out from under the covered way and up and up, up, up and he walked forward and the mother watched the axe and turned with him and she held the boy behind her with one fending arm until he passed.

And he ran and ran until behind him they were just voices, dark and smoke, and he was passing Gospel Oak station all closed up as he ran as fast as he could run until at the entrance to the Lido CORPORATION OF LONDON HAMPSTEAD HEATH GOSPEL OAK ENTRANCE he ducked up the path under the oaks where the witches slept running freely in the pitch black calling Fiona Fiona would she never be would she never be a girl of four a girl of five would he never get to brush her teeth until he left the last tree behind and the playing fields before him and 200 metres in which to die, to see out there in the dark the fallen shape of a body of a man of a boy he ran towards a dog the ridgeback lying full length with its muzzle on its paws in the long grass watching over the approaches and the path and he saw the shape before it as he came, he saw the shape, a smaller figure before the dog in the grass and sodden plane tree leaves everything a-glisten in the dew lay the white and swaddled form of a child and the dog raised its head and watched him sadly as he came to her crying slowing and reaching for her and he picked her up her swaddle dusted lightly with wet blades of grass and slowly crying he turned and walked away from the dog and she was warm and she was heavy and he turned her over and over and touching the blankets away from her face and examined her face and head and she yawned and crooned to him as a baby should and she was fine and the ridgeback rose and sniffed the night and backed away eyeing him slightly before it turned and jogged away onto the darkened Heath half sidelong like they do and James held the baby and watched the dog leave them and up above the ringed-round hill the rain at last began to fall.

The office was empty.

All the desks' chairs were swivelled at their angles of exit. Screens on but dimmed. The quiet all around. It was a Thursday, 11:30am, and not one person was visible from the door. From Susan to Death the cubicles and desks of the *Royal London Journal of Medicine* were bereft of workers and looked like the looted stalls of some terrible book fair. Helen Jackson's desk in particular was just a single amorphous pile of paper with a screen in the middle fringed with Post-its. The occasional embarrassed teacup teetering here and there. No Jane, no Vivien. The blind half down above Birgit's desk clanking gently. The odd desk lamp on. James stood in the doorway with the neat warm package of his last Sorrento BLT in hand. Not a bus to be had, it had taken him an hour and a half to walk from home, Tatia and Fiona through an emptied Camden from Mansfield Road to Tavistock Square, NW3 to WC1. He'd done his bit of work then gone downstairs for a sandwich and now everyone was gone.

So he carried the BLT down the aisle, past Kristian's neat and empty desk, past Harriet's, and Julia's, D2's and D1's and Ibrahim's. Past Helen's. At the corner of Pheromone's and Pitti's paired desks, Pitti's chair tucked firmly away, he saw Simon Smyther-Jones's single child-sized Converse lying on the floor a good metre from Trish's desk.

All was quiet.

He suddenly saw what was going on. It was some kind of super-Clinch in the Goddess's corner office. Through the interior glass walls he could see the tiny room was packed with staff—hair and tweed skirts pressed up flat against the glass—and everyone was facing away from him into the far corner.

There were probably 30 people in there—the full complement of the office workers who'd made it in today. It was way past time for a Clinch. He began to walk towards the office where now the door, he could see, was partly open. They were facing the Goddess's desk, and he could hear the Goddess talking.

She was onscreen on her own Dell. He could see her now and she was sitting in civvies, slightly hunched: a bottle-green gilet over a tattersall shirt, a bandanna holding up her hair. Beyond her a white wall with a window. Two fifths of a battered mahogany tallboy. It was her office at her house in the country or High Barnet, at least. She was home and as if to confirm it a small bedraggled spaniel's snout and paws appeared in her lap and she stroked it absentmindedly. Helen Jackson and John Mayer were standing in the doorway and made room for him to sidle in. John said companionably, ''Ere 'e is,' but made no eye contact, as if he never would again. David 2 smirked knowingly and David 1 pursed his lips and wagged his head from side to side in some freshly coined acknowledgement signal. Kristian in his Cutler & Gross glasses, folded arms and a determined suit jacket stood slightly in front of and obscuring Rob. Helen looked at James, then indicated the door and murmured, 'Don't get stuck behind there,' and before the Goddess resumed speaking

James caught Benjamin look up quickly, his expression one of startled loss.

'I want to say,' said the Goddess, 'that though I believe the record of this moment is crucial, and that we have what I would describe as more than an obligation but a duty to bear witness, a duty to the country, our readers, to doctors, nurses, all healthcare staff, to scientists and clinicians, and to patients, here, the US, India, the rest of the world, that, however—' She was thinking hard. A high rose-bloom in her cheeks and very intensely focused. 'It is your safety that is paramount to me.'

The crowded room was silent.

'Now nobody can be against the general idea of an emphasis on the safety of our staff, but in practice, this means action. It means decisions must be taken early in all our interests and in the interests of the *Royal London* and its continuing obligations to our readers and to the world at large. Obligations to the *record*. And it is for this reason—'

''Ere it cooms,' said Morrissey.

'—we are to close London offices and are asking each of you to liaise with your direct line managers and work from home your regular allotment of hours as is possible and you are able.' A tentative, almost pleased exhalation came from the entire room. 'We're going to keep at it.' She smiled then, and the dog peered interestedly up at the webcam from her moleskinned lap. 'Just not from London.'

The entire gathering, like the last twitch of a wound-down toy, moved then, in a gentle shuffle and murmur.

'Now there, there, there—'

It was a common thing for her, this throat-clearing stutter, and it was part of her repertoire of rhetorical strategies, to sustain attention while thoughts were mustered. Surprising, then, that she would use it at a moment like this. Several of the most senior editors, including Barbara Jones, looked pale and somehow internal.

'—there is an IMT task force assembled to assist those of you who are yet to do so in the arrangement of remote server connections and the other necessary arrangements regarding CMS access at various levels, email and support and the rest, and the various templates, for next Monday, so please speak to them. If you are yet to do so. We still don't, um, cater for Mac, I'm afraid.'

She allowed herself a small smile, and a low titter spread through the room.

'This is a test for us. For our resilience. This is an unprecedented situation for which we have made extensive preparations, but we are yet to see how those contingencies operate in practice. We're lucky. We've had plenty of time and we benefit from the foresight of the many gifted people on our team.'

Her platitudes were delicious because they were hers and had the luxury of being true. They sounded grand and one asked—really? And really listened and bore down and found that at the least there was truth there, and it was hers. What she said was always—re-examinable.

'We've had plenty of warning. We could have been Lyon. We could have been Lisbon. And I want to say that this is a test for us. We are an international journal. Where we publish from is incidental. The relevance of that is only in the eyes of the law.'

Tousle-haired and clear of grey-blue eyes, she looked from the screen at her gathered staff. The little dog sat in her lap now.

'So long as we have each other—'

'And broadband—' Morrissey.

'—we can continue to do the important work we are doing. We can continue to be rather rude and unpleasant about homeopathy—' A room-wide chortle broke the tense silence, and invisible in the corner, seated, the Pheromone guffawed and said hoarsely, 'Hear, hear.'

'We can continue to lead from the front on issues of libel law reform, diabetes in Africa, A&E closures, climate change and public health, vaccine hesitancy, pop psychiatry. To champion open access and speedy release of trial data. To bear up as banner and flag the randomised controlled trial. To speak truth based in evidence to power wherever that might be. I know you are all with me whatever your personal circumstances and I am grateful for that and simply ask that if you have any concerns or personal issues whatsoever that you feel as free as you possibly can to contact me, or Tony, or Trish directly. We expect normal service will resume but we don't and can't know when exactly that will be. So until then we ask you to work at home, try to do the best you can, stay safe and to take care of yourself and your families in the first instance. And to try to start work more or less on time even if you're still in your pyjamas.'

Being so narrow, the kitchen of the *R Lond J Med*, oddly, occasioned and inspired a lot of confidences and in-depth discussions. Somehow, standing alongside another person and being forced out of eye contact, as she stirred a cup of tea and he washed his coffee cup, the ability or requirement to lie, dissemble, hide or simply remain aloof was mysteriously sapped. The blinds lifted, momentarily, away from the silence of the emptying desks out there. But it took a while.

'Well!' James said.

'Well! I know!'

'Heading soon?'

'I think so. Back to Dorset till it blows over.'

'...'

'...'

'What happened to your head!'

'I literally ran into a door.'

'Oh no!'

'Yes.'

'Ouchy.'

'How's Dylan, Susan?' James asked.

Susan did her usual small polite sigh—you can't know, and nor should you, just what it's like. 'Oh, he's fine,' she said. 'And how's little Fiona?'

'She's fine!'

'You ought to bring in some photos for us! You know, when we come back. How old is she now?'

'She's six months!'

'Wow!'

'Yeah. And Dylan?'

'Two and a half.'

'Wow!'

'Yeah.'

'And how's he getting on?'

'Apart from only being able to watch the iPad upside down?' She laughed a laugh that was so completely bitter and unbitter at the same time that it was almost static, almost just that, a symbol or the words: ha ha. 'He's fine.'

'He only watches it upside down?'

'Yea-heahp. I—know.' She shook her head at the folly of it all and bobbed and dipped her teabag.

'How does . . . how does he get on with TV then?'

'He lies on his back with a cushion under his neck.'

'Wow.'

'Yeahp. Well, life goes on.'

'. . .'

'. . .'

'Susan, Fiona . . .' he said, and paused. 'There's always odd things with them aren't there, and it's hard to tell if you're just overtired or what's really happening.'

'Uh—huh!' She nodded vigorously.

His cup was quite clean but still he was scrubbing it—pausing and scrubbing as if he could get the ancient stains off the china.

'Did you have any odd things?' said James.

'Oh too many to count!'

'Ha ha!'

'Yes.'

'Well, we had one.'

'Yes?'

'We had a flood in her room.'

'Oh *no*.'

'But I had the plumber in and . . . there's nowhere for the water to come from.'

'Weird!'

'Yeah.'

'Well where did it come from then?'

'We don't know! There's nowhere. That's the thing.'

She had finished steeping the tea, and lifted the dripping bag above the water and let it hover there, unwilling to break the spell. He stood grinning like a little boy, holding the scrubbing brush in the empty cup.

'Was it . . . rising . . . oh I don't know about things like that!' she said.

'There's a possibility, because there's a river down there somewhere. But it's never happened before. She didn't wake up or anything. It just filled up with water.'

'So weird.'

'Yeah. Water and . . . leaves.'

'Weird! Wait—leaves?'

'Also one morning'—his voice had changed, still half grinning, but his jaw set. He looked hard at the pinboard where there was a pamphlet tacked advertising the *London*'s in-house mental health counselling service. 'One morning I found a . . . dog in her room.'

'A dog?' The two words were said, bright but toneless, as if she'd said something boring but plausible like *A snail*. 'Wait, you *found* a dog?' She laughed, but the laugh was wrong.

'A dog. Found it in her room. Actually when I say morning I mean middle of the night. Still dark. Like 4am or something.'

'An actual dog?'

'A Rhodesian ridgeback was sitting in the corner of her bedroom in the dark.'

'A what?'

'She slept through it.'

'Did someone let it in?'

'The doors were locked.'

She laughed again, not knowing what kind of story this was. 'A real dog, though?'

'A young but full-grown Rhodesian ridgeback hunting dog.'

She decided, in her special way, to both recede, leave this situation completely, and still be maternal. To care, and not to care, in her way. She was still. He was half grinning at the pinboard, poised and ready, it seemed, for her to extricate herself. Pre-armed for her to murmur, *Well must be getting back.*

'Did it, well it didn't try and *harm* her or anything, did it, James?'

'No. No it didn't.'

'Didn't it scare you?'

'Oh absolutely *shitless*.'

'Well, what did you do?'

'I edged around it and stood between it, in front of the Moses basket with my arms sort of like this—' He spread them wide, and laughed at the helplessness of it. It was as if in self-deprecation he could drag the conversation, drag reality, back to somewhere vaguely manageable, an aimless chat. '—and I just stood there.'

'Wow.'

'Yeah!'

'But—'

'I know. It just sat there. I stood there for a long time. And eventually I did what you do with strange dogs.'

'Which is?'

'I let him smell me. I held out the back of my hand. Very slowly. You know, took my time. But I did what I'd do with any dog. He just sniffed it gently like this. Then he didn't do anything and so I took him by the collar and I led him out of the nursery and he let me and I led him down the hall and up the stairs and I let him out the front door.'

'*Wow*.'

'Yeah.'

'Did you . . . call the RSPCA or someone?'

'Nope!'

'Wow.'

'. . .'

'. . .'

'Were there . . . other things too, you said?'

'Yeah, there's been a few. Some other things. Ha ha.'

A long, long pause.

'James, do you have people to talk to about this stuff?' she said, and it was hard for her to come out so far.

'No, it's all right,' he said brightly, and he turned to look at her then. 'It's just hard to assemble it all isn't it. Anyway. I just talked to you.'

'And you've got your partner or your wife, sorry, I don't actually know her name,' she said.

'Wife,' he said. 'It still sounds strange.'

'Yes,' she said. 'Wife, ha.'

He seemed to have snookered her then, and she didn't know what to say. To continue, to help, or to recede if the help had already been given. 'Well that's *very* strange,' she said. 'I don't know.'

'Ha ha,' he said, then at some kind of rest and with not a trace of bitterness in his voice, he put his cup in the dish-rack and the scrubbing brush across the backs of the hot and cold taps where it always lived, and said, and his New Zealand accent was very strong and he sounded quite small, 'Weird, eh.'

They went out together back into the office.

wisp (not whisp)
Wistar rat an outbred albino rat
within normal limits use normal
woebegone
woe betide (two words)
worth while, worthwhile Make two words when used predicatively (the job was worth while) and one word when used adjectivally (a worthwhile job). Something that is worth doing is worth while.

Annabel awoke in hospital bed and looked about, changed. Inadvertedly altered. Static, significant. Irrefutability had showed her that it could. A gasp in her understanding. Scares for scarce; in tense. A causality scared for life, written in a direct style.

    Until at the door, look, for her: came quietly, politely, expectant and concerned as if she had given birth, like shy new siblings sidling in: Oliver Reed, Benjamin Subramaniam, Davids 1 and 2, and Kristian, Birgit, Rob and Jane, and lastly, regally, the Pheromone, bearing balloons of fringed tinfoil, packets of flowers, the extent of their love, and boxes of chocolate, Quality Street.

y axis (ordinate; the vertical axis)
years 1950–2, 1960–70, 1850–1950; from
Yes/No Affirmative and negative answers to direct questions should be printed in lower case and within
yolk sac

back up the system provided back up, a back-up procedure; never one word

Burned to aches around me.

'Does anybody know where the style guide's kept now? I can't find it. Well I mean I found it but it's not it, if you know what I mean. There's all kinds of stuff in there.'
   'Ask James.'
   'Where is James?'
   'Yes, where *is* James?'
   'Oh he's gone. Running home to the wee girl.'
   'But what about his dicky ankle?'
   'Said he's going to "gut it out".'
   'I wonder when we all will see each other again.'

zygotic not zygous

Fiona Beatrice Ballard born 26 October, at the Royal Free, to parents James Ballard and

Later that day came the second to last blackout. The screens all went dark. The hard drives all spun down.

And everyone went '*Oh* . . .' with the same falling middle C.